NEITHER HERE

Other World
Fantasy Stories

Cat Rambo

Hydra **H** House

NEITHER HERE

978-0-9890828-7-7 (trade paperback)
978-0-9890828-8-4 (limited edition hardcover)
Library of Congress Control Number: pending

Hydra House
2850 SW Yancy St. #106
Seattle, WA 98126
http://www.hydrahousebooks.com/

This is a work of fiction. Names, characters, places, and incidents are either the products of the author's imagination or are used fictitiously. Any resemblance to actual events, locales, situations, or persons, living or dead, is purely coincidental.

Cover art by Galen Dara
http://www.galendara.com/

Cover design by Tod McCoy
http://www.todmccoy.com/

Illustrations by Mark W. Tripp
http://www.spiderpig.com/

Text design by Vicki Saunders

"Love, Resurrected" © 2011 by Cat Rambo. First published in Beneath Ceaseless Skies, 2011. • "The Toad's Jewel" © 2013 by Cat Rambo. First published in Abyss & Apex, 2013. • "The Mage's Gift" © 2016 Cat Rambo. First appeared on Patreon, 2016. • "Pippa's Smiles" © 2011 Cat Rambo. First appeared on Daily Science Fiction, April 19, 2011. • "Karaluvian Fale" © 2011 Cat Rambo. First appeared on Giganotosaurus, 2011. • "The Subtler Art" © 2015 Cat Rambo. First published in Blackguards, edited by J.M. Martin, 2015. • "How Dogs Came To The New Continent" © 2015 Cat Rambo. Original to this collection; first appeared on a private Patreon post, 2015. • "Love's Footsteps" © 2013 Cat Rambo. First appeared in Daily Science Fiction, 2013. • "To Read The Sea" © 2013 Cat Rambo. First published in *What Fates Impose*, edited by Nayad Monroe, 2013. • "A Brooch of Bone, A Hint of Tooth" © 2013 Cat Rambo. First published in *By Faerie Light*, edited by Scott Gable, 2013. • "Call and Answer, Plant and Harvest" © 2016 Cat Rambo. First published in *Beneath Ceaseless Skies*, 2016.

First trade edition v.1

Praise for Cat Rambo

Five reasons to read Cat Rambo:
#1: If you like stories about strange places and strange creatures
#2: If you like stories that leave you yourself feeling a little strange
#3: If you like a good love story
#4: especially one with talking cats, deadly mermaids, mind-altering technologies, live coats, detachable limbs, gorgeous descriptions and great leaps of imagination, wit and power
#5: plus travel through space and time
Then this is the book for you.

Karen Joy Fowler

Cat Rambo's futures are complex, and often dissonant and eerie—they evoke the familiar in their careful world-building, intricate detail and recognizable characters, while simultaneously constructing futures flavored with the strange. Her futures are often unsettling, but never so simple as to be dystopic; her stories inhabit complex, ambiguous worlds. Her simultaneously familiar and unfamiliar settings sharpen her portrayals of human relationships. By recasting core experiences against disjunctive backgrounds, she causes the reader to appreciate them anew. People are always at the center: they fall away from each other, cope with betrayals, seek connections. While the inner eye marvels at her immersive images, the body resonates with the subtle, deft emotions imbued in her characters. Cat Rambo's finest stories shimmer in the memory like the lights of the Aurora Borealis: vivid and eerily illuminating.

Rachel Swirsky

Cat Rambo's stories never go where you expect them to. They twist and turn and end up in strange places—sometimes very strange indeed. Both the stories set on the Earth we know (or think we know) and those set far away will surprise and delight you.

Nancy Kress

Neither Here Contents

Love, Resurrected   1

The Toad's Jewel   16

Pippa's Smiles   34

Karaluvian Fale   43

The Subtler Art   69

The Mage's Gift   77

How Dogs Came To The New Continent   85

Love's Footsteps   102

To Read The Sea   110

A Brooch of Bone, A Hint of Tooth   114

Call and Answer, Plant and Harvest   128

LOVE, RESURRECTED

GENERAL AIFE CROFADOTTIR WAS ACKNOWLEDGED THE greatest military mind of her generation—perhaps even her century. No wonder then that the sorcerer Balthus recruited her early in her career, setting her to rally armies of Beasts and magically-equipped soldiers, planning campaign after campaign, until finally he stood the ruler of a vast expanse of the continent's northeastern corner. Once fertile lands, once countries, now only uncontested, devastated territories.

Three years after her death, she still labored in his service.

—————

Aife stood at the window of Balthus' tower, looking out over the desolate countryside. Age and blight had stooped the apple trees dominating the view, and sticky webs clustered in the vees of the knobby branches. The dry grass tried to hold onto the dust, but here, as everywhere, drought and ash and the silty remnant of magic choked away all life. The chalky-white stones surrounding the dry well gleamed in the hostile sunlight.

Decades of sorcerous battle had warped the land. It was dead in patches, or so plagued by ghosts that no living soul could walk it and remain sane.

She rested her fingertips on the windowsill and contemplated her hand. The skin was gray and withered, but still functioned. Sooner or later, Aife thought, it would rot away, despite Balthus' preservative spells. What would happen then? Right now she could pass for a living, but very ill, person, could wrap herself in a cloak and whisper, make some claim to human company. What would happen when her bones began to show through?

Behind her, Balthus said, "You will become a skeleton, but one that

1

walks and talks by magic means. The mere sight of you will strike fear in any heart. What a war leader you will be then, my darling!"

He touched her shoulder, closer than she had thought him. "You will make a beautiful skeleton. All clean-lined ivory. I will commission you a crown, gilt and amber, with the warhawk that shows you general."

She was weary of him reading her mind.

At the thought, he removed his hand. "Is that what has concerned you lately? But I must know your mind, Aife, must be able to glimpse your plans in order to work to aid them."

"Every creature in your employ," she said, words thick. "I know, you must know them all."

He let the room's silence gather, then ventured, "Perhaps …"

"Perhaps?"

She turned away from the window to contemplate him. She might be a monster, but he was little more: yellowed skin stretched drum-tight over his bones. His long, wispy hair was tied back with an embroidered ribbon the wrong color for the crimson robes he wore.

Blotches and scars marked his hands, the relics of past experiments. An olive green patch covered the heel of one hand, an irregular oval resembling old mold or lichen.

He returned the gaze, eyes as glassy as an opium addict's. What spells had he laid on himself, throughout the years? She wondered if he saw her as she truly was now. Or did he let the memory of her slip over it like a mask, making him see her when the blood still coursed through her veins, instead of the slow seepage it engaged in now, as though begrudging her body its energy?

"I will make you a charm," he said. His voice was almost pleading. "One that keeps your thoughts hidden. No other man, woman, or Beast in my employ has that privilege. But I will give it to you."

And with that promise, she gave him her hand, her gray and withered hand, and let him lead her to bed.

But again, she did not know whether he kissed her or the memory of what she had been to him.

He kept his promise. The next day, beside her on the pillow he had left at dawn, a silver chain coiled, holding a dark gem, darker than death or the loss of memory.

She put it around her neck and went to do his business.

⎯⚬⎯

Since her transformation, all living things shied away from her. She had become accustomed to that. But the Beasts accepted her more than the humans did. Most of them were creatures Balthus had created, sometimes by putting living things together to make something new, like the swan-winged woman that acted as scout and courier, or the great Catoblepas, blended of ox and wild pig and turtle and something Balthus would not name, whose breath withered whatever it struck. More often he transformed what he was given: stretching, pulling, augmenting, till something was created that the world had never seen before. If it showed promise that he could use it, he left it alive.

She did not seek the Beasts' company deliberately, but rather, as a cat does, she would sit in a room where they were gathered, not part of the conversation, but letting it swirl around her. There but not there. It reminded her of long-ago barracks chatter, the taunts and gibes and affectionate mockery of fellow soldiers.

This day she sat in the corner near the fire, careful not to get too close, lest a spark singe her without her knowing, because her skin was dead now, and only reported a little when pain struck it. Near her was the swan-woman, who they called Lytta, and the Minotaur who guarded the stables, and a man-wolf who had once been one of her finest soldiers. He was the only one who had looked at her when she entered, his eyes glinting sly green in the firelight as he half-nodded. She had not returned the gesture.

"They say the Falcon is making inroads near Barbaruile," Lytta said to the wolf-man, who had refused any name other than "Wolf."

That news interested Aife. She had pursued the bandit chief who called himself the Falcon for almost a year now, and found him a more than adequate challenge.

"What does he fight for?" the Minotaur demanded, his voice as heavy as a sack of gravel. "He leaves things worse than they are, with no sorcerer to look out over the land."

"He must have magic of his own," Lytta said. "Look at how he has escaped capture, again and again."

"They say it is no magic," Wolf said, "but rather something that dispels magic."

Aife had spent much time contemplating the same question. What was the source of the Falcon's success? Spies sent to gather information never returned. Were never heard from again. Subverted or killed? She hoped, for their sake, that it had been the latter. When Balthus finally captured the Falcon—it was inevitable—he would take him and all his allies, and make new things of them, things that they would not enjoy being.

Any more than she enjoyed the life he had given her.

⚬————⚬

When she had first opened her eyes, after her death, all she saw was Balthus' face, like the full moon in the sky above her. She had shuddered then, not understanding why she breathed.

She remembered dying. She remembered the cannonball slamming into her, the broken knitting needles of her ribs, bright stitches of pain weaving her a garment. Reeling back on unsteady legs—something in her spine was wrong, was numb. Slipping away, like retreating into sleep, defeated but not unhappily by dreams. It had been so restful.

She realized she no longer had to breathe.

"What have you done?" she tried to say, but Balthus' hand pressed her back implacably on the bed.

"Rest, my dear," he said. "You were too valuable to me to be laid beneath the earth."

Her heart, she realized, had not been revived with the rest of her.

⚬————⚬

When Balthus had first recruited Aife, she had stood straight as a spear, muscular but tall, carrying herself like a willow tree. She kept her hair short then, in the manner of foot soldiers, even though she had risen much further in the ranks than that. Her only scar was a burn along her left forearm where it had been caught by quick-fire in a southern sea battle against raiders.

They had heard of Balthus, of course. His demesne bordered the petty kingdom in whose service she battled. Rumors initially said he was a mage, but the stories had grown until they named what he really was: sorcerer, the sort that battled perpetually on these shores. The devastation had not yet spread across the continent. She had thought she could keep the kingdom safe for its Queen-Regent.

But in a single night, everything changed.

When she awoke that morning, the first thing she noticed was the silence. Then the smell of blood.

She alone was alive. She went through the castle, opening door after door to look in, seeing a gaping wound like a second mouth on each throat, the pool of spilled blood, the flies already gathering. In the Queen's chamber, grief nearly brought her to her knees. She had promised to protect the woman who lay there. Now all that was alive in this place was her. Why had she been spared? Had she been merely overlooked, or was there some reason?

Finally she had entered the throne room, expecting no one there. A red-robed man sat alive on the gilded chair, watching her approach.

"Your fame has spread, Aife. Aife of the deadly sword and clever plan. I have come to collect you. Will you serve me, or must I coerce you?"

His eyes were deceptively kind; her mind numb. Her fingers curled around the hilt of the dagger at her waist, felt the ridges of the leather wrapping on the pommel. But what use was steel against a sorcerer?

At the time she agreed, she'd thought to catch him off guard, kill him when he was unwary. She watched for opportunities, made her plans. She could not hope to escape alive after slaying him, but it would be worth it, to avenge her Queen. She waited patiently.

But a year passed, then another, and she found herself enjoying planning his campaigns, being able to use magics, technologies, of the sort her Queen never could have wielded. She had never been able to play at war on such a scale. Her victories pleased her. Made her even more famous.

Wolf had come to her then, sought her out, not as a lover, but as a follower, and been captured by Balthus. Brought to her, he had sworn to whatever changes the sorcerer thought might make him a more efficient soldier. The potion Balthus gave him twisted and elongated his skull, pulled his jaw forward, endowed it with canines the size of her thumb.

All the while he had stared into her eyes, trusting her.

By then it all seemed normal.

She'd been seduced by her pleasure in the puzzles Balthus had set her. How to coax an enemy from a walled tower. How to keep supplies from the coast from reaching their destination. As though the mental chessboard had been expanded, the rules not changed but become more complex. Challenge after worthy challenge, and she overcame them all.

And so when, the next night, he had kissed her, she had not resisted. She was not a virgin. Nor was she the only person to find themselves in his bed. She thought he would miss her companionship. Perhaps it would keep her safe; perhaps he'd hesitate to slay someone who'd touched him, cradled him. Loved him.

Had she known she would become so dear to him that he'd impose this existence on her, she would have tried to kill him that first moment in that echoing, empty throne room, even knowing it meant her death.

———✦———

This half-life dragged at her. She felt weary all the time, a chilled-bone sluggishness of motion that belied the quickness of her thoughts. It was not painful to breathe, but it was tiring, and she began to eschew it when alone and unworried about frightening the living.

She touched the silver chain at her throat. Was it real or some trick? A trinket that did nothing but give her peace of mind? She thought, though, that he would deal squarely with her. Of all his creations, she was the most his.

In the chambers she inhabited, she unrolled the massive map that

6

showed Balthus' territory and spread it on the table. She used a copper coin to mark each site where a raid had occurred and studied them, trying to puzzle out the pattern by which he determined his targets. There was always a pattern, even when people were trying to avoid it.

The Falcon seemed to be working north, but in the past he'd doubled back on occasion, hit a previous target or something near it. When would he do it again? What prompted the decision each time?

Discover that and she'd have him.

She had always walked among her troops, late at night, getting a feel for their worries, their fears. She could do that no longer. She frightened them too much.

So now she relied on her three troop leaders, all uneasy-looking men Balthus had recruited from the Southern Isles. One told her he had come thinking this war-torn continent would provide easy pickings for a man of war. Then, once here, he had realized, as had the others, the importance of placing himself under a sorcerer's command. There was no other way to survive.

Unless you were the Falcon, it seemed. Was it true, was he a sorcerer himself?

If so, only Balthus could catch him.

But her employer—her lover, her resurrector—seemed more preoccupied with the waters to the north and skirmishes with the Pot-King, who might actually be the Pot-King's son, according to one set of rumors.

"A minor bandit," Balthus said dismissively.

"A troublesome one," she said. "He burned your granary at Vendish."

A bold move, but a strategic one. Hungry troops were inefficient troops, whether Human or Beast.

Balthus shrugged. "Is that not why I have you, for matters of this sort?"

NEITHER HERE

Her fearsome nature had its advantages. She could not move easily among her soldiers, but she could walk the land around the castle. No creature would trouble her; no predator would sniff her and think of food. No ghost would attack her, knowing her somewhat closer than kindred.

Sometimes Wolf trailed her, never speaking, but always guarding. It was a comfort, even if unnecessary, to feel him in the shadows, a guardian presence at her back.

She did not take a torch. Her eyes were well-adjusted to the darkness—indeed, most times she preferred it.

In a glade, she found a doe and her fawn, part of the herd of Riddling Deer Balthus had loosed on the orchard. They lay in a drift of fresh green grass. Red poppies bloomed around them, rare vegetation in this scorched land.

The doe's eyes were dark as forest pools. Her nostrils flared and her head jerked, testing the air, as Aife approached. But the wind reassured her; she settled back.

The fawn spoke—how had Balthus managed that? The Deer were his unique creation. He had wanted oracles, had not realized how enigmatic and troublesome they would prove.

"Inside you is your worst enemy," it said.

She did not move, but looked at the fawn, hoping for additional details.

They were not forthcoming. But perhaps—

A branch snapped under Wolf's foot in the underbrush. The wind changed. Jack-knife sudden, doe and fawn were on their feet.

They flickered away into the night, taking with them the answers she sought.

———••••—••◦

She came back to her quarters, smelling of grass and thyme, knowing the boundaries were unchallenged except by the Deer's troublesome words. She unslung her heavy cape, velvet folds as soft as a baby's earlobe. Her boots were black leather with gilt buckles. She undid them one by one and slipped the footwear off by the fire before padding over to the table to contemplate the Falcon's patterns anew.

A black-barred feather lay on her map.

She picked it up with some difficulty. Cold made her fingers stiff.

Who would have dared to leave it here? The Falcon had some ally—perhaps even allies, for she would have never betrayed just one ally, unwilling to lose the advantage it gave her, unless she had others in place, and she reckoned the Falcon her equal in cunning, in planning out each move in a long game.

Twirling the feather, she watched its dance. She would use it as her test of the amulet. Surely if Balthus plucked it from her thoughts, it would spur him to some action.

But he did nothing when he saw her the next morning. Instead she laid the feather beside the map and continued her study of the Falcon's appearances. She tracked the phases of the moon, the weather, anything that might prompt his decisions.

It seemed to Aife that in the last few months, such a pattern had emerged. But why, puzzlingly, had one recently appeared?

Still, she was there in the village he had half-burned before, lying in wait, when he doubled back. She sent the surviving townspeople away, filled the houses with archers and swordhands. In the remnants of the town hall, the Catoblepas crouched, waiting for her orders.

She chose the Mayor's house for her headquarters, finding it the best appointed for her needs. She told herself the decision was not motivated by the way the man had flinched when she first rode in.

As expected, in the night the bandit band appeared, slinking in through the shadows, slipping into houses. Their deaths would be quick and as silent as she could manage. She had ordered them killed; she had no need for anyone alive but the Falcon.

But she waited in vain, and the breath in the Catoblepas's lungs withered only the small grasses among the stones where it crouched. When her archers and soldiers came, they said the Falcon's men had been only illusory wraiths, melting through their steel.

At that, she expected the courier's arrival to bring word that the castle was under siege. It did. She had been outmaneuvered. It was not a customary sensation for her.

By the time she arrived, several dozen of Balthus's choicest Beasts were dead, and a full troop's worth of seasoned mercenaries who would be difficult to replace. Balthus uttered no reproach, but she felt the weight of his unspoken disapproval and disappointment. For the first time, she wondered if there were worse things than her current existence.

In the months that followed, she found herself experiencing another uncustomary sensation: irritation. She played a game where her opponent had her outwitted at every turn, as though he could read her mind. As Balthus once had.

Her opponent taunted her. Every few days another feather appeared. Laid atop her pillow, on the tray beside her breakfast, drifting on the windowsill. A marker in her book, turned a few pages beyond where she had been reading.

She burned them in the fireplace but said nothing to Balthus.

Inside you is your worst enemy. What did that mean? The thought ate at her like a parasite. Was she at odds with herself? Was she overlooking the obvious, making mistakes she should have realized? She found herself outside her actions, watching them with a critical eye.

She faltered sometimes. The fine lines around Balthus' eyes meshed and deepened when he frowned at her, but he said nothing aloud.

But he wanted the Falcon captured, and soon. He was angry about the losses, the time that would be necessary to create more Beasts. For the first time he did not communicate his plans, but expected her to guess them in a way that left her scrambling to catch up at times, trying to figure how to incorporate each creature he created. He did not consult her. She could have used more winged Beasts, to replace lost scouts, but she did not dare request them. Or dray animals to move supplies, and yet, as though mocking this need, he gave her a troupe of Unicorns, too fine-boned and delicate to be hitched to wagons.

It shocked her when Balthus, finally making a move, caught the quarry she had sought so long. Little consolation that his victory came by cheating, not the sort of thing she would have ever embarked upon.

She could see why Balthus had moved with such efficiency, though. Was not all fair in war, as in love?

It was through an exchange of hostages, one of the sacred customs. By doing it, she thought to pay the Falcon tribute, let him see she respected him as an opponent, perhaps lure him into complacency. It was not until they had been dispatched that Balthus revealed that one had been a Siren, a woman created to entice, who would cast her magic over them.

"She even looked a little like you," he said with a smile. Then added, "As you were, I mean."

She made no reply aloud, but had he been able to read her thoughts, his smile might have faltered.

———————

Aife went to the cell where they kept the Falcon. She took two guards with her, trailing her like hounds as she made her way down spirals of stone. On the third landing, a torch burned beside his door.

Her hand spread like an elderly starfish on the door's surface as she leaned forward. She found herself trembling like a hound ready to be loosed on the scent.

He had been sitting on the bunk. He sprang up as her shadow crossed the rectangle of light on the stone floor, approached the door till he was inches away from the bars and the hood's edge shrouding her face, but not far enough. He recoiled as he saw her fully, recovered, stood still, but this time not as close.

She looked at him all the while. Rumors had not lied about his handsomeness. Slim and brown-skinned, his hair as black as ink, a few white strands at the temples somehow making it seem even darker.

Aife could have loved this man, long ago, in her soldier days, before the weight of death had settled on her shoulders. He was young and beautiful, so beautiful. So alive. She wanted him as she had not wanted anything for so long. She put a hand to the bars, looked at him, hoping to see the same recognition there.

Only horror and revulsion.

She had thought her heart dead, but that was not true, else how could she feel it aching now?

Still, she had to question him. She took two guards in with her, but motioned them back when they would have seized him. Leave him his dignity for now.

"How did you know what I was doing for so long?" she said.

He sneered. "Are you not a dead thing, to be commanded by magic, like all dead things that walk must be? I have had my necromancer working for months, trying to find a way inside your mind. On the night of the year's third moon, he succeeded.

"After that, all was clear to me. His magic let me take control of you from time to time. We could not risk it for long, though, so I used it to trouble you, making you lay down clues for yourself: a feather to stir your thoughts, send them in the wrong direction. And it worked, until your master chose to trust you no longer."

Had Balthus realized what had happened? That closing her mind to him had opened it to other magical controllers? Surely he had not known it at first, but only later, had used it to infiltrate the Falcon's camp, discover his plans in order to catch him?

"Your compatriots," she said, "including any magickers with them, are dead. You are here in Balthus' castle, and will be wrung of information as a sponge is of water. Will you yield it up easily or will you force him to twist you hard?"

She watched him as he considered her words. She thought that it would be hard to kill him, but she'd do it nonetheless. She had killed pretty men before, and seen many of them used to coaxing their way from women die as quick and efficiently as the ugliest man.

Sometimes they were a little more theatrical about it all. He seemed like he would be the theatrical sort.

She touched the silver chain. She had refused jewelry for so long. It was something that made you a target, or gave enemies a chance to grab at it. And here it had happened, just as she had always feared. Her worst enemy had been in her head, and it was not herself.

She thought, though, that if she could have freed him, she might have. He was that pretty. It would have made her happy, to know that he lived somewhere, that he knew it was by her mercy. If only that was possible.

12

Footsteps, coming down the stairs. Who?

The Falcon twisted at the air with his hand. She felt the chain constrict around her throat, puppet fingers slipping into her brain.

"It seems my necromancer's magic lingers after all, after all," he said. "I suspected you could not resist coming close enough that I could control you, even without his assistance. What shall I have you do? Kill your master seems the most obvious step, doesn't it?"

"Perhaps," Balthus said from where he stood on the stairwell.

Aife was pulled upward, her limbs someone else's, a loathsome intimacy that made bile burn in her throat. The guards were on their knees, choking, hands at their throats, trying to pry away invisible cords. She was thrust towards the door, trying to keep her arms out to maintain balance.

Balthus raised his hand, palm towards her. The green blotch had grown like a bracelet around his wrist. A blob of silvery liquid covered the center of his hand, like the moon, pulling her forward, a mystical tide washing through her, making her heavy, restoring her to herself. She shuddered, shaking off the last of the netting over her senses.

"You are not one sixteenth as clever as you think you are, puppy," Balthus said contemptuously.

"Enough to rid you of your most powerful tool," the Falcon exclaimed. She twisted away as he flung something at her that dispersed in the air, a handful of motes. She felt it settling on her back and shoulders, saw red sparkling dust riding the breeze, falling on her gray skin and setting it smoldering wherever it landed.

Where was water, anywhere close at hand? The privy pot in the cell was dry. The guards were recovering, as she had, and so she discarded the thought of quenching anything in their blood.

Fire blazed along her skin, burning deep, too deep to extinguish. She staggered towards the door, where Balthus stood. His face was stricken. She saw herself, a fiery angel, reflected in his pupils, saw the thick velvet of the cloak gone lacy with flame. She opened her mouth to appeal to him and felt it fill with flaming dust, go hiss-flickering out, the heat stealing any chance at words.

Fire, and more fire, and then final darkness.

Neither Here

‹——·····⊙

Only to awake, agonized. Balthus' face above her yet again.

Was that all it would ever be, from now on?

She was bone now. Bone and some sort of spectral, invisible flesh that netted her limbs into order and gave her the power of sight. She moved her fingers and they clacked and clicked against the planes of her face as she tried to touch whatever held her together.

Opposite her a standing mirror, green-lit, presenting her rippled and obscured as though drowning. Her skull, wavering in the reflection, capped with a tiara—a golden hawk, wings stretched out to cup the bone.

Wolf was there past the mirror, pressed against the wall of the chamber. Watching her with loyalty. Whatever she became, he would follow. It was reassurance. She would always be a leader, no matter what.

Truly a monster now. She would have to give up some of her illusions: the pretense of meals and cosmetics and clothing. What good would armor be, except to hang on her as though she was some sort of display rack?

"I have made you a present, my dearest," Balthus said. His fingers stroked her skull, bumped along her teeth. He released her and stepped aside.

Undead, skin already graying. Ah, the fine dark hair, the silver strands like penmarks in reverse. The once-piercing eyes now blue and cloudy marbles.

Marbles full of hate and spite and helpless malice. Hers forever more, her handsome toy, given her by her master, perhaps to torment, perhaps from love and an impulse to please. Would she ever know his motives, would she ever understand if she was puppet or lover, source of amusement or font of something else?

Endless days stretched before her, in which she would never find the answer.

Afternotes

Almost a decade ago I was part of a terrific workshop run by Walter John Williams and Connie Willis in the Taos Ski Valley. It was a talented group, and the two week session was a happy blur of lots of writing, lots of critiquing, and lots and lots of shop talk, plus assorted movies and a lot of wine.

One of the participants mentioned that he planned to start a literary fantasy online magazine. Since he happened to like the stuff I was workshopping, I figured that would be a surefire sale. So as soon as he opened up the magazine, I fired off a submission.

And he rejected it, because he didn't feel it had the right flavor for his magazine.

That's one of the things I respect tremendously about that editor, who was Scott Andrews of Beneath Ceaseless Skies. *It was, in fact, not till the fourth submission that he took a story, which was this piece, set in the same world in which the novel I'd workshopped at Taos, Tabat. For people who know something about that world, this one is set on the Old Continent during the peak of the wars between sorcerers that destroyed it; it is set at roughly the same time period as "A Twist of Flame," which appears in my collection* Eyes Like Sky and Coal and Moonlight.

One-sided love is a frequent theme for me; here it happens in an uneasy triangle of Balthus, Aife, and the man known as the Falcon. My favorite image of the story remains the silver-crowned skull of Aife; I believe the Riddling Deer that appear here originally came from the manuscript I was working on at the time that would become Beasts of Tabat.

THE TOAD'S JEWEL

THE TOAD KNEW THERE was a jewel in her head. She had not been told so by the philosopher who had written, many years ago: "It is a repugnant and venomous beast, but contains a stone of great value in its head which cures bites and poisons." He had gone on to speculate about cosmological Prima Materia and symbols of the First Matter of the Great Work. All of this would have been lost on the toad.

Rather, she knew the jewel there in the same way that one knows one has a hand or a foot or a tongue. She could feel it in her head. A fierce light shifted beneath her warty skin, the gem's facets changing their plane of inclination as though contemplating some other angle of thought.

The toad was a clever toad. And, furthermore, a toad that lived on the borders of the land of Faerie, between it and the swamps of Wick, inhabited by reptiles and insects, which feed upon each other.

No animal—or human, for that matter—can live near that place without being somewhat touched by it, and so the toad had more subtlety of thought than most of her counterparts. When she looked at the sun, she thought more of its beauty and roundness than its light or heat, and in the evenings when the fireflies played over Faerie's rolling lawns, she did not hop out to catch as many as she could, but rather sat in a damp patch near a tree's roots and watched them while eating less aesthetically pleasing grubs.

Because she was self-aware, she could not help but puff up at the thought of the sight she made, or would have made if split open, with the splendidness of her gem and the intelligence of her actions. In this sort of thinking, she was like all other thinking creatures.

But thoughts of this sort entered the gem. And in there, they could not escape, but rather bounced from one edge to another, trapped and unable to break free of the toad's mind. And so she grew more and more puffed up with pride, to the point where her appearance was a little odd, as though bloated with too much air or mayflies.

As she sat watching the fireflies, it came to her that she was more intelligent than they. "They are little machines made of chitin and ichor," she thought. "All they do is shine on and off. If I directed them, think of what I might create—a symphony of light that stretched as far as the eye could see!"

Absorbed in such speculations, she thought harder and harder. The idea came that she might direct the fireflies to feed on specific things and thus alter the color of their flashes. With color came possibilities of syncopation, and after that she thought of enlisting the help of nightingales, who she respected more than the fireflies and would be willing to court a little, with sweet flatteries and endearments in the speech of animals, a language of gesture and scent and thought and sound.

This scheming was not as far-fetched as it might seem. The toad was clever and, given that fireflies are easily bullied, might have some hope of coordinating their pulsing signals. She would not have been able to make them colored—such experiments are always risky— but she would indeed have been able to entice the nightingales into accompanying them and the thing she might have achieved was something no one else had ever dreamed of in the world.

It was the freshness of the toad's dream that attracted the wizard.

———•———

Pettigrew, a wizard of some notoriety but little actual power, was out walking in the morning in order to catch a mist sylph. He was less a magical scientist than a tinkerer, and he had designed a device, a pearl of prophecy, that required a sylph's tongue to function.

His luck had been better than the sylphs', for he had caught not one but two. One had been injured in the taking, and sat sulking at the bottom of the collecting jar. The other, uninjured but much perturbed, fluttered against the lid, clinging to the air holes punched there (Pettigrew valued freshness in his ingredients) and uttering imprecations that might have been more effective had they not been too high-pitched for the wizard's ears.

While some consider mist sylphs interchangeable, the sylphs themselves find it an entirely different matter. The sylph beating at the top of the jar, for instance, thought of herself very differently than the sylph sitting disconsolately at the bottom. Peony (for this was her name) was irritated by Alaric Prosperine Tailwind's (for that was his name) lack of action, but underneath that lay a touch of social awe. Sylphs are actually quite family conscious, and while Peony was of little account, this was far from true of Alaric.

Had sylphs had royalty, one might have thought of him a duke, or perhaps a sub-prince, one removed several times from ascension to the throne. His family was expressed in his name's length and complexity.

The jar jostled about. Peony cried, "Come and help me! Perhaps we can twist the top off from within, if we both fly in the right direction at the right time."

But Alaric was having nothing of the sort. "I can't do anything with my arm like this," he complained, clutching the bruised limb. "It's broken and agonizingly painful."

Peony eyed the air holes. If they were larger, she might have tried to make her escape through one of them, but she could tell that they were simply too small for her to do more than insert a spindly arm through as though to wave.

She clung to the lid's underside, wings fluttering, as it swayed. Pettigrew was ascending a hill, and his strides threw her back and forth against the walls. Alaric had laid down flat and clutched at the jar's floor with his good hand while uttering cries of dismay and terror.

"We're dead," he shouted. "Captured by a wizard! Our bones will be ground up to make love potions. Ah! Why did I ever agree to go hunt for fermented mulberries?"

Peony snorted. Drunk on mulberries. No wonder he had been captured! She herself had been out working, gathering dew that would be used to distill beauty potions by her aunt. The two of them depended for survival on the trades that could be made with the vials of liquid.

She had seen a few glittering beads beneath a large fern's arching leaves and gone to investigate. She had not seen Pettigrew crouching behind a nearby shrub until his net had swished over her head, stunning her. She had come to her senses only once she'd been placed inside the jar.

She glared and stared. Her companion in misery might have resigned himself to his fate, but she was determined to go down with a fight.

Pettigrew was oblivious to the drama taking place inside his collecting jar. Sylph interactions did not interest him. He had never been one of those wizards fascinated by magical creatures, even to the point of being willing to grant them their own sovereignty. What was the use of being human and a wizard, if not to rule over lesser creatures? Sylphs were a natural resource, meant to be consumed. Why else did spells exist that required things such as their tongues or wings?

Up ahead, he saw the border to Faerie. It gave him pause. The one wizard who dwelled in Faerie was jealous of his tenure there and killed other wizards, draining them of their power to add to his own. Pettigrew was not a particularly powerful wizard, preferring subtlety to brute force.

But he knew things could be found on Faerie's borders that could not be found anywhere else. Forces acted there. Plants never seen before grew for a day, and then withered and vanished, never to be seen again. The birds that flickered through the trees there had learned to speak human words, and they sang songs that told all of the secrets of this world and the next, if only one had time enough to stand and listen to their song's entirety.

So he edged closer, thinking to himself that Faerie was a wide realm, after all, and that there was little to no chance that his rival would actually be there, at the same spot overlooking the wide lawns and a copse of black-barked trees.

As he huffed and puffed his way up the hill, he sent his thoughts out before him, like a catfish's whiskers, searching for danger in the air.

It was thus that he came across the toad's aura, which shone on the psychic plane. It glimmered like netting around some phosphorescent fish drawn from the depths. Psychically, it tasted like lemon and glitter. It made Pettigrew's mouth water and his eyelids itch with anticipation. He congratulated himself on having the courage and perspicacity to visit Faerie's borders, despite the dangers.

He felt through the underbrush for what he knew must be lurking there. He hadn't expected it to take the shape of a toad, but he was quick enough, once he recognized it, to snatch the toad up and pop her in another jar. He capped it and decided to search to see what else he might find.

Pettigrew's collecting jars were of his own design. Each had a hook set in the metal lid, by which he could fasten them to a belt. He did this now, and Peony stared in wonder and terror at the toad's distorted image, only an inch or so away from her face. To Peony, the toad's pebbled, grainy skin and great golden eyes blinking at her seemed menacing and full of further danger. She retreated to the other side of the jar.

The toad was bemused to find herself in this odd, new place, and irritated that she had been pulled away from her schemes of fireflies and nightingales and orchestration. She was not clear what had happened, because living on the border of Faerie, she had encountered a wizard only once before. She was not afraid, but she was annoyed. The sunlight through the glass walls dried out her skin. Pettigrew had not thought to line his jars with grass or earth, since he did not care much about their inhabitants' well-being. Quite to the contrary.

He was hunting through a drift of leaves, having spotted an oddly colored mushroom, its gills the sullen purple of a bruise. The jars clinked and clattered together. Alaric held his hands to his ears and moaned that the din would kill him long before the wizard did.

Peony gesticulated through the glass, trying now to catch the toad's attention. Together they might be able to work out some plan of escape. In any case, the toad looked like a more helpful companion than Alaric. But try as she might, the toad simply blinked at her as though contemplating some insect that it had found inedible.

"Hateful thing," Peony said at last, and let herself slide down the glass to bump shoulders with Alaric. At some other time, she might have enjoyed the proximity, since he was both young and handsome, but right now it felt as though nothing could cheer her.

Meanwhile, the toad was chewing things over in her ruminative way. She didn't know why the wizard had picked her up, but a naturally cynical nature assured her that it certainly was not for any purpose that she would like.

She licked the glass in order to find out more about it. Across the way, the two sylphs shrieked in horror at the sight of that long tongue, but she ignored their complaints. Inside her head, the jewel revolved, presenting possibilities and permutations of the future, most of them dismal. The glass puzzled her, air that had hardened and chilled to impenetrability. She croaked.

Pettigrew was picking through mushrooms, sorting them into a collecting bag. At the resounding croak, he said "Shhhh."

This had no effect on the toad, who continued her plaint.

"Shhh!" the wizard exclaimed again. He didn't want to kill the toad until he had examined her, for he knew from experience that sometimes magical phenomena depended on a creature's being alive. He looked around for something to stuff into the jar and muffle the toad, and finally dumped his mushrooms in with her, swearing under his breath. He was only a minor wizard, and he would not survive a showdown with the wizard of Faerie.

As the mushrooms tumbled down around her, the toad attempted a jump that would take her out of the jar, but she only hit her head on the glass. She subsided and studied the sylphs. They resembled particularly fat dragonflies, and she was growing a little hungry by now. She hunted through the mushroom bits and found a few stray grubs, which the horrified sylphs watched her eat.

"He's going to feed us to that ... thing!" Alaric exclaimed.

"Or that thing to us," Peony mused. Her sense of absurdity was lost on Alaric. "Look," she said, "we have to get out of here."

But Alaric had lapsed into stupefied depression. Peony stared at the toad.

The toad stared back. It was learning all sorts of things in its contemplation, and it was curious about these talking dragonflies.

Much could have been solved at this point had the toad acquired the power of speech along with thought. But alas, it had not.

———•

When Pettigrew finally skulked away from the forest, casting many glances over his shoulder lest someone be sneaking up on him to end his encroachment, he returned home and to his study.

He placed the jar with the sylphs high on a shelf, figuring that they would keep while he absorbed himself in his new curiosity. Taking up the toad, he put it in the bottom of a large metal box, its sides too high for the toad to jump out of, and furnished it with handfuls of grass and a small bowl of water.

The toad explored its surroundings while Pettigrew attempted to discover what, exactly, he had caught. Unlike the toad, he could not sense the jewel, only the odd jumble of thoughts that it caused in the toad's mind.

"Perhaps it is some sort of crossbreed," he thought. "Some magical reptile in its ancestry." He measured the creature and recorded its dimensions in a small red-bound notebook. After that, he went to fetch his tea. He was a man who loved his comforts, and had enspelled his kitchen to produce a pot of tea and several crumpets each afternoon, and rarely missed collecting the china plate on which the food was presented.

Peony examined what she could of the room whose shelf they sat on. It was cluttered but well-lit, stacked with books and bell jars and small stuffed animals. She nearly shrieked aloud when she realized that close at hand, a stuffed sylph stared at them with despairing eyes.

Pettigrew took taxidermy as a hobby. He prided himself on presenting his specimens in tableaux depicting their natural habitat.

The stuffed sylph was poised, through a clever arrangement of wires, above a bouquet of silk daisies and laburnum. It did not look entirely natural in the angle of its wings, and to Peony that only increased the horror of its appearance. She wondered if the wizard planned to stuff them, and if so, what sort of flowers he had planned for them. She hoped that it was roses. She liked roses.

The edge of the shelf lay inches away. If she pushed hard enough, perhaps with Alaric assisting her, could they rock the jar and make it fall? She shoved experimentally against the glass. Yes, she decided, she would need Alaric's help, slight though it might be.

The toad, watching the sylph's performance, did not think much of it. She had decided that the wizard had selected her because of some great work, in which her highly individual nature was required. She was pleased and flattered by this conclusion (who wouldn't be?) but she was not sure what part she was meant to play, and still had reservations.

She was also acquiring the concept of language, from hearing the sylphs talk back and forth, and Pettigrew's mumblings to himself, and her own need to communicate with something other than insects and birds.

She was a vain creature, but not to the point of foolishness.

Pettigrew came into the study with a tray on which a brown-glazed teapot steamed, accompanied by a white mug thick to the point of unbreakability. This mug had accompanied Pettigrew through wizard's college, and post-college, and early years, up to this point, where he might be reckoned middle-aged in the terms of wizards, or early middle-aged, still unlearned in some areas and with a hint of brashness about him that was fading into caution.

He dreamed of a great discovery. Either a spell that he could horde throughout his lifetime, teaching only to a favored few, who would in turn propagate it and his name throughout the ages. What form this might take, he was not sure. Pettigrew's Potent Philter or Puissant Potion were two he had considered.

Or the other, which was to realize a Truth. While wizards generally kept their discoveries to themselves, there were some spells that all knew, the building blocks of magic, so to speak, as well as some that were simply so useful or basic that they had become common, like Lope's Infinite Step or Ripley's Refreshment, which produced a glass of cool water and a random piece of fruit. There were things to be learned by taking such spells apart and studying the basic Laws that lay at their roots. There were Truths, axioms of magical practices that would be studied for centuries to come by apprentices who might build on and refine such work.

He was not sure what would come out of his study of the toad, whether it was more likely to be one than the other, but his hopes were high. There was something about the toad's aura, the flux of thoughts in its eyes, something about the way it felt, so strong and alluring that Pettigrew, who had never played a hunch in all his life, would have bet that life that the toad would yield something both amazing and career-advancing.

He put aside all thought of his pearl of prophecy. It would keep; the sylphs were capable of living for at least a week in their jar, longer if he kept them supplied with water and fresh flowers.

He considered the toad, rolling a pithing needle back and forth between his fingers. He laid the tool back in the jar of murky blue fluid that had contained it, and shook off the flecks of liquid accumulated on his fingertips. They sprayed outwards.

One landed on the surface of Peony's jar, as sudden as a snake striking. She gasped and backed away from the glass before advancing again to peer through it. Seen through the droplet, the study was blue and charcoal chiaroscuro, and the type on the backs of the leather bound books wavered like daddy long legs, unintelligible even if Peony had been able to read.

Pettigrew peered down at the toad while the toad stared up at him. From Peony's vantage point, it seemed as though they goggled at each other, bulge-eyed as certain goldfish, puff-cheeked and plump. She wondered what the wizard saw in the toad, because it seemed a monster to her.

She turned to Alaric. "If we wait until the wizard is gone," she said, "We could work together to topple the jar, breaking it, and escape out that far window."

"Are you insane? We'll be smashed to bits!" Alaric said. He cradled his arm and moaned. Then he eyed her. "You could come over and make it all better," he said throatily.

Peony did not find him half as attractive as she might have under different circumstances. She sighed and turned her regard back to the toad and the wizard.

Pettigrew squatted down, ignoring the creaking in his knees. He said to the toad in the wizards' tongue, which is as close to pure language as anything can come, and which is spoken by demons, elementals, and angels alike, "What is your name?"

The toad regarded him and blinked her eyes, one slow blink, catlike in its length and disregard.

He frowned. "Can you not speak?" He snapped his fingers and went to his shelves, searching through racks of vials. He pulled out one that roiled with dark purple, put it back, and took out another that gleamed green, an alarming foxfire shade, which might have illuminated the room had it been darker.

Setting it down, he went to the shelf where the sylphs' jar sat. Peony fluttered against the side in alarm while Alaric curled whimpering on the bottom. Pettigrew's fingers hesitated over Peony, then reached for Alaric. She tried to follow him out of the jar, but the lid slammed down before she could escape. Pettigrew had worked with sylphs a thousand times before. They were ingredients to a number of useful spells.

26

Alaric dangled unresisting between two fingers. Pettigrew reached for a needle-tipped syringe in the blue liquid.

"Fight!" Peony shouted. She beat her fists against the glass and screamed until she was hoarse. The toad listened from its metal box and croaked as though distressed.

The other sylph hung, eyes glazed and fixed on some internal landscape.

When the wizard inserted the needle, Alaric twitched as though stung by one of the fierce wasps that live on lizards and small birds in the desert.

Peony had to look away.

When she glanced back, she could see Alaric deflating, like a balloon being drained, skin folding inward in protest against absence, as Pettigrew drew the syringe's plunger back.

He shook the wisp of Alaric from the tip. It drifted like a dry leaf to the floor. Pettigrew unstoppered the vial and added several drops of vital fluid from the syringe. An herbal scent came from it, clean and strong as mountain air, smelling of yarrow and pine and coriander. In the jar, Peony sniffed and felt her heart lift despite the horror. Her jaws and tongue felt strange, tingled as though kissed by magic.

The toad felt something in her head other than the jewel. The new thing nudged itself around the jewel, which felt newly reformed as she thought of it in terms of words: glittering and faceted and splendid. It made her even vainer, to think that such amazing things resided in her head. She opened her mouth and croaked out "I!"

"I?" the wizard said, nonplussed.

The toad continued to croak, lost in a solipsistic reverie, contemplating something that had been lost on it up till that point, the idea of a word that communicated its existence: "I. I. I."

The wizard replied, "You?"

The toad paused, trying to introduce this new concept, which seemed at cross-purposes with the idea it was currently celebrating. It said, more doubtfully, "I. I. I?"

"Indeed," Pettigrew said. He returned to the desk and ate his crumpet, staring at the toad.

The chime beside the door sounded, and he started from his reverie, leaving the study in a scuttle of robes and rustle of papers.

The visitor turned out to be a pretty village maiden, come seeking advice on elixirs to preserve the dewy freshness of her skin. Pettigrew swelled as much as the toad, taking the liberty of stroking her cheek with a reverent forefinger as she fluttered her eyelashes at him.

Back in the study, Peony rocked back and forth on the shelf, alternating runs at the glass jar with fits of sobbing.

When evening crept over the garden outside, the wizard insisted on seeing the maiden home, and stayed to drink a glass of brandy with her father, who fancied himself a country philosopher, even though his most determined resistance to any of the wizard's arguments was to challenge him to define his terms and then to say, in a tone simultaneously mysterious and awed, as though at his daring in plumbing such depths, "It always boils down to where you draw the line, don't it?"

Replenished by brandy and the goodwife's frumenty pudding, which held even more brandy in its gelid depths, Pettigrew staggered home and fell into bed without a further thought of his captives in the study, collapsing still dressed in his outer garb.

⌐——•••—◖

Down in the study, Peony had finally given way to despair. Around her were scattered the silvery leavings of her tears, which Pettigrew would no doubt be delighted to discover, for they were integral in several esoteric spells he had always meant to try.

The toad had given up croaking. Some quality of the echoes to her

"I. I." had put her off, as though chastened by some reprimand. She wondered why the wizard had not returned, for surely he could have no greater fascination to pull his attention from the phenomenon that was herself.

Moonlight drifted in through the windows. The curtains were dusty lace, inherited from Pettigrew's landlady, who had initially put them up in order to achieve a genteel atmosphere. Later, giving up on the gentle-mannered gentry she had hoped to attract, she resigned herself to the wizard, who at least was a steady source of income and unlikely to relocate, particularly given the amount of clutter he had accumulated in the intervening years.

The lace, a floral pattern, interrupted and reinterpreted the light, cast it in ornate shadows across the worn carpeting. The light, crossing and recrossing, seemed to shudder at intervals, as though it were a spider web, plucked by an exploratory spider's leg. It pulsed, taking on a rhythm reminiscent of a human heartbeat.

As it beat, moment by moment, it took on more solidity. At length, that solidness translated itself into something, like a picture coming into focus to show that an integral element of its landscape was, in fact, something quite different. It revealed a hawklike face, a scalp that quill-like tufts of white hair rode, spiky and owl-natured.

Peony stared downward, mouth agape and tears forgotten. The toad, trapped in its zinc box, could see nothing, but she inflated her throat and hroomed out a vast, melodic note that quickened Peony's breath as though it had electrified the air.

"Ssssh," the man who had coalesced there said. It was said quietly, offhandedly, but the toad felt bands of steel clamp around her head until she could make no sound at all. Peony pressed the heels of her hands against the glass and hoped. She didn't know who this was, but she could tell that he was no friend of Pettigrew's.

He or she. For as the figure moved around the study, it sometimes seemed like a slight, aged man, and other times like a slim woman whose age could not be told, but whose shape was that of someone just entering puberty. Sometimes it seemed that the figure's fine, cornsilk hair fell to her ankles; other times it seemed to fall only to his neck, loose and flowing as river waves.

Whoever it was, it was clear that they were new to this room. They examined it with great interest, running a finger along the spines of the books and reading the titles, fingering the leaves of the desiccated aspidistra in the corner, paging through the notes on the desk. At the last, it chuckled and cackled to itself, as though amused.

When it peered up at Peony's jar, his face (for it seemed a he at the moment) was clearer. It was not an entirely human face, but one that might have begun as human and become distorted and changed by other forces. He took the jar down and unscrewed the lid.

Perhaps he was touched by the sylph's plight, but it seemed more likely that he was after the trove of tears Peony had left, scattered like mouse droppings along the bottom of the jar, for once the sylph had fluttered out, he collected these drops and tucked them in her pocket and turned back to the box that held the toad.

The toad stared up at her, her great golden eyes shining like coins in the moonlight, and would have said something, but the steel bands still held her tongue.

"Little bait," the interloper whispered. "Little trap, little trick, are you ready to go home?"

"I," the toad would have said, but it couldn't speak. The figure seemed to understand though, for it leaned forward and plucked the toad from the bottom of the box. Its fingers were cool and sure and sinewy.

Up above, Pettigrew had tried to ignore the noises from his study. When you experiment with living creatures, you should expect noise, and he had grown accustomed to the toad's booming "I." But it had fallen quiet and been replaced by other noises, noises that seemed more alarming: a distinct rustling for one, as though papers were being scattered by a breeze and then a sound that had reminded him of laughter.

He remained in bed. The linens were warm, and like most wizards, he knew what really could be lurking beneath the bed, and was careful with his toes accordingly. But the noise didn't die down, and it provoked all sorts of visions in his head: a creature escaped from a collecting jar was wreaking havoc in revenge for its imprisonment; a misplaced curse had emerged from its den below the armchair and was changing all his experiments; magic had seeped into some commonplace household object, now knocking about in a misdirected effort to fulfill its purpose.

Then he thought, "What if it's a thief?"

He knew that was unlikely. Thieves avoid wizards, for the same reason that they avoid houses with very large dogs. They do not want to get hurt. But on occasion, a thief might be employed by some rival wizard, and dispatched with the appropriate protective spells, in order to take some treasure or bit of useful research.

Had someone discovered what he had found? Did they know something about the toad and were anxious to get it back before he unfolded its secrets? He jumped from bed and flung on his dressing gown. The toad might represent his only chance at fame. It could not be lost.

When he entered his study, he was horrified to see the figure, sorting through a rack of vials.

"Stop!" Pettigrew shouted. He drew himself up to his fullest height. "Stop or face a wizard's wrath!"

"But you invited me, brother," came a silken, epicene voice. "At least you brought my creature in, and was that not meant as invitation? I took it as such."

Pettigrew's eyes flitted to the jar that was no longer sylph-filled.

Peony, seeing no way out the closed window, had taken to a higher shelf and was awaiting any opportunity to make for the outside.

"Sylphs are a pence a dozen," he scoffed. "Tricky to take, but easily replaced. You came chasing one of those?"

"Ah, no," the figure said, and now Pettigrew saw that she was a woman, and a beautiful one. "You took my toad."

He was flustered and bewildered. To have entered his cottage, she must have some magic about her. Was she a rival wizard? But she was so beautiful! He stammered something out and stepped forward. When her lips met his in a kiss that was sweet as ice-wine and as fiery as a red-hot coal, he lost himself in it.

The toad could not see what was going on, but to the horrified sylph it was clear. Pettigrew shriveled as he clung to the other's lips, deflated as though, minim by minim, his fluids were being drawn away. His features shrank inwards, he grew wrinkled as a raisin, until he was only a leathery scrap. The woman plucked it from her lips and dropped it to the floor.

Now she flickered from male to female and back again as though uncaring of gender, as though it were some outside force, like wind or rain. She picked up the toad and tucked it in her pocket. She was pleased with herself. It had been a clever ruse, for it was hard to lure wizards to the boundaries of Faerie, where she might feed upon them while eliminating any threat they might form in the future. She hummed to herself, and there were echoes in her voice of the toad's thoughts and words.

She opened the window, and the sylph darted out, swift as a fleeing cat and just as careful to stay out of reach. He smiled a little as he watched Peony go, and touched the trove of tears in his pocket. It had been a good day, and so she left.

As she walked, she talked to the toad, and the toad replied, and they schemed all the way home, of how to coordinate the fireflies.

Afternotes

When I was a child, I spent summers on my grandparents' ranch in Kansas, and one of the things I remember most vividly about those summers were the toads. As the sun set, they'd begin stirring, hopping around through the long grass, and I and whatever other kids were around (usually my brother and some cousins) would chase and catch them, a variety of sizes ranging from the size of a small platter to a thumbnail. We kept them in an old bathtub behind the garage, where we had set up a palatial toad compound.

I remember the beauty of their eyes, which were golden and textured like the intricate folds you see when you look closely at Damascus steel, and the contrast with their dusty, warty skin. They've always fascinated me.

I'm not alone in that; alchemists believed that toads had a magic stone in their heads that acted as an antidote to poison and the genesis of this story was encountering the passage about that belief that is quoted near the story's beginning. I wrote the beginning and then kept going to see where the story would take me. Pettigrew emerged, along with the hapless sylphs he had already collected, and then the eponymous fairy that comes to collect Pettigrew.

The image where the fairy drains Pettigrew was inspired by a moment in Annie Dillard's Pilgrim at Tinker Creek *in which the narrator encounters a frog in the process of being killed by an insect. I read it around the age of twelve and it's always stuck with me.*

PIPPA'S SMILES

MARCUS HADN'T THOUGHT marriage would be like this after three months. He had expected to love her, but he hadn't thought she would love him so much, that she would follow him from counter to till in his tiny shop where he sold souvenirs and curiosities: stuffed mermaids, filagree jars, and great shark jaws set with more teeth than a carved comb.

Was it that he was all the treasure that Pippa had? Would her need diminish with time, as she felt more secure?

His mother had wanted him to marry Gerta the innkeeper's daughter, who could run a household with easy efficiency, could scald a hog or bleach linen, and who had wide hips that could bear a score of infants. His father had wanted him to marry Lisa the banker's daughter, who came with a hefty dowry and land of her own, and who had wide hips that could bear two score infants. Maybe more.

But he had seen narrow-hipped Pippa the day she'd arrived in the seaport town of Spume, in the pinnace that had rescued all that remained of a capsized galleon: Pippa in her drenched skirts and two sailors, one with a scar across his eye and the other a rangy man with only one hand who claimed that a kraken had eaten the other.

The sailors had moved on quickly, taken other ships, but Pippa had stayed behind when Marcus had asked her to become his bride, enchanted by her small, brown-skinned form, her dandelion fluff of hair, her mismatched eyes, one sea foam green, the other as blue as summer sky, the tiny smile that she only let escape in moments of true delight, and which she kept clutched inside at all other times.

She loved him too. At night, she touched him, laying her hand along his back, to make sure he wasn't dead. They were both light sleepers. Wakened by some outside sound—the last of the late night drunkards stumbling home from the tavern in the next street, the cobblestone clatter of a cart, or the apothecary's dog barking at some imagined monster—they would both lie there for a moment. And then Pippa would turn over and lay her hand on his back or side, feeling for his warmth, and then, reassured, would go back to sleep.

It was because she feared losing him, he knew. It wasn't easy but he hadn't expected marriage to be easy. He knew he was a man set in his own ways. His own mother said, "Marcus was a grown man before he was ever a boy." He had followed a different path than his farmer father, had been lured to become a shopkeeper, though not just any shopkeeper. He did not sell merchants' doings, but the odd things sailors brought from other shores, which had fascinated him since he was a boy, and had first seen a gleam of porcelain luck-beads in a traveler's palm, offered for a bag of apples.

To Pippa, he was a greater treasure than anything in the shop. She'd sit watching him as he dusted, telling her each item's name and making her repeat it to him in her soft, slurry accent. He taught her names of spices that were rarely used in local cooking and the adjective for each historical dynasty's antiques, and left her to pick up the simpler things on her own, like "salt" and "water" and "bread."

She rarely left his side in the shop, but would sit there, tatting lace and watching him with those bright eyes. Sometimes she was so pretty he could not help but come and kiss her, and then she would give him a little smile, brighter than any coin. It worried him that she gave only him those smiles. In front of his parents, he'd coax and joke, hoping to elicit one, hoping that she'd show them why he loved her so, but she hoarded them and would only spend them when they were alone together.

Alone together, and never alone, truly alone, by himself. She was always there. He felt suffocated. He grew impatient. He tried to hide, to catch a breath to himself. But she followed him, bright-eyed and curious, even in the most private moments. He wondered what she saw when she looked at him, what her eyes saw, to make her love him so.

It was too much. It was all together too much.

———————

And so he waited until he saw her drinking the willowbark tea that she took to relieve the ache of her courses. That way he knew she was not with child, for he didn't want to leave her that way. He made love to her that night despite her protest, for he did want to remember her that way, with a wondering smile on her face. And he did not look back in the morning, because he didn't want to remember her that way, bewildered and crying, clutching the key to the shop in her hand.

He took a backpack of clothes and a stout walking stick and a purseful of coins he'd meant to use to buy pearls when Jacobo, a favorite sailor, passed through again. And he went out into the world to escape the love that weighed on him so unexpectedly. His mother had not loved his father so, although they were the best of friends. He had thought that was how his own marriage would be patterned, that it would not come to resemble a yoke around his neck.

He had walked for a month and a day, and seen more wonders

than he could count, when he came to a pool beside the road where a waterfall spilled out on great green boulders, which churned the surface into milky foam. He saw naiads splashing in the water, and they waved to him with long, languid arms, their blue hair spilling out around them like weeds, and sang to him, a sweet and unknown song whose meaning he could only guess at.

He had meant to remain true to his wife, for he would not have it said he had been fickle and left her for another woman. But the song called him, and he laid his pack and staff down beside the pool (and hid his purse underneath a stone, for he was a prudent man), and dove in.

But there the women seemed not to notice his presence. He swam down, down in the water and there on the pool's floor he saw skeletons, skulls gaping up at him and grinning at the joke that he might join them. He felt hair drifting around his ankles, his wrists, soft and fine but strong as rope. He panicked and swam upwards despite their pull, and when he broke the surface he clambered gasping onto the bank, blue strands still clinging to his ankles.

The naiads shrugged and combed each other's hair as he walked away. Far below their song, the skulls continued grinning.

⌐·····◑

The road wore him down. It cracked his heels and sifted dust into the seams of his clothing, so he could not wash it out, no matter how he tried. He began to think longing thoughts of his shop, of Pippa leaving his side long enough to make him tea and bring it to him, hot and sweet as he preferred it. He thought of the lace she made and how many yards she must have finished in his absence.

He wondered if Jacobo had brought the pearls he promised and if Pippa had reluctantly turned him away, or whether she had managed to scrape together enough coin to buy them. They would have proved a good investment, because merchants' wives loved pearls, and claimed them tokens of true love.

He wondered why he never thought of Lisa or Marta when remembering that vanished life. Only Pippa. And even now, the thoughts made him feel that he was being smothered—or drowned—overwhelmed with the love that she no doubt still held, hoping he would come back.

He thought he would, when he was done walking. But he'd teach her to be independent, to spend time without him. He'd make her go to his mother and learn to sew, learn to sit in the circle of women and natter as happily as they did, stitching away on their husbands' clothes.

Fog overtook the road one day and he walked in silence, thinking that he heard sounds, footsteps somewhere in the white darkness, accompanying him. He saw faces in the mist, mostly Pippa's face: frowning, yearning, wanting. Never smiling. He thought he heard a scrap of song that took him off the road, and he blundered through the forest, wondering if the wood-wives would come to him, try to make him stay there with them. That was how they reproduced, catching travelers and keeping them, he knew.

He kept watching for a trunk to split, a green-skinned woman emerge to claim him. He was young and strong, and few men walked in the woods here. They must have summoned the fog to snare him, were waiting for him in the cloudy air, waiting for him to discover their hiding place. Surely word had gone out the minute he stepped into their forest: a man, walking, the prize they spent their lives waiting for, arrived at last.

But no trees spoke to him, no arms reached for him, and when he stumbled into daylight, he found himself on the edge of the forest, and back on the road again.

He had walked for another month and a day when he saw the castle far ahead. It sat on a mountaintop, and the road spiraled up to meet its gates. When he knocked there, a guard opened the gate, dressed in gilt and lilac armor, asking what he wanted.

"Whose castle is this?" Marcus asked.

"The Sorceress Alyx," the guard said.

It all made sense now. She had magically summoned him, that was why he had left his wife and come to her. She had glimpsed him, in a scrying mirror or crystal ball, and decided that he would be hers. He would rule in the castle by her side, and see to setting things right. Women had little idea how to govern, and she had probably realized she needed help.

But when Marcus said he had come to see the Sorceress, the guard only laughed, although not in an unkindly way, and said that Marcus might sleep that night in the kitchens, warm and fed, but that the Sorceress held no audiences.

The soup was good and thick, and there were bits of chicken with it, and slices of well-crusted bread, and even a tankard of cider to wash it all down. Full-bellied, Marcus lay down upon the cot he'd been given, but could not sleep.

At least, he dreamed he could not sleep. He would stir, and wait for Pippa's touch on his back, and the little reassured sound she made when she felt him breath. At length he went wandering through the castle, slipping through the hallways unnoticed, for the guards were outside, protecting the castle from those who would enter unlawfully.

He passed tapestries woven of bone and iron, and wonderful things that he would have liked to sell in his shop: hourglasses that told when sunset would occur, and great narwhal horns, and a clockwork woman who told fortunes when you put a coin in her nose. He gave her a coin, and the little pasteboard ticket he received in return said, "She would have waited forever."

He smiled at this assurance and wondered what Pippa was doing, right then. Surely she was sleeping, dreaming of him dreaming of her. Or did the card speak of the Sorceress, and her devotion to him, so strong that she would have waited forever, had he not responded to her call?

He went up a winding staircase and found himself in the sorceress's chamber. She sat there on a high-backed chair, looking out over the land, her golden hair about her like a curtain. He told her he had come, and expected her to turn and smile and greet him, but she ignored him, still looking out the window. He frowned at this. He was the hero of this dream, and she was meant to turn and smile at him.

He thought, "Perhaps she cannot hear me, or perhaps she is shy and wishes me to initiate things." Going to her, he leaned and said in her ear, "I have never kissed a sorceress."

She pushed a button and he was pulled from the room by soldiers. He realized that he was only a nuisance, like a fly buzzing, for she had shown no rancor on her face, only impatience. As though he was interrupting very important business. As they took him away, he saw her lean forward towards the window again, her face intent. She had already forgotten him.

He had been wrong. She was not waiting for him, or any man.

He thought they might imprison him, deep below the castle. But instead them simply put him out the gate, and even gave him back his stick and pack, and a bundle of bread and cheese. He felt small and unimportant, and above all, impatient as he went back down the mountainside. He would return, and Pippa would give him smiles again, and this time he would teach her better and she would learn when he wanted her to stare at him and when he wanted her to leave him alone.

He had walked very far, and it was almost a year before he saw the walls of the seaport again. They glimmered in the sunlight, for the day was fair and bright, as though everything rejoiced to see him returned, to see him back in his proper place. He half ran down the street, past familiar faces that looked startled to see him, and sometimes filled with another emotion that he thought must be envy, that he had gone so far, was so well traveled now, and was returning to his wife, who had no doubt kept things well till his return, and would give him the keys along with another purse of coins, even fatter than the one he had left with.

But when he came to the window of his shop, he looked in. There was Pippa, but not as he expected. She held a baby in her arms and he thought with great regret that he had erred that last night, that he had left her with child despite his efforts. He felt a twinge of guilt and thought, "I'll make it up to her, though." He set his hand to the door knob and then he saw through the cloudy glass, amid the strings of glass balls that are said to hold the souls of witches, illuminated by a lantern carved of ivory and fish bones, amid trinkets and trivialities, the lace upon her shoulders and Jacobo's pearls gleaming around her throat, and Jacobo's arm around her waist, and he realized then, bile biting in his throat, that she would never spend her smiles on him again.

Afternotes

Sometimes gloriously, wonderously, inexplicably—and sadly, somewhat rarely—I wake up with a story in my head and all I have to do is write it down. This was the case with "Pippa's Smiles."

As I wrote the story and the three encounters that Marcus has along the way, I wanted the encounters to be with symbols of femininity that weren't really there to act as counterfoils to the protagonist, but who had their own existence and agendas to pursue, first the naiads, then the wood-wives, and finally the sorceress Alyx. Marcus makes the mistake of thinking that he is the center of the story, and forgets that everyone is the center of their own narrative, and this costs him something that he doesn't really value till it is gone.

I don't believe this one is a Tabat story. It seems to exist in a world that's a bit more of an archetypal fairytale existence.

KARALUVIAN FALE

"ALLOW ME TO PAY FOR YOUR DRINK, LADY Kara," Leksander Oash drawled. "I know Fale has trouble at time with the bills." Coins rang on the dust-gritted tavern table as the young nobleman stood with an unpleasant smile, staring at the woman a few tables away.

Behind him, his half-brother Alge guffawed, and one of the courtesans with the men tittered, a sound as brittle and false as the gilt bangles adorning her olive-skinned limbs. Her nails were tinted to match the bracelets and her dark eyes were kohl-shaded to give her the appearance of a midnight rendezvous even now at midday. The other courtesan held her fingers over her mouth, making it unclear whether she was amused, shocked, or sympathetic.

Karaluvian Fale knew she'd think of a thousand witty things to say as soon as Leksander and Alge exited through the hanging bead curtain of the inn's entrance. She stared at her friend and servant Ionna's sympathetic but speechless face across the table and finally, desperately, erected the public persona that stood her in good stead on these occasions.

"Dear Lord Oash," she trilled, half-turning, pitching her voice to an annoyingly high pitch and letting her lavender bangs fall over guileless eyes. It was her "thinking of kittens" expression. "How kind of you! It's so rare to see an Oash paying a bill. Shall I direct my house to take this as a declaration of interest?"

Leksander Oash had been resisting matchmaking for several decades now. His father had sired a fine crop of bastards, such as Alge, and Leksander devoted himself to building a household from them rather than starting a family. Kara was amused rather than offended at the grimace of distaste crossing his face.

"Given the swift workings of the Allanak rumor mill, let me quash that one straight out," Leksander said with grim satisfaction. "The day Oash marries into Fale, both moons will fall from the sky."

"See, we have so much in common already," she said in the most dulcet of tones, so sweet it made her teeth want to leap out of her mouth. She was rewarded with the faintest flush of anger, perhaps embarrassment, on his aquiline face. He turned and left in a clatter of beads, his sibling and women trailing after him.

"Well," Kara said, looking at the handful of coins on the other table. "At least I'm sure we can pay now. Although I note he neither paid for you nor included a tip. Trust Oash to pinchpurse even on their public insults."

"He's getting worse," Ionna said. "Had Gracchus been here, he wouldn't have dared. If knowledge is too public about Fale's lack of coin, will the Highlord allow the House to continue to stand?"

"There's a good chance he might not," Kara said, "and remember … it's Beneficence Gracchus. Now that he's been elevated in office, we must be less informal with him." She smiled tightly at her friend. Around them, the clatter and gossip of the Inn, fallen to silence at the Oash's words, had renewed itself to an even livelier hubbub. "You might do well if you talked to Oash about them hiring you now, rather than wait for later. If they thought you'd be of help in bringing us down, they'd pay you better than I do."

Ionna touched her fingertips to the back of Kara's hand with an affectionate look. "Never, Kara. Who plucked me from the streets and taught me to read and write—not to mention how to eat a honied cochra! Who created the official position of a Whatsit for me?"

"Well, I had long needed a Whatsit, to remember things for me," Kara rejoined.

Ionna tilted her head and touched her hair. "Who else was clever enough to dye my hair green so she and I together display the House colors?"

"Is that clever or simply mad?" Kara said.

"A little of both."

Kara could not help but laugh. "Very well. Run along ahead of me, and make sure that the loaves are taken from the oven in time. My heel is broken and I must walk a little slower, but I will catch up with you at the estate."

"Very well, m'lady."

———

Swirls of fine red dust flowed like water over the cobblestones of the street. An eerie hiss rose from all sides: the sound of the grains sprayed by the wind against the obdurate stone buildings.

The airborne sand tinted distances like mist, but she knew the red robe coming towards her. He was a burly man, broad-shouldered, bristle-bearded, with a scowl that changed into a smile as he saw her.

"Lady Kara," the Beneficence said, extending an arm. "Walk with me?"

Gracchus Kasix was a stout-shouldered, burly man, with a beard that bristled as fiercely as his temper's reputation. The red robes of his rank that swirled around him were made of expensive northern silk, and around his neck was a gleam of gold, rare anywhere in Zalanthas. Red dust ran like blood in the folds of his heavy robes.

She fluttered a hand at him before slipping it through his arm. Her voice pitched itself up slightly; she'd found people more likely to take her for a featherhead that way. "Will you walk slowly? I have broken my heel."

"You are poor at being a noble, Kara," he said slyly.

"I beg your pardon?"

He arranged her hand on his arm. "I mean that you spare servants where others would not. But I am glad I ran into you. It has been at least two days since I had anyone chattering nonsense in my ear."

She smiled lightly as she walked beside him. "I had dispatched Ionna to look out from the southern edge of the city to judge the weather because I was contemplating a trip down to Red Storm to see the sunset over the silt flats."

He snorted. "A trip to buy smoke, you mean. The Highlord forbid the Fales go without their illegal luxuries."

"I don't do that sort of thing."

"Then you are surely a changeling, Lady Kara, for I have never met a Fale who turned down intoxicants."

"No," she said. "But smoke makes you something other than you are, and I would hate to lose myself. Imagine, what if I became someone else, and then I met my old self! We would quarrel over who got to walk with you." She gave him a look through her lashes.

"I hear Leksander gave you trouble earlier."

"Oh, was that what that was? I thought he was trying to court me."

Gracchus snorted out a laugh. The enmity between Fale and Oash had lasted for decades.

"May I come and see you tomorrow, when the sun is down?"

"You are always welcome, you know that," she said, smiling at him. "We will steal little cakes from the kitchen, and Ionna will bring us mint-water and we will admire the last of the sunset over Allanak."

"So you will postpone your trip to Red Storm?"

"For you, of course."

They walked along the sun-laden street in companionable silence. After two blocks, Gracchus cleared his throat.

"I saw your brother this morning, looking very fine in new fighting gear."

Her foot wavered sideways on the broken heel and her lips thinned before she found a smile. "Is that so. I rarely keep track of the fads he follows."

Gracchus looked at her sideways, the white of his eye rolling, his jaw set in amusement. "I mention it only because his tailor was trailing him about, importuning that his bill be paid."

They walked for another few blocks before she said, tightly, angrily, "Sometimes it feels as though you try to catch me out, Lord Kasix."

He stopped, astonished, caught her hand when she would have hurried onward. "I beg your pardon, Kara, I intended no such thing." He stared down into her eyes, shaded by pale purple bangs, holding her hands close to his chest, trapped within his own. His voice softened. "Surely you know that, pretty Kara."

"Is that you speaking, Gracchus, or the newly appointed wielder of Tektolnes' power?"

"Can't it be both?" He twined his fingers through hers, looking her in the face.

She extracted her hands nonetheless. "I need to get home. I promised Ionna I would oversee the meal."

"That seems very domestic for you, Kara. I can see you in the kitchen, singing to the fire and letting all the cakes burn and pots overboil."

She had practiced that trill of laughter. "But how will I learn to oversee banquets, pageants, and festivals without such training? A Fale must know the ins and outs of producing extravaganzas!"

"Then I will speak to you tomorrow." At the gate to the Noble's

Quarter, they paused and bowed to each other.

"Tomorrow then," Gracchus repeated.

"Tomorrow." She turned and walked away, feeling him watching her. Her ankle ached from the strain of trying to maintain an even pace, but she kept it up until she turned the corner. There she stopped and shed her shoes, relishing the coolness of the pavement underfoot and counting on her skirts to conceal her feet until she had made the short way home.

The Fale estate was on the west side of the Quarter. A few ancient hedges lined the gateway, their branches huddled inward as though to protect themselves from the constant wind. Lanterns of purple and green glass hung on either side of the main gate, made of wide slats of thornwood. No one stood at hand to shift the massive weight. The north breeze had slowed, and the sand in it murmured against the dry wood.

Kara entered instead through the smaller servants' gate and went down the dusty hallway and into the kitchen. She hummed to herself as she went.

Thadeus Fale was there, sitting at the table, hunched over expectantly. At her entrance he looked up. His sun-mottled scalp was pink and wisped with grayish hair like cobwebs, his wrinkled face set in a smile at the sight of her. Ionna had taken the loaves from the oven. They sat in a golden-crusted row, sending out their sweet scent.

"Papa, there is bread and fruit-paste in the cupboard," Kara said.

His smile turned to a frown. "That's not what I want!" he snapped. "I want honeycakes and a tandu meat roll with ginka sauce. Wake the cook! I have been calling for her for hours!"

Kara sighed. Steam wafted up underneath her knife as she sliced through the loaf's crust. Ionna entered, standing in the doorway. "There is no cook, Papa, and you are lucky that I baked this morning," she said over her shoulder. "Lunaris spent the last of the housekeeping money gambling and the stipend from the Highlord will not come for another three weeks. But I will bake cakes tonight, when it has cooled, and there will be some for you."

He blinked at her as she spread paste on the bread and handed it to him. He turned his attention to the food in his hands and after another few blinks, began to eat it.

Once Thadeus had been settled with food, Ionna followed Kara into the ballroom. The furniture sat contained in linen sheets to keep it free of red dust, fine and persistent as ash. Ionna and Kara had worked to shroud it a few months earlier, after the ball that the Fales traditionally celebrated their yearly stipend with. Officially it was called the Sand and Pearl Festival, in honor of two Fale ancestors whose story and lineage had been, like so much of the family's history, extremely complicated.

Kara flopped down on a covered lounge, sending up a dust cloud and a flutter of disturbed insects. "If Leksander pushes further, I have no way of proving his accusations of pennilessness wrong. Not that they're false in the first place. And I thought I had enough to keep us looking well afloat, up until Lunaris found where I'd hidden it. This time I don't know how we're getting out of it."

Ionna peered down at her employer and friend over the sofa back. The two women were similar in height, but Kara's hair fell in lavender lengths, while Ionna's curlier hair rippled in waves of green. Ionna's eyes seemed to combine the two shades: the right was a brilliant amethyst, the left emerald. "We could dig for treasure in the back garden."

Kara laid her head back and contemplated the dust-caked molding of the ceiling some twenty feet overhead. The three chandeliers were contained in sacks, and the red dust accumulated in rusty shadows on the yellowed folds.

"We could find you a templar to wed, one who would shower you with gems and housekeeping money."

Kara's lips thinned. Two small scorpions, midnight-carapaced, moved over the nearest chandelier's covering, and she thought she could almost hear the scratching of their legs against the cloth. Colored lights danced across her vision.

"We could ..." Ionna started again, but Kara held up a hand, gesturing for silence.

"I'm getting a headache," she said with weary patience. "Go and bring dampened towels and a basin to my room."

"Of course, my lady." Contrition was evident in the Whatsit's tone. Kara closed her eyes and listened to the slap of Ionna's bare soles against the marble floor. The wind howled outside the high arched windows that overlooked the neglected garden, and delivery carts and carriages rattled on the street.

As she passed the arched windows overlooking the courtyard there was a clash of weapons and a gleeful shout—Lunaris, showing off for his friends again. She let out a sigh, shielding her eyes from the painful sunlight with the back of her arm.

Her room was located in an otherwise deserted wing considered past repair. Through hard work and patience, Kara had reclaimed it from disrepair, sanding out gouges in the floor where an ancestor had housed her hounds, mending worm-eaten tapestries, and furnishing it with the best pieces scavenged from other rooms where storms had torn away walls or roof.

Settled in her bed, she put her head under her pillows and sighed. What to do? Fale's precarious financial state would be exposed, creditors would call in their bills, and the house and all its holdings, even sold for ten times their worth, would not be enough to satisfy those debts.

Marrying well had been a traditional means of salvation for Fales in the past, but currently there were no eligible nobles, with the exception of the loathsome Leksander Oash. No sane woman would have her equally loathsome sibling. If only she could marry a Templar! Gracchus liked her well enough, or liked the version she gave him, at any rate.

The door opened and Ionna's quick steps sounded her arrival. "I have damp towels for you, Lady Kara."

"Put them beside the bed."

The bed creaked as Ionna sat down beside her and began to rub Kara's neck. Groaning, Kara rolled her shoulders and extended her neck, feeling the touch coaxing cramped muscles open, loose.

"Kara, you don't have to carry the weight of the entire House," Ionna said.

"But who else will carry it?"

"We'll run away to Luirs and become entertainers at the Tan Muark tavern, the Silver Wheel. You'll sing and play the guitar. I'll pass the hat and badger the stingy until coins fly from their fingers on wings of shame."

"Would that I could gather coins with my music."

"Kara, I'm telling you again. You should confide in Gracchus. One of the Highlord's Beneficences would have enough coin and influence to drive off Oash."

"One, Gracchus's friendship with me is half of why I'm a target for the Oash. They can't stand the thought of a Beneficence without their collar on him. And two, he'd cast me aside quickly if he knew I was penniless. And three …" She fell silent.

"Three?" Ionna prompted.

"Three, I'm never quite sure what Gracchus wants from me."

"He likes you because you don't bow and scrape the way the rest of them do. I swear he'd ask you to marry him if he could."

"Pah. He's from House Kasix, and Kasix does nothing that is not calculated."

The next day, the wind was from the south, carrying with it evil intimations of ash, the depleted residue of magic, the spoor of sorcerers. It made the head ache and dried the eyes and lips.

Kara could hear the usual clack of blade on blade well before she rounded the corner to the Fale courtyard and its garden of statuary. Lunaris danced in the center with the captain of the Fale guards, a toad-bodied man who had embraced flab in his declining years and who was showing the effort now of sparring with his charge. Red spots mottled his cheeks, and he was bent over, concentrating on catching his breath, more intent than a night-waker who finds a ghost draining their lungs.

"At least if Lunaris drove him to pitching over, we'd be able to hire a young captain at a lower price," she thought.

Lunaris smirked at the older man, saluting him with a sweep of the wooden weapon. He turned with a practiced swirl of cape and midnight blue hair.

"Kara, how unpleasant to see you," he said, and giggled with another smirk.

"Lunaris, where did it all go?"

"All what?" He preened, flicked imaginary dust off his cape.

She eyed his snakeskin and silk outfit in horror. "You spent it on fancy clothes?"

"Of course not," he said. "I bought a sword from House Salarr as well, but it is not due to be delivered till next Abid."

His hair glittered with the iridescence of a beetle's carapace. He was just as hollow, she thought, and bit back tears. He could not help who he was.

When she and Ionna opened up her cupboards, trying to figure out how they would keep her wardrobe up to date, moths fluttered out. Kara could have wept, seeing her hopes for finery fly away on tiny parchment wings, like pamphlets of lost dreams.

She pleaded headache and went to lie down. She lay among the cluster of bright dresses marked with the meandering tracks of moth grubs and sank into misery. The House would fall. Her father would be reduced to begging outside the Traders Inn. Lunaris would no doubt be treated badly by the Oash, which was a mildly cheering thought. She didn't know what would happen to Ionna, but Kara had no right to hold her servant to her if Ionna would do better elsewhere.

The door creaked as someone opened it. "Beneficence Gracchus is here," Ionna said.

"Gods and moons." Kara pressed her hands to her face, trying to wipe away tears. "Bring me a cool cloth and then tell him I will meet him in the garden in a little while."

The ash-laden wind had died down and sand-colored bats fluttered back and forth in the last of the sun over the Quarter. Gracchus stood peering into an elderly fountain that sporadically slurped out green-colored water, his hands clasped behind his back.

"Are you looking for the ghost?" Kara said.

He turned away from the lily pads mottling the surface to look at her. "What ghost?"

"A servant was supposed to have drowned herself after being spurned by an ancestor, several generations ago. I've never seen it, though." She sighed. "It would be so interesting to see a ghost. Do you think it would appear wearing the House colors, all purple and green?"

He reached out to run the ball of his thumb along her face, as though feeling the drag of moisture there. "Kara, why have you been crying?"

"It has been a long and dreary day," she said, putting aside her customary prattle for a moment.

"That's all?" He stepped closer.

She let herself give into the urge to nestle her head along his shoulder. He felt comfortable and solid.

"There were moths," she said.

She felt the chuckle as much as heard it. "Moths."

"I won't have clothes for this season. I've spent all my budget."

He stroked her hair. "What if I said I had confiscated a wagon of Kadian silks—the driver had a pouch of smoke on him—and that you might have your pick of them?"

"Really?" She stepped back to look up at him, resting her palms on his chest. "Truly, Gracchus?"

She thought he would have kissed her then, but instead he released her, stepping back. "Yes, truly, sweet Kara. I'll have the wagon sent round in the morning, and you shall decide which bolts you want. Take enough to outfit Ionna as well. Not Lunaris, though."

They both laughed at that, but then Lunaris said from the garden entrance, "Not Lunaris what?"

His color was high and rosy, and there was a slur to his voice, a drag to his eyelids that betrayed he had been drinking.

"Lunaris, go away," she said, even as Gracchus said, "I may extend favors to your sister, but I will fund no business of yours. Are we clear on that, Lunaris Fale?"

Lunaris stepped forward, tottered, danced with a high stone pillar for balance before he recovered himself and, clutching it, said with a haughty grimace, "As though I would want your funds! I have friends, well-pocketed friends."

"If you speak of the Oash, you are riding a dangerous horse in that race," Gracchus said.

"Better the Oash than a corrupt old slug sniffing around a bony rack in hopes of table leavings!" Lunaris pointed at Kara.

"That doesn't even make sense," she said. "Lunaris, go to bed before you embarrass yourself."

"Too late for that," Gracchus murmured.

Lunaris staggered forward. "You keep your mouth off me!"

Gracchus's eyebrow twitch, Kara's involuntary laugh, were all the prompt that Lunaris needed. He swung, and Gracchus ducked below the clumsy blow. Kara gasped. Striking a Beneficence was high treason, even for a noble! She pushed herself in between them, shoved Lunaris down. He staggered back, hitting his head on the bench, and sat.

"Ionna!" Kara shouted.

Ionna appeared at the gateway. "My lady?"

Kara pointed at Lunaris. "Go and call the head of the guard and have him taken away and to bed."

After Lunaris had been hauled away by the arms by two guards, with Ionna supervising, Gracchus poured the last of the mint water into the goblet at his side and sniffed at the film of ash on its surface.

Trying to regain her equilibrium—what would Gracchus choose to do about Lunaris?—Kara began snipping old roses from the bushes surrounding the fountains.

Gracchus set his goblet down. "This is charmingly domestic again," he said. "I thought just last month you told me you thought you would become an assassin."

"I still maintain I would make an excellent one," she said. "I can move quietly, I have learned to throw a knife …"

Gracchus interjected, looking alarmed. "You have learned to throw a knife? How?"

"Through practice, how else? And Ionna gave me some tips. Look, I will show you." A knife appeared in her hand and he looked twice as alarmed.

She used the knife to cut a rose from amid a tangle of thorny leaves, then flung the blade overhanded. It landed in the old wooden statue that the Fale children used as a playmate, quivering in the triangular

55

patch that served the dummy as nose. With a grin at Gracchus, she fastened the rose in her hair.

He watched her thoughtfully. "Kara," he said. "Just when I think I have you figured out, you turn all my notions on their heads."

She simpered, while her thoughts raced. Perhaps this was the time to reveal herself to Gracchus, to show herself not the chattering socialite he thought her, but a mind as sharp and steeped in Allanak politics as his own.

She opened her mouth to speak, but he spoke first.

"They want me to plan a Festival that will rouse the city spirits."

The moment had fled. She retrieved her knife and clipped two buds.

He said, "Perhaps you might do some of the helping with the planning?"

She turned to blink at him. "You want me to help?"

"The city's pockets are deep, as long as there is much to gawk at and games to keep people entertained. You have a genius for that sort of thing." He laughed. "Remember the party last year where you had the coach races and the party guests pulling them with the mounts inside, sticking their heads out the windows and rolling their eyes at the spectacle? And you can use the Kadian silks to make yourself a new dress for each day of the Festival."

"Well," she said, cutting another desiccated rose bud away. "I suppose I could put off becoming an assassin a little longer to help you out." Her heart sang. New clothing and a Festival to plan! And in the process of spending the City's money, would anyone notice if a little went astray here and there in order to help Fale keep up appearances?

———◦———

Within three days, she found herself regretting it, despite the deliv-

56

eries of food for testing to the Fale kitchens, the tailors working at stitching ornamental banners as well as new outfits for herself and Ionna, the new hired carriage standing ready to take her all over Al-lanak on her errands. Her mind was awash with details, with lists and schedules and prices.

"Are you sure you're all right with all this? I would have expected you to put all numbers in the hands of a scribe," Gracchus said. He looked at her across the table. They sat in the Trader's Inn, towards the back, listening to the clink of glasses, the hiss of the wind outside. Papers lay scattered across the table.

"I'm all right," she said. "The weather has been bad for my headaches lately."

He gave her a sympathetic look. "Should I put away talk of the refreshments for now?"

"No, no," she said. "The sooner all of this is figured out the sooner we can put it all away, but not till then."

He shuffled the papers, dry leaves covered with numbers. "Very well. I could understand these figures for pastries, to be dispensed in the Great Bazaar, but what are these bushels of honey candy for?"

"Ah!" She brightened. "I have had a magnificent idea. I have hired wind mages to fly above Meleth's Circle and throw down candies."

He eyed her in alarm. "Kara, are you seriously suggesting that I license mages to fly above crowds pelting them?"

"Tossing, not pelting."

"Kara, I must put my foot down at this. Mages are dangerous and unpredictable, wind mages a hundred times more so." He frowned.

She eyed him. She knew that he'd always had an unreasonable (or so it seemed to her) fear of magic. But as a Red-robed Beneficence, wouldn't the Highlord's power protect him?

"Then I suppose you don't want fire mages and fireworks along Merchant Road," she sighed.

His face reddened with temper.

"Very well." She made an airy gesture with her hand. "I will forego the fireworks." She flashed him a charming smile, trying to extract the same expression from his face.

"And the wind mages," he said coldly.

She dimpled, still trying to catch a matching spark of amusement in his eyes. "Oh well."

He relented and took her hand, drawing it through his, fingers closing to shackle hers with fondness.

"Well now, this is a pretty scene," a voice sneered.

Gracchus did not release her hand as he looked up. "Lord Oash," he said.

Leksander Oash blocked out the patterned rectangle of light that was the doorway, his retinue behind him. "Another tax levied for your Festival," he said to Gracchus. "Will you tax the sand from our robes?"

Gracchus stroked his beard. "A sand tax, an amusing conceit."

"Perhaps you would let your companion pay hers in sand. That sounds to be the only way her House could pay it." Leksander's attention was trained like a gimlet on Kara.

Beads clattered as Lunaris entered, sauntered over towards them.

"Leksander," he said with a studied friendliness.

"Fale," Leksander said. "Come and drink wine with me."

Lunaris's grin was a triumphant puppy trying to pretend it was a jackal. "Very well."

Kara watched them anxiously. The Oash would use Lunaris somehow, she knew with a sinking heart. He was a danger to the House. What could she do to protect it?

"Smile, pretty Kara," Gracchus said. "The Festival will lift your spirits and take all your cares away."

⌲┈┈┉◉

"Tell me," Kara said to the first bard. He was a gray-eyed Northerner, an exile who kept quiet when not playing. "How many times do you need to hear a new song before you can sing it at the Festival?"

"Once," he said. "I am Tuluki-trained, lady."

"And do you fear to sing political songs, as some bards do?"

"I would not sing against the Highlord," he said quickly, but she shook her head.

"Songs against higher-ups, but not so high up as that," she said. "The Beneficences are not targets."

He looked unconvinced.

"I have the ear of a Templar," she said. "At most you'll spend a night or two in the cell, and I would pay you well for that inconvenience."

He hesitated. "Play me the song."

"There are several. Here is the first, called, "The Oash Are A-Hiring.""

Her fingers coaxed a quick melody out of the guitar. He listened and a smile trembled on his lips as the family in the song hired more and more unsuitable servants. He drew in a breath when the song moved from unsuitable to treasonous servants. Dangerous sands to tread. He considered the lady and she looked up and gave him a smile that would have made even the smartest man stupid.

"You promise me you'll pay well if I'm arrested?" he questioned.

She nodded.

He grinned. "Very well, lady Kara. Teach me your songs."

─────·····─○

Lunaris found Kara in the kitchen, sorting through sacks of lentils to remove pebbles and grit.

"Kara." He leaned in the door with a creak of leather, a tilted smile. "How is your Festival planning going?"

"What do you want, Lunaris?" She poured several handfuls of lentils into the soup roiling in the fireplace. Sand spoke idly on the wooden shutters and gritted underfoot.

He touched his vest, tugging it down to better fit his figure. "I was thinking that you might need honor guards for the parade."

"Honor guards." She sorted an onion from a bag and diced it with neat, precise strokes of the knife she held.

"My friends and I thought that if we were all outfitted suitably, we would be a fine honor guard."

"I see. A gang of shiny young men and women, marching at the front of the parade." She sizzled the onion bits in the pan and watched their dance rather than look at him. "And I should spend Gracchus's money on this because?"

"What do you care? It's not your money." He peered into the boiling lentils and wrinkled his nose. "Peasant food," he said dismissively. "Why not get a few more crates of good stuff sent around here?"

"Because you and your friends ate your way through the last, before I even had a chance to see what was being offered. I am not buying uniforms or more pastries for you and your friends," she said flatly. She covered the onions with a lid, muffling their heated whispers. "And when your tailor came round this afternoon, I told him the House would not cover your bill."

His face darkened. "You'll regret this, Sister Karaluvian."

After he had gone, she held onto the table for support, breathing.

⚓

"This part," Kara said. "Personally I would accompany with a drummer, were I so bold as to be arranging it."

The gray-eyed bard nodded. By now he had recruited several others, readying them for the Festival.

New songs were hard to come by—a new one each day was unheard of.

"Lady," he said slyly, "who writes these songs, and why does he not come forward to sing them himself?"

Kara put the guitar on which she had been demonstrating the latest down on her lap. She was a seasoned player, the bard noted. Calluses marked her fingers—something few noblewomen would have allowed.

"Someone for whom it would be inappropriate to play in public," she said dryly.

He looked at her servant, hovering in the doorway behind her. If he had to pick between the two as candidates for author of these ballads, so wry, so pointed, so catchy, he would put his money on Lady Kara.

"Whoever they are, they are very talented," he said, meeting her eyes.

She rewarded him with a smile.

"Indeed," she said. "Let us go over that chorus again. It must sound like dancing."

———••••—◦

The day of the Festival the air was clear and bright, soaked with sunlight. The purple silk Kara had selected for her dress was figured with harps and guitars.

"Bold," Ionna said, looking it over. "That is a Northern print, isn't it?"

Kara twirled, arms outstretched. "The coffers of Allanak and Gracchus's festival yielded enough for the finest seamstress in the city."

"So you think you have skimmed enough off to keep the House afloat?"

61

"Afloat for at least two seasons!" Kara gloated. "I have padded expenses and taken kickbacks, skimmed and dipped, all in the name of the Highlord."

"You don't think Gracchus will say anything if he notices?"

Kara smoothed the silk down over her hips and went to the dresser to get green ribbons to tie through her lavender hair. "Gracchus thinks me too much of a featherhead to be capable of such deviousness." She tugged at a knotted plait.

Ionna coaxed the tangled hair loose and took up a comb, smoothing Kara's hair to fall smooth and straight. "Then we don't need to flee to Luirs," she said.

Kara smiled at her maid's face in the mirror. "Not yet, at any rate."

———•◦

Outside the Traders' Inn the archways all along the circle stood swaddled in jade and black bunting, the city's colors. A small stage had been erected near the Inn. Kara paused long enough to check the banks of vendors, the crispness of the bunting, the assembled bards, the troop of soldiers ready for crowd control. She swept on with Ionna in her wake.

"Where are we going?"

"I've directed the parade to assemble in the Merchants' Quarter and come up Temple Way."

The streets were crowded and cheerful. They made their way through sellers and buyers, peasants come to Allanak for the day, troops of soldiers going between the gates and the Beneficents' Quarter. The parade, gathered just outside the Beneficents' Gate, was a conglomeration of carts, some bearing celebrities and military figures with their guards, others laden with tableaux of painted clowns and side show freaks: a half-man, half-mantis; a two-headed toddler;

an ox-sized albino beetle.

Kara beckoned Gracchus over. He looked nervous but freshly washed and groomed.

"We're in the second cart, in the place of honor," she told him. "Go up there."

He looked around at the collisions of crowds and carts. "This is chaos," he muttered.

"It will all turn out," Kara said cheerfully. "Go on the cart. I'll be along soon."

Ionna had always known that her employer's guise as fluffhead was deceptive, but in the next ten minutes she perceived the depth of that deception as Kara re-ordered the wagons, checked the timing, settled two squabbles, and prevented the half-man, half-mantis from eating the toddler. Then, with a squeak of glee, the noblewoman allowed a burly soldier to hand her up to the wagon and the waiting Gracchus.

Kara's arm flashed up as she waved the first cart forward, and then she clutched at Gracchus's arm for balance as they lurched forward. The crowds shouted. Kara and Ionna threw honey candies from the baskets in the front of the cart while Gracchus waved benignly at the faces surrounding them in the sunlight. As they neared the Trader's Inn, the first group of bards began to sing.

"Oh the Oash are a-hiring …"

"What's that?" Gracchus said to Kara.

She listened intently as the song grew louder. "Ah, that's a new song that's been going around about the Oash hiring northern spies."

Gracchus glanced back. Several carts past, just beginning to come within earshot of the bards, were Leksander and other glowering Oash. Gracchus laughed.

"Ah, you plan a good Festival indeed," he said, and patted her arm. They rolled onward, and the little stage became visible. When they stopped, Gracchus dismounted, striding towards the stage. Kara watched him go before letting Ioanna help her down off the cart.

"Why are you smiling?" Ioanna asked.

"Because the Oash will find themselves the subject of public entertainment for months to come. My bards have a good score of new—and catchy—songs to entertain the public with."

Ioanna grinned. "Come on, let's get some of those tandu sausages."

But before they could go farther, Leksander Oash interposed himself in their path. He was dressed in crisp white regalia, and the harsh sun danced on the stiff fabric.

"Lady Kara," he said between gritted teeth. "You have arranged quite a charming Festival."

She beamed at him. "Indeed, Lord, are you enjoying yourself?"

His eyes narrowed at her innocence.

She kept smiling. "Keep listening to the music, Lord. You will find quite a lot of it new."

He swore. "I knew that it was all a big-eyed, simpering act! Believe me, Lady Fale, you'll find yourself regretting this." He strode off through the crowd. Kara saw him catch at Lunaris and pull the other in his wake.

She turned to Ioanna, smiling. "There's a couple of songs in there about Lunaris as well."

They made their way through the crowds. Together, they bought bangles made of green and purple glass and tied green and black feathers in their hair. They had their fortunes told—twice—and bet more than they lost at the wrestling pit near the city entrance. They stopped at the booth outside the Temple of the Dragon and bought cold water mixed with fermented fruit juice and meat and cactus bits on skewers, roasted over a pan of charcoal.

When they came into the Traders' Inn, they sat on either side of Gracchus and pestered him with questions, bantering back and forth, a conversation light and free of information as froth.

"Kara!" Lunaris, in the doorway, midnight blue hair a mirror of

Kara's cut. His clothing was a little worse for the wear—it looked as though he might have been rolled, to tell the truth.

"Oh dear," she said.

Gracchus followed her gaze. "Don't worry," he said. His hand clamped over his her wrist, holding it to the table so she could not rise. He signaled, and two soldiers near the front of the Inn stepped towards Lunaris.

"Lunaris Fale, you are arrested for high treason," Gracchus pronounced. He gestured at the soldiers. "Take him away to the jail."

Leksander, in the doorway, gaped as the young Fale was dragged past him. Gathering his composure, he advanced on Grachhus with a swagger.

"What are the charges?"

"The spreading of seditious songs and chants. I believe you were the first to press for me to discover the perpetrator, Lord Oash."

"How can you think he was the origin of the songs? Some of them were about him! It was his sister!"

Gracchus shook his head sorrowfully. "A cleverer subterfuge than one might expect from a Fale, to be true. Do you really expect the gentle Lady to have come up with such savage wit?" He gave Kara a fond smile.

Kara looked in bewilderment between them. She was pinned by Gracchus' hand. Lunaris was gone, dragged out the door.

Leksander's gaze fell on Kara. She expected him to say something but then, with a twist of his lips, he stepped forward, took her free hand, and pressed a kiss atop it. Gracchus's grip tightened to the point of pain.

"In a different world, lady, I would have enjoyed understanding you better."

A soldier entered and whispered to Gracchus.

"Ah," Gracchus said. "It seems the young lord has implicated you in treason against the High Lord, Lord Oash."

Leksandr released Kara's hand, stepped back, saluted her. "I would have expected nothing less, Beneficence."

He was not dragged out like Lunaris, but left paced by his guards. Kara stared at Gracchus.

"You need not look so surprised, Lady Kara," Gracchus said. "Someone had to shoulder the blame for the songs, given how much fuss the Oash were making. And now he will no longer drain your household, and what you have embezzled will keep Fale flying high and pretty for another year."

Kara felt limp and drained, as though she might blow away in the heat and sun. "You knew …"

"I thought you would probably use the Festival to your advantage, as I would have in your case," Gracchus said. "Paying a bard to write songs about your adversaries, knowing that all the crowd would be out and listening, ready to pass them on—another clever ploy."

His fingers on her wrists were like steel. "We will work together well, you and I, now that the pretenses are over."

"Lady Kara, your father is ailing, and asks that you take him back to the estate." Ionna was beside her, her eyes on Gracchus's hands.

The Beneficence released her. "There will be a quick trial and tonight's arena match will be finished with the death of the traitors. I will see how they fare against each other, I think."

Lunarius would go first, Kara knew. And then Leksander standing between the high sandstone walls, wind blowing across the sawdust of the floor. Would he face his death well, knowing that the crowds were watching him? The thought of that straight-backed figure, falling among the arena sand while vendors called out, selling souvenirs and cactus-beer, stiffened her own spine. "I must tend to my father. I will speak with you again soon, Lord."

"Very well," Gracchus said. His eyes were hooded, his smile

satisfied. "I will go and enjoy my Festival a little more. I will call on you soon, Lady Kara."

Walking down the length of Merchant's Road, one of them on either side of the slow-moving Thadeus Fale, Ionna said, "The offer to flee to Luirs is still open, you know."

Kara glanced over. "Not yet," she said. She thought of Lunarius, no longer dragging down the house, of life without watching out for Leksander Oash.

"He didn't realize I wrote the songs," she said to Ionna. "He thinks I paid a bard to do it. I think I am still a little cleverer than he thinks, after all. There will be grievance paid for Lunarius."

She touched the knife at her side, the sheath woven into the fine silk. She thought of things that a noble could do that might be questioned in a commoner. Gracchus had laughed at the idea that she might be an assassin. True, she had underestimated him and how much he understood of her situation. She had thought herself much cleverer than she had been.

But what really made a woman clever was learning. Learning to play to her adversary's blind spots and perhaps even use them against him. Learning how to use the power void that Leksander would leave.

There were still many things a clever woman might do, before running off to play guitar with the Tan Muark. She rubbed her bruised wrists. At home, Ioanna would wrap them with cool cloths, and Kara would go over the festival accounts to be paid one last time, to wring out the last drops of graft. She wasn't done with Allanak, or Gracchus, quite yet.

Afternotes

This story is very loosely based on game events from the world of Armageddon, which produced the title story for Eyes Like Sky and Coal and Moonlight, *as well as "Mirabai the Twice-*

NEITHER HERE

Lived". Kara, who was originally inspired by a Brom painting, is a favorite character: all fluff and silliness on the outside, but holding a dagger's deadliness hidden within that giggliness.

Sometimes people ask me why I don't play Armageddon anymore, and it's simply that the game is just too good. Its stories end up obsessing the players to the point where, whenever you're not logged in, you feel as though you're missing out on important parts of the narrative. I know my personality, and it is easily addicted. In some ways, I'm surprised I ever broke free of the game, particularly after a decade and a half of working with it.

The game still exists; explore it at your own peril.

THE SUBTLER ART

ANYTHING CAN HAPPEN IN SERENDIB, THE CITY built of dimensions intersecting, and this is what happened there once.

The noodle shop that lies on the border between the neighborhood of Yddle, which is really a forest, houses strapped to the wide trunks, and Eclect, an industrial quarter, is claimed by both, with equally little reason.

The shop was its own Territory, with laws differing from either area, but the same can be said of many eating establishments in the City of a Thousand Parts. But the noodles were hand shaved, and the sauce was made of minced ginger and chopped green onions with a little soy sauce and a dash of enlightenment, and they were unequaled in Serendib.

It was The Dark's favorite place to eat, and since she and Tericatus were haphazard cooks at best and capable of (usually accidentally) killing someone at worst, they often ate their meals out. And because the city is so full of notorious people, very few noted that the woman once known as the best assassin on five continents on a world that only held four and her lover, a wizard who'd in his time achieved wonders and miracles and once even a rebirthed God, were slurping noodles only an elbow length's away at the same chipped beige stone counter.

Though indifferent cooks, both were fond enough of food to argue its nuances in detail, and this day they were arguing over the use of white pepper or golden when eating the silvery little fish that teem every seventh Spring in Serendib.

"Yellow pepper has a flatness to it," The Dark argued. Since retirement, she had let herself accumulate a little extra fat over her wiry muscles, and a few white strands traced themselves through her midnight hair, but she remained the one of the pair who drew most eyes. Her lover was a lean man, sparse in flesh and hair, gangly, with long capable hands spotted with unnatural colors and burns from alchemical experiments.

"Cooking," said another person, newly arrived, on the other side of her, "is an exceedingly subtle art."

"Cathay," The Dark said, recognizing the newcomer. Her tone was cool. She was both acquaintance and former lover for both of them, but more than that, Cathay was a Trickster mage, and you never knew what she might be getting one into.

Tericatus grunted his own acknowledgment and greeting, rolling an eye sideways at The Dark in warning. He knew she was prone to impatience and, while Tricksters can play with many things, impatience is a favorite point to press on.

But the conversation Cathay made was slight, as though the Trickster's mind was elsewhere, and by the time the others had tapped coin to counter in order to pay, most of what she'd said had vanished, except for those few words.

"A subtle art," The Dark repeated to Tericatus, letting the words linger like the pepper on her tongue. "It describes what I do, as well. The most subtle art of all, assassination."

Tericatus leaned back in his chair with a smile on his lips and a challenging quirk to his eyebrow. "A subtle art, but surely not the most subtle. That would be magery, which is subtlety embodied."

The Dark looked hard at her mate. While she loved him above almost all things, she had been—and remained—very proud of her skill at her profession.

The argument hung in the air between them. So many words could go in defense of either side. But actions speak stronger than words. And so they stood and slid a token beneath their empty bowls and nodded at one another in total agreement.

"Who first?" The Dark asked.

"I have one in mind already, if you don't care," Tericatus murmured.

"Very well."

⸺⸺⸺

Serendib has no center—or at least the legend goes that if anyone ever finds it, the city will fall—but surely wherever its heart is, it must lie close to the gardens of Caran Sul.

Their gates are built of white moon-metal—which grows darker whenever the moon is shadowed—and their grounds are overgrown with shanks of dry green leaves and withered purple blossoms that smell sweet and salty, like the very edges of the sea.

In the center, five towers reach to the sky, only to tangle into the form of Castle Knot, where the Angry Daughters, descended from the prophet who once lived there, swarm, and occasionally pull passersby into their skyborne nests, never to be seen again.

Tericatus and The Dark paid their admittance coins to the sleepy attendant at the entrance stile outside the gate and entered through the pathway hacked into the vegetation. Tericatus paused halfway down the tunnel to lean down and pick up a caterpillar from the dusty path, transferring it to the dry leaves on the opposite side.

The Dark kept a wary eye on the sky as they emerged into sunlight. While she did not fear an encounter with a few Daughters, a crowd of them would be an entirely different thing. But nothing stirred in the stony coils and twists so far above.

"This reminds me," she ventured, "of the time we infiltrated the demon city of S'keral pretending to be visiting scholars and wrestled that purple stone free from that idol."

"Indeed," Tericatus said, "this is nothing like that."

"Ah. Perhaps it is more like the time we entered the village of shapeshifters and killed their leaders before anyone had time enough to react."

"It is not like that either," Tericatus said, a little irritably.

"Remind me," she said, "exactly what we are doing here."

Tericatus stopped and crossed his arms. "I'm demonstrating the subtlety with which magic can work."

"And how exactly will it work?" she inquired.

He unfolded an arm and pointed upward towards the dark shapes flapping their way down from the heights, clacking the brazen, razor-sharp bills on the masks they wore.

"I presume you don't need me to do anything?"

Tericatus did not deign to answer.

The shapes continued to descend. The Dark could see the brass claws tipping their gloves, each stained with ominous rust.

"You're quite sure you don't need me?"

A butterfly fluttered across the sky from behind them. Dodging to catch it in her talons, one Daughter collided with another, and the pair tumbled into the path of a third, then a fourth …

The Dark blinked as the long grass around them filled with fallen bodies.

"Very nice," she said with genuine appreciation. "And the tipping point?"

Tericatus smirked slightly. "The caterpillar. You may have noticed that I moved it from one kind of plant to another …?"

72

"Of course."

"And when it eats jilla leaves, its scent changes, attracting adults of its species to come lay more eggs there."

"Well done," she said. "A valiant try indeed."

The Home for Dictators is, despite its name, a retirement home, though it is true that it holds plenty of past leaders of all sorts of stripes, and many of them are not particularly benign.

"Why here?" Tericatus said as they came up Fume and Spray and Rant Street, changing elevations as they went till the air grew chill and dry.

"It grates on me to perform a hit without getting paid for it," The Dark said, a little apologetically. "It feels unprofessional."

"You're retired. Why should you worry about feeling unprofessional?"

"You're retired too. Why should you worry about who's more subtle?"

"Technically, wizards never retire."

"Assassins do," The Dark said. "It's just that we don't usually get the chance."

"Get the chance or lose the itch?"

She shrugged. "A little of both?"

Tericatus expected The Dark to go in through the back in the way she'd been famous for: unseen, unannounced. Or failing that, to disguise herself in one of her many cunning alterations: an elderly inmate to be admitted, a child come to visit a grandparent, a dignitary there to honor some old politician. But instead she marched up the steps and signed her name in bold letters on the guestbook: THE DARK.

The receptionist/nurse, a young newtling with damp, pallid skin and limpid eyes, spun the book around to read the name, which clearly meant little to him. "And you've come to see …?" he said, letting the sentence trail upward in question as his head tilted.

The Dark eyed him. It was a look Tericatus knew well, a look that started mild and reasonable but which, as time progressed, swelled into menace, darkened like clouds gathering on the edge of the horizon. The newtling paled, cheeks twitching convulsively as he swallowed.

"Simply announce me to the populace at large," The Dark said.

Without taking his eyes from her, the newtling fumbled for the intercom, a device clearly borrowed from some slightly more but not too advanced dimension, laden with black-iron cogs and the faint green glow of phlogiston. He said hesitantly into the bell-like speaking cup, "The, uh, Dark is here to see, uh, someone."

The Dark smiled faintly and turned back to the waiting room.

After a few moments, Tericatus said, "Are we expecting someone?"

"Not really," The Dark replied.

"Some thing?"

"Closer, but not quite," she said.

They glanced around as a bustle of doctors went through a doorway.

"There we go," The Dark said.

She tugged her lover in their wake and up a set of stairs where they watched the doctors gather in a room at the head. An elderly woman lay motionless in her bed.

"The Witch of the Southeast," The Dark murmured. "She's always feared me, and her heart was as frail as tissue paper. Come on."

They drifted further along the corridor. The Dark paused in a doorway. A man in a wheelchair wore an admiral's uniform, but his eyes were unseeing, his lips drawn up in a rictus that exposed purple gums.

"Diploberry," The Dark said. "It keeps well, and just a little has the effect one wants. It is a relatively painless means of suicide."

Tericatus looked at the admiral. "Because he heard you were coming?"

The Dark spread her hands in a helpless shrug, her grin fox-sly.

"And you're getting paid for all of them? How long ago did you plant some of the seeds you've harvested here?"

"The longest would be a decade and a half," she mused.

"How many others have died?"

"Three. All dictators whose former victims were more than willing to see their old oppressors gone."

Tericatus protested, "You can't predict that with such finesse!"

"Can I not?" She pointed at the door where three stretchers were exiting, carried by orderlies in the costume of the place; gold braids and silver sharkskin suits.

She smiled smugly. "Subtle, no?"

Tericatus nodded, frowning.

"Come now," she said. "Is it that hard to admit defeat?"

"Not so hard, my love," he said. "But isn't that Cathay?"

The Dark felt another touch of unease. You never know what a Trickster Mage is getting you into. And there indeed stood Cathay at the front desk, speaking sweetly to someone, a bouquet of withered purple blossoms in her hand, more of it in her hair, a smell like longing and regret and the endless sea.

The Dark murmured, "She always loved those flowers, and yet did not like contending with the Daughters."

Tericatus said, "She had lovers here, I know that. No doubt she has five inheritances coming."

Cathay turned and smiled at them. The Dark bowed slightly, and Tericatus inclined his head.

Neither Here

—•••—◁

"But," The Dark finally said into the silence as they walked away, headed by mutual accord to the bar closest to the noodle shop, "we can still argue over which of us exercises the second most subtle art."

Afternotes

This was the first Serendib story that I wrote, and it was in respond to a call for an anthology called Blackguards: Tales of Assassins, Mercenaries, and Rogues, *put together by J.M. Martin for Ragnorak Press. It clocked in at a neat little package of 2,000 words, thereby making it the shortest story in the book, and freeing up a couple of other authors to go longer as a result. You're welcome. In subsequent stories, I've tried to shoot for similar lengths, making each one a brief glimpse into the city. I don't know that it's a location I'd want to set a novel in; part of its charm is in its fragmentary nature, in my opinion.*

I liked the idea of a long-married couple arguing over whose work was "subtler," with the implication that it therefore was more artistic, and it also seemed to me that probably the book wouldn't have many stories featuring older characters. (And indeed, it did not.)

I wanted the story to be quick and light, which ended up being a challenge. I struggled a bit when combining humor with the fact that The Dark is killing people, and that led to a lot of thought on my part about how to make assassins sympathetic— and whether I actually wanted to be doing so. The conclusion I ended up reaching was that assassins are amoral by nature, and in truth Tericatus is just as ruthless (and egotistical) as his mate, but less overt about it.

The Mage's Gift

THIS IS A STORY OF SERENDIB, THE ORIGAMI city where dimensions intersect and where you step between worlds as easily as turning down a new street to hear the stars singing overhead or the clanging steps of automata on patrol or centaur hoofs clattering over concrete. Everyone that comes to Serendib has a story, and sometimes those stories continue well after they've come to stay.

Once she'd hopped the glass-edged wall using gloves made of fish-leather from the deepest deeps, it had been easy enough to defeat the bloodsucking ivy and the centipede hounds contained in the first set of barriers. After that, she paused to change gloves to a new set, this time made of technology stolen from ancient Atlantis, fashioned of ebon clay and silver circuitry.

The Dark rarely stooped to thievery nowadays but it was how she had started her professional life, long ago in a city whose name she had deliberately forgotten.

There she had been a child born to both privilege and indifference. At fifteen, she had left the school where her parents had deposited her and sauntered off to make her own living. This took the form of burglarizing her parents' friends, at least those whose estates and townhouses she'd had occasion to reconnoiter in earlier years.

This was not as novel a revolt as it might have been, for that city accepts its criminals to the point of licensing them. The true revolt manifested in flouting paperwork until she came of age at sixteen.

Nimble, fearless, and adept in unexpected strategy, she did quite well by this. Well enough that she was able to spread the largesse to many of those less comfortable than her victims, and in doing so, became known as "The Dark Angel."

When, thirteen months later, the infamous guild of assassins that had noted her exploits came to recruit her, they demanded she rename herself (for licensing purposes, since murder was as strictly regulated as theft), which she did by truncating the former name to the alias she had gone by several decades now.

She had kept that knowledge to herself as, over the course of those decades, she'd met any number of unusual characters, including her spouse for two of those decades, Tericatus the alchemist-mage; her sometime-enemy, sometime-friend Chig the Rat God; and quite a few fellow thieves and assassins who often failed to live up to the high standards she held when it came to both of her professions.

Of that group, only Chig knew of her thiefly beginnings. The Dark had kept meaning to tell Tericatus, but he did not come from a city where burglary or murder were government-sanctioned and so held a number of different opinions on such matters. In her secret heart, The Dark found her spouse a trifle sanctimonious at times and preferred not to give him license to pontificate.

She had retired from assassinations—aside from the occasional wager-related killing—some time ago. And now she returned to thievery not so much for entertainment but also because she was impelled by the yearly conundrum of a suitable anniversary present for a man who could, literally, conjure almost anything his heart could imagine.

The next wall was made of fricklebrick, which sounds amusing but involves a number of razor-sharp edges shifting frequently and somewhat randomly in their orientation.

She held her hands near the wall, palms in parallel to let the gloves sense the vibrations of the bricks and adjust themselves to countershift accordingly in a gentle grinding born of magic and machinery.

Casting a glance upward to make sure none of Serendib's possible moons hung too high in the sky, she thought about Tericatus' imagination and—not the for the first time—contemplated her luck in a mate who had long ago grown blasé with outer appearances and preferred inner qualities of fierceness and determined loyalty.

She wriggled upwards, features smeared with coalblack to match the midnight shadows around her, a silver box bumping on her hip. This year, she planned to snare something lovely that could not be bought. Her philosophy of presents was that such things were far better assembled when by effort than by coin.

This garden, located on one of the great terraces built along the mountain slope bordering the city to the north, belonged to a recent arrival to Serendib, a merchant/scientist whose name The Dark kept having tremendous difficulty remembering. This spoke of certain magics laid upon the name to avoid notice, and that was intriguing. More intriguing yet were the rumors of the contents of the innermost garden, center of three sets of walls, which held a worthy anniversary gift.

Not quite atop the wall, she used a mirror-tipped steel strand to survey the territory. She frowned. She had expected to deal with golems, their lips lined with acid spitters, armored in Tesla coils, but they lay scattered about. Someone had preceded her.

Her lips firmed in an uncharacteristic surge of temper. She had throttled back anger since, as a young thief, she had first accidentally-on purpose knifed someone as they grappled.

Not a death she regretted more than any other. The young man (he and his twin sister had been her schoolmates) had followed her to blackmail her. His death had been very painless, very swift. She prided herself that every subsequent kill had also fallen in that category.

But still—she had learned not to give way to impulse.

And it was not as though she had been able to lay claim to this place. Serendib has no organized institutions of thieves. Indeed, it is one of the few forbidden things, and so there was no established way of marking a place as being the target of someone very dangerous to cross.

Sparks from the farthest golem's body still smoldered, sending up bitter smoke from the felted leaves, which meant that her predecessor had beaten her by moments. She moved across the space with assurance, still clinging to the shadows, careful of the snarls of razor-edged grass, ornamental and deadly, lining the pathway.

The stones of the inner wall were cemented with soul stuff, and she had never been good with that magic, so she relied on a wholly technological approach, letting a wand of phlogistonic radions spill its lavender light out along the pink-veined surface, soothing it, till she could climb without complaint.

She saw no sign of the intruder as she came into the garden's inner heart. That was a very good thing, because it was such a pretty place that it stunned her momentarily, a phenomenon that rarely happened to the phlegmatic and sometimes a little cynical woman.

Here in the lambent center, lit by living lanterns, a thousand flowers swelled and bloomed, silky petals dappled and daubed with iridescence, each sending out great invisible clouts of perfume, each different, dizzying with its intensity: cinnamon and carnation, musk and mossrose, vanilla and vetiver.

Mechanical dragonflies and bumblebees, hummingbirds and hovering moths, flitted from one great head-sized blossom to another, posing for seconds in the scented depths as the biomagnetic fields recharged visitors, letting them continue to dart about on patrol.

Crouched at the wall's foot, The Dark lost no time setting the contraption she had carried at her belt on the ground and touching an ivory dial on its side. It unfolded spindly legs and began to totter about, looking like a walking cage made of silver wire and light, staggering towards a flowering bush circled by whistling bees.

She ignored it and looked for tracks, searching over the soft earth. As she moved, flying creatures sensed her and veered, but as each neared with tiny laser-lit eyes flashing and razor sharp mandibles and stings at the ready, it swung away, disoriented and warded off by the complicated magnetic field of The Dark's earrings, fashioned of rare and subtle earth magics by her husband for their last anniversary, who had intended his gift for protection rather than pilfering.

The Dark knew how to read subtle signs: a bent leaf, a displaced butterfly, a flower turned to an unnatural alignment. Whoever it was, they were of a certain height, and a certain weight, and wore a robe that flickered out just so … A frown grew on her face, and each time the moonlight licked her mouth, her lips were turned further down.

By the time she found the intruder, standing to watch carp seethe beneath the surface of a tiny pond, she knew enough to say, her tone irritated, "But I was getting a present for you." And then, "You always have said thievery is a base form of art."

"Well, that is true enough," her husband said in a mild tone intended to smooth the rasp from hers. "But you must admit that you are very hard to find presents for."

"Hrmph," she said. "Well, enough, let us collect what we have come for and return home to exchange gifts a trifle early."

He inclined his head.

But when they reunited some moments later in the garden's center, The Dark held her walking cage, twisted and rent asunder by some force, and Tericatus had scraps of similarly shredded mist, smelling of ozone, clinging to a handful of glowing threads. The Dark eyed that device curiously, for it was not a spell that had occurred to her, but she said only, "Someone else is here, and they do not mean us good."

"Two thieves for the price of one," a voice fluted, "but I am only interested in the one. Man, you may go now, if you leave swiftly and without interference."

The figure that stepped from the shadows was hard to see, for the mechanical insects whirled and fluttered around the slim form, not as though to attack, but to protect. It was a face that The Dark had forgotten, but she realized now she had remembered it all her life, for it was that of the young man who had been her first kill.

Then another step forward and she realized—not him, but his sister, who The Dark had known but little, and last remembered seeing at the very uncomfortable funeral.

"Alas," Tericatus said, and his tone was still mild, but this time steel flowed beneath it. "I do not choose to leave my wife behind."

"Your wife!" the lady exclaimed. The Dark remembered her curls as dark as her own, but now silver threads outmatched the ebon ones, vanquishing, and age and disapproval thinned the once-plump lips. "Not just a thief, but a killer, and a noted one, fattened on her murders over the years. I see that crime treats you well enough."

"In all things," The Dark said, "I have always acted within the boundaries of the law." She glanced at Tericatus.

"That does not matter," the sister, whose name The Dark still could not quite recall—Elissa? Alyssa? Elison? Whoever she was, she thrust her clenched fist out, tight knuckles upward, and let her fingers fly open as she slapped downward a few inches, releasing an alarming number of gnarly black tentacles that plunged for seconds then writhed upward with a swordblade's swiftness, flashing up at the pair.

By mutual accord, they separated, stepping simultaneously in opposite directions. The Dark vanished into the shadows beneath a tree's outgrasping branches while Tericatus thumbed three vials open with practiced swiftness, vapors from the first two combining to solidify around him while the third released a thimbleful of glittering motes that swarmed to halo his head.

But the tentacles moved unerringly only for The Dark, altering course and somehow picking up speed in the process, perhaps assisted by the mother of pearl moths, their wings edged with perilously sharp flakes of crystal, orbiting her head in paths that curved in to slash at her cheek, then shoulder.

Tericatus stepped forward, striking the tentacles with a lacy golden blade that shimmered with sunlight, but they ignored him.

"They only judge those who are truly guilty!" The noblewoman laughed, the sound high-pitched, relief achieved after decades.

Tericatus said, "My wife is not guilty. She tells the world she stepped down from her path for love of me, but I know it was because things weighed on her too heavily. She has worked to atone, and anyhow who are you to judge her and pronounce her fate?"

He moved between The Dark and the tentacles as he spoke, and they fell away from him as the sparkling motes danced over them, becoming more and more sparks in the process.

"I have been told of her misdeeds, over the years," the woman said, and glittering beetles danced in time with her words, fever-quick. "She learned nothing from killing my brother, has gone on to kill again and again. I have spoken to her comrades, her companions of the blade."

"Perhaps you had a particular informant," The Dark said, coldness counterbalancing the fire. "Perhaps they were narrow of face and dark of hair."

"That could describe many," the noblewoman said.

"Much like myself, they dressed in blacks and greys, with the occasional touch of silver."

The noblewoman shrugged. "That is a style, like any other."

"And possibly from time to time, when you glimpsed them from the corner of your eye, they appeared to have ... whiskers."

The woman wavered. "That," she said, "is both idiosyncratic and true."

"Chig," The Dark said without intonation, but her husband muttered it under his breath in a very different tone.

"You are a pawn," Tericatus said and glanced at his wife, "in a game that has been playing for a very long time, and which I thought was over."

"If so," The Dark returned, "and I am neither confirming nor denying such things, I would have anticipated such a contingency but would welcome your sage advice on the subject of my imprisonment."

"Given my knowledge of magic, I would suspect that the things holding you might be dispelled by truths."

"Or magic of one variety or another," The Dark suggested, feeling the tentacles tighten around her.

But as he sighed and readied two new vials, she said, "My dear, the truth of it is that I began my working life as a thief, and I have never told you that because I thought you would think the less of me."

Tentacles withered and fell. The woman gaped, and somewhere from the deepest shadows came a murmured curse, the slither of a great tail and a plomph of displaced air that might signify a rat god vanishing.

"I personally would count that truth a gift, but perhaps you might remove one of the flowers and several of its attendant insects for our garden, as I had intended, as a token for our trouble. Take your present, my dear, and go ahead," The Dark said. "I'll be along in a little while." She eyed the woman.

When she caught up with Tericatus at the outermost wall, he said, "An assassin who had repented might stay their hand from killing someone who they thought might pose a future danger sometime."

"That is true," The Dark said, cleaning some substance from a silver stiletto. "And it is also true that even such a one might think it best to avoid future trouble if it might affect others that one cared for."

"That is indeed another truth," Tericatus said and reflected, not for the first time, on the value of growing blasé with outer appearance and preferring inner qualities of fierceness and determined loyalty in a mate.

Afternotes

This story is set in a location that, like Tabat, originally started as a game setting. I love the idea of places where universes intersect, and the idea of a city where multiple technologies, cultures, and even laws of physics co-exist, and the challenge that it would have presented to code made it even more interesting. Alas, I had the ambition but lacked the technical skills, so Serendib remains a fictional location only.

Tericatus and The Dark first appeared in "The Subtler Art," though they were inspired by an RPG I played as a teenager. One of the reasons I enjoy writing stories with them is that while we've got plenty of fantasy stories full of vigorous, young heroes, we don't often see what happens to them after they retire from the adventuring life, as is the case with this pair. While I never intend to write about their earlier adventures, I do mean to keep mining their retirement. I have at least two other stories (one featuring Chig the Rat God) in the works in which they will play a part.

The title—and the story to a very small extent—is a play on O. Henry's "The Gift of the Magi," although it doesn't otherwise draw directly on that text. The insects in the garden owe their existence to a conversation with Peter Bakker.

How Dogs Came To The New Continent

THIS IS, OF COURSE, BUT THE BRIEF-
est preface to a longer, more de-
tailed study. To my best knowledge, I
am the first scholar in either Tabat or
Verranzo's New City to set down the history of dogs on this continent (aside from the sundry jottings of Beastkeepers). I have written
hastily, despite its lack of decorum, in order to pay tribute to my
cousin, closer than any brother, recently deceased. In these pages, I
will answer the charges made against him as well as myself and my
father.

The following 1512 pages contain detailed lineages for the city's
significant dog lines, along with accounts of their exploits and
advances. While I have neglected many of today's lesser breeds,
Appendix G lists the current species available, ranked in order of
popularity, from teapot poodles to the dangerous miniature basilisk/
greyhound mix. It is indicative of the softness of our society that the
lapdogs known as Mops top the list.

At any rate, this work is indeed a scholarly effort, but also one that
details the lineage of the heart dearest to me in all this world.

Neither Here

When the man the history books know only as Verranzo's shadow twin established the city of Tabat, he opted for differing territory than his brother Verranzo, whose New City lay on the Eastern seaboard, an advantageous but sometimes dangerous proximity to the Old Continent.

Taking separate ships, both brothers had fled that dangerous land, driven away by sorcerers. They hoped to establish cities on new shores. Verranzo picked an island to the north, along the eastern coast. Fertile land, inhabited by Centaurs, easily driven west into the mountains.

His twin chose a far more southerly site. Local tribes feared the place, and claimed an earlier sorcerer had visited there and thrown an existing city into the depths. If true, this would have been the only known visit of a sorcerer to the New Continent before its settlement, but no signs remain to corroborate the story. The cliffs sheltered a sizable inlet, while quarries and forests close at hand offered ample building material. Within a year, early settlers cleared the northern forests of infestations of fairy hives as well as ill-natured little scrub dragons and the spotted panthers that hunted them.

As the city grew, the shadow twin guided another member of his party, the Duke of Whisp, knowing himself childless, and Whisp proven fertile seven times. In time, he passed all power to the Duke. The Duke had come from his lands with wife and mistress and all his household, including a pack of greathounds.

These greathounds had always been a part of the Ducal household. Their breed was reserved for royalty: shaggy hounds standing shoulder high, brindle brown and capable of taking down a lion. Such a greathound guarded each Ducal heir's crib. The dogs watched over the babies as carefully as any nursemaid. The children grew shoulder to shoulder with the hounds. If rumor held true, they ate from the same plate.

Several of these hounds accompanied the Duke, therefore, as he went about on daily rounds of the city.

Much work presented itself in those early days. Tabat grew quickly as refugees from the Old Continent landed and set to building the city to come. The Duke planned the city with an eye that looked to the far future. This was laughed at when crews found themselves building sewage systems, canals, and avenues through the wilderness, but in the century to come, the Duke's layout would prove his remarkable foresight.

Over five years, the eastern swamp was drained, creating rich farmland. Deposits of fine-grained alluvial clay were discovered among the stumps, and the first factory began to produce brick and roofing tile in the region later become known as the Slumpers. Neighborhoods sprang up and found themselves efficiently and neatly arranged. Along the cliffs, terraces were smoothed, and staircases and winding roads laid out in careful order.

Between the cliffs and the forest, merchants funded the brick houses of trade town, posts, and warehouses that handled river traffic as well as overflow from the sea docks.

The Duke's vision focused on the promise of trade made by the two great rivers that met the sea near the city. The continent-cleaving Northstretch river emptied out in a waterfall spilling down a ridge and over the Lazylake to the sea, while the looping Lazylake River, upshore so broad that a boat in the middle often could glimpse neither bank, here narrowed, plunged beneath the ridge, and then anticlimactically ebbed its way into the marshlands. A few traders made their way up and down it, but the founders of Tabat knew that their furs, medicinal herbs, and gems only hinted at trade to come.

With this in mind, the Duke set up expeditions while his counterpart oversaw the construction. The first five years, the Duke, his dogs, and his troops roved the territories by horseback and in small boats around the burgeoning city, mapping and documenting. Those first maps, with meticulous notations and annotations of land grants, hang in Tabat's Hall of Law.

A year later, two exploratory parties set out, each numbering a dozen and named for a quality of soul, Mercy and Tenacity. A pair of Ducal greathounds accompanied each. This action diminished the pack to ten, a risk, yet the Duke wished to signify his investment in the exploration's fruits.

Mercy's greathounds were Cavall and Laurens, both young males. They accompanied the leader, a scholar-warrior named Mikka Fenmerry, and a handful of soldiers. The youthful group enjoyed their trip along the river's western edge, drinking wine and living off fish and game they caught and gathering fruit, more and more bountiful as summer wore on and autumn approached.

Fenmerry's journal details wonders: hot springs and the sulfur-colored snakes living in their waters; a talking face carved into a hill side; vast quantities of game; plants rumored to cure snakebite and miscarriage and greed (none of these survived their trip back to Tabat, alas); an ancient road of gray stone, warm and greasy feeling to the touch; ghosts that rode horses; flower-bearing clouds; and an island which floated in the sky.

Fenmerry estimated the island might have been as much as a mile above them. They shouted up, but it appeared unoccupied, although both dogs barked as though scenting prey or predators. Vegetation was visible on its sides, but they were unable to obtain samples. They walked through its shadow for three hours. Future expeditions never sighted the island again.

The final incident is unjournaled, and known only from a survivor's account.

Scout Pippin Epselm, making his way back to the city four months later with companion and sister Weiga Epselm, stated that he and the others came to a marsh where crocodile-headed beings lived in grass huts. These huts were built atop great wooden legs, which walked about at the direction of the village's shaman.

The huts proved the expedition's undoing, for at the comical sight of two huts walking to a new location, they erupted into laughter. The unfamiliar sound enraged or frightened the natives, so that they fell upon the expedition and killed all but two. The dogs stayed behind them, fighting, their fate unknown until decades later.

Epselm's story of the attack the group had brought upon themselves was used to caution future expeditions, urging them moderation in all emotion, no matter the circumstance. The calm placidity with which leaders to come were wont to meet death was a point of pride in the history lessons, and inspired generations.

The second expedition's dogs were Pomene and Maue. Tenacity was led by a soldier named Ann Natterly, (who may or may not have been the same as a pirate of that time, Tattered Nan). She and her crew ventured as far as the central plains, where they traded for furs and spices, as well as many plant specimens, which were transported back to the city along with Natterly's maps and journals, and seeded the current Ducal gardens.

Natterly herself remained behind in the settlement that would eventually become Cloudmarch and raised a family that became leaders in that city's government and banking. Again, the dogs did not return to Tabat, although three of Pomene's pups were shipped back to the Duke the following spring.

The second flight of expeditions was mounted by more merchantly minds. Outfitting took at least a year—in the second's case, a year and a half. The first, Valor, was jointly funded by the Duke, Verranzo's shadow twin, and a merchant consortium, the second, Perseverance, by merchant family Silvercoin.

Khanda Kanto led Valor. Able second Nella Call organized the outfitting and saw the expedition equipped with a variety of supplies, including: trade goods (blue, white, and green glass beads, fireworks, cloth, and liquor); powdered soup in oilcloth packets, dried apples, figs, pears, and raisins, four pounds of baking powder; tea, coffee, pepper, bags of corn and flour; sacks of dog biscuit; 12 glass-bubbled messenger demons; waterproof brass compasses; notebooks, inks, and pens, along with watercolors for what Kanto called her "miserable talents in this regard"; waterproofed playing cards, and a case that doubled as backgammon or chess/checker board; fishing tackle, including line ranging from a pound to 100 pounds, with fishhooks sized accordingly.

The poet Tullus accompanied them. Kanto's journals deemed him "a poor shot, prone to whining while pretending not to do so," although she warmed to him by the trip's end, and more so when his Khanda's Ballad was published.

A mage, Aloy Taskter, also accompanied the Valor. While Verranzo's New City outlawed any form of magic use, Tabat was more lenient. Both the Shadow Twin and the Duke spoke out about the difference between clean magic and evil sorcery, which twisted the mind until it was incapable of knowing right from wrong.

The remainder of the expedition were soldiers and two scouts, all in all numbering fourteen Humans. Only Valor was accompanied by Ducal greathounds, a mated pair, Artos and Gwenhyfar. They traveled westward along the coast, hoping to eventually reach its end.

The second expedition, Perseverance, was led by Aldo Silvercoin, seconded by Josef Honey. While it had no mage, it did take a matched pair of Minotaurs, whose brawn was eminently useful in pulling boats along the river, and who also proved invaluable in impressing the tribes of the interior.

Back in Tabat, little was heard from the expeditions except for a monthly demon-carried message from the Valor. Accounts of the latest adventures spread quickly, and when word came of one soldier's death, the city declared a day of mourning.

At the time of the last message of the dozen, they thought the western coast within reach, but the land was dipping southward, so they could not estimate their time of arrival. No word had returned of the Perseverance except for two messages carried back by fur traders, which simply stated their arrival at Cloudmarch and then at a place where the river split, and where they were debating which fork to take.

At this point, a year and a month after the Valor's departure, the expedition later be known as "The Beast's Expedition," set forth, organized by an independent scholar, Fabula Nittlescent. Where earlier expeditions sought to map which lands were inhabited by Humans and which contained only Beasts, Nittlescent's expedition thought to find lands where Beasts had formed their own governments. Such early Abolitionist thinking was seen as aberrant at the time. Several plays satirized the expedition and its improbable mission.

While Nittlescent's findings were discredited almost immediately upon publication, many of her writings and observations would be used by Abolitionists in following decades. She observed that many of the interior Beasts mirrored sorcerer-created versions on the Old Continent, raising the question whether the sorcerers had actually created or summoned them.

Although no Ducal hounds companioned Nittlescent's expedition, it contained two dogs from the Southern Isles, whose like had not been seen on either Old or New Continent before. They were striped deep red and orange and black, with thick fur particularly evident over their shoulders, given to eating carrion. Nittlescent had acquired the pair, which she called Paprika and Cinnamon, on an earlier voyage to the Isles, and they were devoted to her and her manservant Jandro.

Nittlescent's expedition chose to not follow the routes laid out by earlier travelers, but rather struck out across the vast interior plains, inhabited by buffalo and mammoth. Hers would have the most success trading and negotiating with the tribes and other Beasts she encountered. By the end of the trip, she had noted seventy-two different groups.

Like other expeditions, Nittlescent's group encountered Shifters. Where the others had steered clear of such creatures, Nittlescent infiltrated the groups, recording their location, numbers, and whatever customs or other information she could gather, in a special journal. Like others of her generation, Nittlescent feared the threat to the natural order posed by the Shifters, and devoted later years of her career to helping wipe them out.

At the time the first expeditions set out, Tabat's citizens numbered over four thousand, an equal number of Beasts living beside them. Like their owners, these early Beasts labored to build a city for the ages. The site for the Ducal castle had been located, the stereotomy of its block drawn out, and the first granite blocks quarried and cut with simple margins and pulled via mule team to its destination.

By the time Perseverance returned, the Duke's pack had grown to thirty, and the castle walls were taking shape.

Where Valor had chosen to go via horse and wagon along the coast, Perseverance chose the river. They traveled along the Lazylake's northern shore, hoping to reach the western mountains and find a way across them.

They rode in sturdy pirogues (the boats' construction created their departure's delay, for they had hoped to launch before Valor), but when the wind was against them, they resorted to poling or having the Minotaurs tow the two boats from the shore. The pirogues proved invaluable. Depending on the territory, each could make six to ten miles per day.

Two weeks in, Perseverance found itself floating in the midst of a sea of feathers, a glittering mass of white, black, and gold covering the water's surface for nearly a mile. Turning a bend, they found themselves among cliffs covered by birds in their summer molt: white pelicans, and golden songbirds, and a host of black swallows of a kind no one had seen before. The noise the birds made was so deafening that the crew stopped up their ears with lumps of tallow lest they be driven mad. They gathered bushels of the feathers, and at their next trade stop, sent back several sackfuls, which were used to make feather ornaments for Tabat's elite.

The most troubling report that returned with Perseverance was word of many Shifter tribes inhabiting the interior, co-existing with Beasts.

On the Old Continent, the delineation between Human and Beast had been clear-cut. On this expedition, explorer Aldo Silvercoin found himself faced with a puzzle this continent would pose for its new inhabitants, when it became clear that the tribe he was trading with were not Human, but shapeshifters.

Early on, the tribes did not hide this fact from explorers, but rather changed form freely before them. While knowing themselves in the midst of dreadful peril from such abominations, Aldo and his fellows remained calm, and escaped, although all recorded how shaken they had been by the encounter.

Word traveled before them though, and they found themselves surprised by Shifters more than once. They learned to distrust all large animals—even the herds of elk, buffalo, and mammoths turned out to have Shifters in their midst. Debate sprang up in the councils of Tabat as how best to deal with the menace such creatures posed.

The expedition was not a complete success. Upon reaching a place where the river forked into three separate tributaries, they chose one fork and followed it into a series of high walled canyons. There winter snowed them in. They lived a miserable existence, subsisting through trade with Centaurs living in the mountains. The Beasts traded them corn and dried meat, but the expedition found themselves at the mercy of politics—showing one too much favor would send others into a rage.

Things got sticky when the Humans stole several elk from a hunting party. The presence of the Minotaurs saved them. The Centaurs held their two fellow Beasts in awe. An elder one said they had met such beings far to the north in earlier days. The Minotaurs were thereafter used to exact tribute from the neighboring tribes.

When spring came, as the expedition made plans for return, the ungrateful Minotaurs snuck away on a moonless night. The Centaurs refused to assist in their recapture, and the expedition left soon after, tracing their route back and arriving much thinner than they had left.

The Duke observed that if they had had a hound or two, the Minotaurs might have been captured.

When messengers brought word, another year later, of Valor's return, crowds formed to meet the expedition, which was unprepared for the heroes' welcome awaiting them in the city, where their legend had grown with each sporadic report of their progress.

Classes in Tabat's schools were cancelled for three days, and the brass band that had been preparing for the expedition's return since the previous year was finally given their chance. Merchants churned out replica "Explorer's Hats," complete with a rainbow of feathers in a fanlike formation at the front, the first of what would become Tabat's signature feather cockades.

Valor's cargo was of the utmost importance to the Duke and his government, which had invested heavily in its outfitting. Their expectations were met. It included gold and silver bars; sea and freshwater pearls; pelts of many unknown birds, animals, and Beasts, including two Selkies; ten gallons of water from a healing spring; plant seed, root, and cutting specimens; song-opals; a clutch of Dragon eggs; two gold and blue macaws; crates of phantasmerie collected from tribes; and rock specimens.

They also came back with inlaid bracers of chitin of a type prized to this day, although only a few pieces remain.

Notable among their finds were the purple reeds that are used in dying. Transplanted to the marshes, these would spread and overtake less hearty vegetation, until the marshes shone lavender and cobalt in the sunset. The poet Tullus observed of Tabat's marshes, that his heart was "less lonely there than any place on this earth."

But most important were journals and maps, particularly when combined with Perseverance's. Space was laid out in the half-completed castle's main hall for what would eventually become the Great Map, showing the continent's entirety.

Valor reported it had traveled along the coast, finding alkali flats and poisonous nymphs, as well as a city of intelligent wasps, who were eradicated by means of sulfur smoke and salt of lead. At times they were forced inland to find a place where they might ford larger rivers, but whenever possible, they stuck to the water's edge, mapping as they went.

Khanda Kanto spoke of hatcheries of Harpies, who screamed at them in an unknown tongue and flew high above them in order to void their bowels, causing the explorers to move along and leave the creatures' territory uncontested.

On the salt flats, while looting the wasp city, they spotted what seemed to be humanoids dressed in spined armor, but were unable to track any down. Finally, the dogs brought a representative of the species back to the city, and they discovered it to be an ambulatory cactus, sized like a ten year old human, but covered with bristles and thorns that made it difficult to handle.

They were forced to bandage the mouths of the hounds and use spears to force the beast into a cage. They tried to speak to it, but it made no sound other than plaintive whistling. They gave it meat and water; it ignored the meat but drank down the water eagerly.

In the morning they found the cage broken and the humanoid gone. Khanda gave the Duke a handful of thorns broken off in the struggle to escape. Valor had seen nothing more of the Thornwalkers, who would harry later settlers with warfare that stopped at no barbarity.

For the most part, their dealings had been peaceful. Valor had made contact with dozens of tribes, and gathered word where it could of what lay inland. Khanda's interest in linguistics led her to fill notebooks with rudimentary grammars, subject-verb order diagrams, and notes on tribal similarities.

Like Perseverance, Valor's members found themselves in an odd situation. In the few Human settlements they visited, the men were often in high demand for the infusion of new blood it brought into families. Both expeditions left an impressive number of bastard children behind.

More problematic were the tribes of Beasts, not to mention tribes who appeared Human but turned out not to be. While procreation rarely results in offspring, many Humans shun such contact, deeming it to be unlucky and unseemly. The men of Perseverance took it upon themselves to defend the prowess of Tabatians, for the most part. Only one Beast/Human offspring is known to have resulted from this—the child was raised by the College of Mages and its descendents still live in its menagerie.

But even more than the Humans, the dogs had been in demand, for many tribes hoped to crossbreed them with their own hunting animals. They had proven surprisingly fertile too—on Valor's trip back, they encountered instance after instance of puppies greeting them. The Duke remarked that the dogs sported a remarkably smug demeanor.

In the craze for all things expedition-related, dog ownership became highly fashionable, although only the Royal Household and those favored by it had greathounds. Several traders took to dog breeding and established the varied lines of Tabat, beginning with mastiffs and finally arriving at the terriers, poodles, and sundry ornamental dogs plaguing us today.

Fabula Nittlescent's expedition returned to little fanfare, but much interest on the part of Tabat's government. More than any other expedition, she had established trade possibilities, having found no tribes overtly hostile to her and her party.

Weather, however, had proved their enemy. They found themselves at first greatly enamored of the plains they traversed. Plentiful game included the mammoth that supplied not just meat but hide, bone, and tusk. The soldiers whittled spoons and pipes from the latter; a display of them hangs in the City Museum.

Nittlescent kept careful records of the species she encountered; of her some three hundred illustrations, over sixty proved to be Beasts, animals, birds, plants, and mushrooms of types not yet catalogued by science. Unfortunately her family saw fit to sell her drawings immediately after her death, breaking the collection up. Some examples survive in private libraries; the majority are housed in the Duke's archives.

Future expeditions discovered the fate of the missing Ducal hounds, as well as the puppies they had sired or whelped. In the north, Cavall and Laurens had bred with local wolf packs, which had formed an alliance with the local tribe of Shifters. Over generations, these interbred until some Shifters took on canine, rather than lupine, form.

Many dogs made similar accommodations with native Beasts, particularly Centaurs, who bred packs sired by Nittlescents' dogs, now known as prairie dogs. Trade in these dogs has always been strong, as with the other dogs bred for specialized tasks, such as tracking or rat-killing.

In Tabat, the Ducal pack continued generation by generation. (See

Appendix L for a complete listing.) But unknown to the Duke, some dogs brought back from elsewhere were not what they seemed.

When I was a lad of five, my father brought me a puppy, which the Duke had given for his services, one of the highest honors in Tabat. I named him Cavall in honor of a story I had heard at my nursemaid's knee, and he and I grew apace together. But he matured more quickly. By the time I was thirteen, he had saved my life on three occasions: once from snakebite, once from drowning, and a third by Mandrake. My father loved him as well as I did, and called him in jest a second son. More than once I saw him regard the dog with affection mingled with deep gratitude.

Throughout my childhood, I knew my canine brother a match for me in intellect, although he lacked the powers of speech. He comprehended it as well as I did, and I would talk to him by the hour, telling him all my hopes and dreams.

When I reached adolescence, my companion fell ill. He was put in the stable, where the stable keeper nursed him. Over the next two days, I went to visit him whenever I could, and sat reading to him from a book we had both been enjoying, a detailed account of Valor and its travels. We made our way from the wasp city to the western coast while he lay panting, white froth around his eyes.

That midnight my father roused me. His face was troubled. We went to the stables. My dog was gone. In his place lay a boy my age, blonde where I was dark-haired.

He opened his eyes and they were Cavall's eyes. He struggled to sit up, pushing away the blanket covering him. Naked legs beneath it, spindly and thin as my own adolescent limbs.

"Easy, son," my father said, and laid a hand on his shoulder. At the touch, the youth calmed and sat looking between the two of us, his expression trusting.

"Cavall?" I whispered.

He smiled at me and half-croaked a response. As though the sound he made frightened him, he flinched back, then recovered himself. "Ca-vall."

The stable smelled of dogs and horses and the bitter medicine that they had dosed him in dog-form with.

"He is a Shifter," my father said. "Do you understand what they are?"

"Someone who can be both Human and animal."

He shook his head. "An animal that uses magic to take Human shape, which means it is a Beast."

He looked sadly at Cavall, who tried to croak again but was not understandable.

"Shifters are killed on sight," he told Cavall.

Cavall nodded. Pushing the blanket away completely, he tottered to his feet, then to my father. He moved more gracefully by the end, smoothly enough that he simply rolled over at my father's feet.

He lifted his chin to expose his throat to my father's knife.

I interposed myself before my father could act.

Never have I been as eloquent as I was that night, pleading for my brother's life. I reminded my father how he would have lost me three times over, were it not for Cavall. We could hide his infirmity, I said. I would personally take charge of it. In human form, he could be my cousin, sent south from Verranzo's New City.

And so Cavall came to be in my household, where we shared all things, and have done so all my life. In dog form and in Human, he has run with me and guarded me from all perils.

When I was twenty-three, we traveled together to Verranzo's New City. There are many Abolitionists there and we attended several lectures. After one, I told him that I would be glad to fund him if he chose to seek out others like himself.

He laughed, and asked me how well I thought he would acquit

himself in the wilderness? He told me he had grown fond of the advantages that civilization offered and preferred to stay with me. He made me chuckle, positing ridiculous examples of how he might live in the wild, but he was earnest when he told me he preferred to live with me.

Only a few times have I denied what he is. The first to a young lady we both admired, who inquired of me if I did not think him (she referred to his Human form) a little odd. I denied this strongly, and praised him to her. It only occurs to me in retrospect that this was her way of telling me her preference. My life has been marked by such dunderheaded moments, though Cavall has saved me from many of them.

Have I wronged Tabat by keeping him safe from its hunters? Have I damaged the order of things, encouraged abomination to walk on this earth? But how could one who loves me so be capable of anything but truth and honesty?

It was, and still is, a hard choice, one I struggle with daily.

But it has been taken from me. I am forty now, and while Cavall was still my age when he walked in Human form, in canine shape he grew grey muzzled and slow-walking.

Finally, last night I knelt beside him for the last time in that shape he could not forsake, as much as I implored him to.

He licked my hand. He closed his eyes.

His last breath shuddered from him, but even then he grinned as only a dog can, promising to run before me and find the path.

All that I have left of him is this tribute, this work. Does my acceptance of him make me an Abolitionist and even worse, a traitor to my race? Perhaps it does, but I have known a devoted soul, and it was as Human as my own.

And so to all the Cavalls of this world—run freely and love deeply, my friends, and know that you will be loved in return.

Afternotes

I love stories that are disguised as other things, and so this is a story disguised as a scholarly monograph from a Tabatian scholar, whose underlying story is much more interesting than the pedigrees of the dogs he's discussing.

This story is linked to the second novel in the Tabat Quartet, Hearts of Tabat, *and is the final manuscript that Scholar Reinart gives to Adelina. It is modeled on several early American explorers' narratives, and is intended to underscore parallels between Tabat/the New Continent and early America. (Verranzo's New City is analogous to New York City, although I have yet to write a story set there.)*

One of the joys of sitting down and writing this story was the pleasure of creating more of Tabat's history and the antecedents of a number of things, such as the feather cockades used to signal one's political alliance that appear through the Tabat Quartet, and which have their beginning in the feathers brought back by the Perseverance expedition. Understanding the material conditions of the landscape has enriched Tabat for me, and often details mentioned in one story will spark others. For example, there is a murder mystery connected with the statues on one particular street, and I know some of the details of that, but have yet to sit down and write the overall story of Sparkfinger Jack.

The story explores the relationship between Beasts and Humans and especially the group that both sides fear, the Shifters, who can pass as Human but also are magical in nature like the Beasts, a theme exemplified by Teo's experience in Beasts of Tabat.

Love's Footsteps

 A T THE TIME HE DID IT, THE WIZARD MOULDER found the idea of removing his heart, applying a calcifying solution, and storing it in a safe place, all in the name of achieving immortality, quite reasonable.

He performed the ritual in the small but ominous tower he had built in one corner of his parents' amber-walled estate, watched over by dour-jawed stuffed crocodiles and glassy-eyed owls and his faithful servant, Small, who held out the iron receptacle to hold his heart, her face impassive and unjudgmental, and laved his hands afterwards with cold water.

For thirty years, the practice served him well enough. A heart is the seat, the root of change, and it is as the soul changes that the body degrades, which is why childhood to adulthood is so marked with its physical transformation.

Small, who was twenty-five to his twenty-one at the time he performed the ritual, changed, although not as much as one might have thought. She was a neat-boned woman whose stature matched her name, who remained sparsely fleshed and wired with muscle.

Like all of her family, she had been pledged to serve Moulder's family from her first breath, and at four she had been shown the babe she would accompany all her life. If she questioned this fate, she kept it to herself and never spoke of it, to Moulder or anyone else. Trained to a tee, she was bodyguard and valet, cook, groom, barber, confidante, and a thousand other things to her stiff-jawed and undead master.

When Moulder reached his fifties, although he remained the same physical self he had been at twenty-one, he was seized with the desire to change, an uncomfortable, thwarted impulse like constipation, seated low in his dissatisfied gut.

He tried long walks and sour laxatives, candles infused with poppy and hemp, a diet of flax seed, lettuce, and asparagus-water, but the sensation remained, deepened, drove him to longer walks, more stringent medicines, and sticky, hallucinogenic pellets of the sort the most dream-addled smoked, all to no avail.

"Small," he said accordingly, on a crisp fall day when the sky was a cold blue bowl inverted overhead. "Prepare to travel."

"The destination?" she said.

"Unknown."

She harrumphed, but packed a range of clothing suitable for tropic to blizzard, along with various clever contrivances for a comfortable life, assembled in a great gilt-chased steamer trunk that she insisted on loading herself onto the carriage.

Moulder eyed the trunk and the space it took up, but said nothing. Small made life comfortable, and the price one paid was that sometimes the needs of Small's equipment overrode other considerations. Moulder might have set aside human emotions, but he still appreciated the thought Small put into his creature comforts, the behind-the-scenes choreography that produced robes with knife-sharp creases, steaming breakfast tea, and the little jar of pomade somehow always, almost magically, full to the brim and fresh with fragrance.

Moulder gave his order to the coachman and they rattled down the hill towards the docks.

"If we are bound by sea, perhaps I might have the name of the captain," Small said. On another person's lips, it might have been a reproach.

"We will secure a captain as we find him or her," Moulder snapped.

Small considered this. She was well aware of the ways of wizards. This, she realized, was the beginning of a spell, although not one of a sort she'd encountered before, rooted in random whimsy. She did not trust such magic. But she said nothing of that.

At the docks, Moulder rejected a small galleon bound for southern trading, and an exploratory sloop headed for the New Continent. Instead, he chose a third vessel, a vessel bound west along the coast, towards the Rose Kingdom.

Small busied herself setting the cabin to rights, chasing out fleas with the smoke of aromatic grasses and polishing the single round window so the moons' light might pour through it, unimpeded, whenever so desired.

At night she served fish broth and tea, which was all the sustenance her master required. She took her own meals with the crew, where several men lost their hearts to her, for she had been raised with four brothers and could keep up with the vinegar and vulgar talk of the sailors capably enough to make even the cook blush. She spent her days on the deck, watching the horizon and wondering at Moulder's intentions.

The wizard himself kept to the cabin. He found extremes of heat or cold unpleasant and the musty air of the cabin suited him well as he read through the texts he had brought, a ball of magelight bobbing over his shoulder to illuminate the page.

More than once, Small tried to coax him into conversation, towards some hint of his plan, but the most he would say was that their first stop was in the city of Delaborn.

"Delaborn," Small said. "Where the dragons are?"

"Indeed, they haunt the coastline there."

"Will we also be haunting the coastline?"

But Moulder bent his head back to his books without replying.

She sensed embarrassment lurking behind his silence, the sort of wounded pride he evidenced when she was right but he felt she had no right to be. She left well enough alone. The truth would emerge in its own time. She kept to her chores, and amused herself embellishing his wardrobe with an excess of embroidery.

In Delaborn, she realized that they would be hunting a dragon when Moulder sent her to the outfitters there to purchase the necessary gear. She returned with flameproof net and a stout bow capable of driving the short but sharp iron arrows through the softer parts of its hide.

She was relived to find Moulder had put some thought into the hunt, providing potions that resisted fire and a paralytic agent with which to poison the arrows. Still, she could not help but feel that she had gone far and above her duty as she dragged the reptile, easily as long as she was tall, if not longer, back to his feet as dawn touched the cliff where he had made camp.

Moulder regarded the animal for a long moment. Kneeling with a long, leaf-shaped dagger, he began to dissect it, peeling away layers to reveal the still throbbing heart. As he pulled it free, blood rushed over his second-best boots, which Small regretted packing.

She didn't speak as Moulder raised the flesh to his lips, gnawed and chewed and swallowed before lowering it. Blood covered the front of his robes as well, masking the silver silk stitching of swords and roses Small had set there. She stirred the fire into new heat, and set a kettle in the ashes.

All the while he stood there. She stole glances at him, uncertain whether or not to speak.

He sighed and threw the heart down on the corpse.

"The dragons are magical, born of pride and anger," he told her. "They hold it in their hearts, they are that emotion walking, set into motion. How could it fail?" His voice dropped away, as though he spoke the last words to himself.

"How did it fail?"

"I should feel it, now that I have taken it in. Feel anger, pride racing through my veins. But there is nothing there. My blood is quiet as ashes."

"You put emotions away with your heart," she said.

"I should still be able to stir them, if only through artificial means." He could have been angry, but his voice was flat and expressionless. "Tomorrow we leave for Illuray."

She would have protested—not the destination but the travel to it, which passed near a Siren colony, the only sort of its kind, making it an allure as well as a peril. But the dragon's heart lay in the early morning sunlight, and she had done that, and would face sirens as well.

When they were a half day's sailing from the sirens, the Captain summoned the passengers and offered this choice: they could, if they wished, retire to their cabins and stopper their ears with beeswax. In fact, that was the course the Captain advised, for he had been told that the song would linger with you ever after, stirring regret, and sorrow, and despair. He himself was immune to it, being deaf like the rest of his crew.

For those who had specifically said they wished to hear the sirens—and here he looked at Moulder—there was a second option, where their ears would remain unstopped, but they themselves would be entirely restrained, lashed to a mast, bound head and foot lest they give way, as the foolish and infatuated had in the past been known to do.

Small knew immediately that Moulder wanted to hear the sirens. She would watch over him while he did so, but she would stopper her ears. Even so, when she explained this to the Captain, he insisted that she be restrained as well. She acquiesced, but chose to be bound facing where she could see her master.

As they approached, she could see the moment when he first heard the song, for his brows rose and he lifted his chin, angling his head to better hear them.

As they came closer still, she heard it, seeping through the imperfect seals of her ears. It wrenched at her, it filled her with longing. She must go to its source, she thought, and she struggled against the ropes so strongly she bruised herself.

But Moulder looked at her and spoke a single word. She sank into sleep, although haunted by the music, which she chased and chased through her dreams. As she slept, tears marked her cheeks with silver trails and sometimes Moulder watched her and sometimes he watched the sirens as they swam past, singing, for he felt as little emotion for one as the other, which told him that this foray had been as unsuccessful as the first.

When they were out of earshot, he spoke another word. Small woke and was silent as the sailor loosed her. She did not speak of what she had heard and gave no sign of it haunting her.

Moulder concerned himself little with that. He had tried emotions like anger and despair, and in his third attempt, he would move to another range: Love.

"Love?" Small said with upquirked eyebrow.

"There are two things at the heart of the Rose Kingdom," Moulder said. "The first is its gardens, which are unparalleled. A section of thorn lines the mountain and there, it is said, a flower grows, rarer than most, for it will bloom only in the footsteps of true love. It is said to be small, and sweet, and to emit the sound of a singing bell."

"And the second thing?"

"I will test the second with the first," Moulder said. "For the Queen of the Rose Kingdom is so fair to look upon that she engenders love in the hardest heart."

They had to wait three days for a public ceremony at which the Queen would appear, but finally, there was the dedication of a new park and Moulder, in attendance with Small waiting on him, was finally able to gaze his fill.

The Queen was indeed beautiful, with amber skin and dark hair caught up in an arrangement with golden and silver roses. Her eyes caught his and he felt something stir, surely, that had been unfamiliar. Some emotion.

"Come!" he snapped at Small, and they left without a backward glance for the Queen, rushing through the crowd of citizens and peddlers and tourists, catching a carriage to the garden he had spoken of.

Alighting from the carriage, Moulder walked boldly along the path. He did not dare look behind him and he forgot to breathe entirely. It felt as though a warm haze suffused him. The more he considered it, the surer he was. This was emotion. This was love, surely.

He stopped and turned, still holding his breath.

Only to see his path unmarked by any sign of bloom.

He stood, examining the ground, and then his own internal functioning.

Not love. The overheated workings of his imagination were as close as he had come, would ever come.

It had been a foolish pursuit.

"We will go home and not speak of this again," he said.

Small nodded and followed him as he headed home.

In her footsteps, little flowers nodded, but their song, like her love, was held too heartdeep to be heard.

Afternotes

While Moulder is not modeled on my spouse, I did steal the name from one of his World of Warcraft characters, an undead sorcerer (his companion was another undead, this time named Skully). In keeping with this, I named his servant after one of my own characters from a different game. The idea of sorcerers or other magical beings who remove their hearts and put them somewhere for safekeeping has always intrigued me because I wondered what sort of effect it would have on a person.

Here the lack drives a quest to fill the void left by the missing heart, while the heart's absence makes it impossible to realize that the solution is close at hand in the form of Small's devotion.

While pieces of this seem to belong to the Tabat stories, it may actually exist in the same space that "The Dead Girl's Wedding March" does, being a story told inside that world as well as about it, drawing on its mythology and acquiring a less realistic texture than stories like "Primaflora's Journey" or "I'll Gnaw Your Bones, the Manticore Said."

To Read The Sea

 Yes. You've come to the right place, captain. Meager huts, but they do belong to the ones you seek, the Oracles. Have you brought an object?

Yes, you say. (And think I do not see your sly grin.)

A silver comb. Tie it into this leather pouch. Draw the strings tight. Give it to me.

These are the four winds I gesture to; these are the words I whisper to the world tortoise's heart. This is what you offer; this is what I take.

Now we must wait for a vision to come to me. Sit here and drink lemon tea, it's been brewing over the fire for an hour. The vision will come before the morning.

That is our profession, the Oracles. To read the objects you bring.

And from that to tell your fate ...

I am old to be sitting out in this weather, you say? Perhaps. When I was a child I stole a skin from a shapeshifting seal. Its thick hide keeps me warm, while its other properties keep me protected.

That surprises you? I was a beautiful girl in my prime, almost as beautiful as my mother. The Oracles found her on the beach. Still alive. Twice alive: swollen, gravid, as though the sea had taken up house in

110

her womb, but it had been a pirate.

I am sure you have seen them from your shipdeck. They haunt these shores for the ships that go back and forth between the twelve great ports. It's why there are so many objects for us to interpret. They all wash ashore here, somehow.

So do the dead. The seal maiden had drowned, somehow. Kelp tangled her long dark hair, clung to my fingers as I pulled the sodden flaps and folds of her skin loose.

The skins are more magicky than shapeshifters let on. I was a child no longer then, for I could take on any other form: a slim young man or a gnarled elder or a wild wart-hog. I lived in the forests in that last form for nigh two years.

That was the first object the sea brought me …

The night is holding its breath. Do you know that expression? A moment of import, when forces of fate collide. Certainly you must have crouched inside one before? No?

You need not look at me as though madness has set in.

You have visited here before, have you not? You say no, but I sense your blood has.

What was the second object the sea brought me?

You have to remember that these shores are special. Often the objects that appear on the sand, which people bring to us to be read, to tell them their fates, are magical. One in a hundred, perhaps. That is why sometimes people come that wish us ill. That come thinking they will slay an unwary Oracle and take the objects accumulated over decades of reading.

Not you, of course. Drink your tea. The vision is almost upon us.

I knew the second object was special when the girl laid it into my hand. She didn't ask me anything, just crouched back on her heels and watched me with nervous jade eyes.

It was a little figurine, carved of horn, with a tuft of coarse,

111

springy hair, now crusted with tiny seashells, sprouting from the mottled surface as though growing from it. White salt stains crusted it, showing the grain.

Witches use these things to call men to them.

I told her what it meant for her, which is another story. Afterward I put it away.

I knew to call a man I needed some part of him. Hair or seed or blood.

Or something close to those.

My mother died in my birthing, but she told the woman who nursed her the story of a ship called the Blade, and the captain who'd taken her as plunder, plucked the silver comb from her hair.

Did you say something? No?

You know it, I know it. You were that Captain and I your daughter, even though I look like your Elder. The magic of the skin is not confined to seals, as I said. And a child raised among the Oracles knows how to use magic to hide her youth.

I could call my mother's rapist to me; his blood ran in my veins.

I picked the third object from the sea this morning, a great sharp clamshell, wicked as any knife. I knew what it meant. Every Oracle knows how to read the sea.

It talked to me, said my father was coming, that he'd heard the rumors of Oracle treasure I'd whispered to the figurine. Told me to brew lemon tea and mix in it the vial of spinefish venom, which turns a man's flesh as hard to move as stone.

Yes, that is why you cannot move. Cannot reach the knife you have hidden.

I will not use your knife to kill you. The shell told me how to hold it. How to hack away with its sharp edge at the loose translucent skin even as you make a noise and heave yourself upward as though resisting all contact with the earth, as though you were trying to jump to the moon trembling over us and I wait for you to fall back, so I may drag you down to shore again for someone else to read.

Afternotes

This flash piece was originally written for an anthology centered on fortunetelling. I loved fortunetelling that involves reading found messages, such as tea leaves or dream-reading, and the idea of reading objects seemed a natural counterpart of that. How would objects end up somewhere? The waves seemed a natural mechanism for gathering them, and once I had that and realized it was a sea captain visiting an oracle, I was able to figure out what had brought him there and for what purpose.

This world is not one I've written in before, I think, or else it's a corner of Tabat's world, tucked away somewhere. I doubt that I'll visit it again—but who knows what will happen?

A Brooch of Bone,
A Hint of Tooth

THE CHILD RAN CLATTERING through stone walled corridors and then, softer, softer, through the tapestry lined chambers where The Queen once dwelled. Princess Esmerelda was eight. Baby fat still clung to her limbs, but her face was a cherub's: blonde, blue-eyed, pierced with a dimple that deepened as she ran, giggling, through the palace.

Courtiers and servants scattered out of her way. A few servants laughed, echoing the glee on her face. But laughter was scarce, or worse, only a crippled, forced version, as though most were scared to take much notice of the girl.

Only one person spoke to her. He stepped in her path deliberately. She collided with his silk robes with a surprised oof. Backpedaling for balance, she stared as though confronted with a creature she had never seen before.

The smile on his lips was a withered worm.

"Softly, princess!" he said. The tortured worm twisted. "Your Highness will injure yourself. It would be more suitable if you sent a servant running for whatever it is you are looking for."

"But I am looking for the wind, and I can only find it when running!" she chortled, and was off again. The frown he threw at her heels did not slow them. She grinned back at him and he imagined a certain toothiness about her expression, like a dog that has scented something long dead or a fox picking morsels from a wire brush.

But the two court ladies that grabbed her by her hands and swung her along as she kicked her heels and giggled must have seen something different. Their laughter echoed hers, fair faces all alight.

Released, the child ran on. Sir Lyonel, advisor to the King, followed, slowly. He muttered to himself about bad blood and fingered the bone brooch at his neck. The coin-sized round was carved with a sword laid over a crown, as though to protect it from harm.

———————

In an echoing room, the King sat on his throne, listening to treaties. When the child ran in, he gestured to his court for silence. He lifted up his arms and caught her and folded her against him in a rush of laughter!

"Have you caught the wind yet, my pet?" he asked.

She shook her head, making her fine blonde hair float in the air around her. "When I run, I feel it, and when I stop, it stops!" she exclaimed, having just made that discovery this morning. She had tried it at various spots in the castle. It was always the same, whether she tried it up on the roof along the parapets, or down in the tunnels where no one but she ever came.

"She will tire you out, your Majesty," Sir Lyonel said as he entered.

The King stroked Princess Esmerelda's hair as she leaned against him, feeling it soft as silk under his fingertips.

"Nonsense," he said. "She is the best medicine I could have, full of life and sweetness, like her mother." But dark shadows lay under his eyes, and a cough shook him as he set her back down.

"Run along, my fleet-footed one," he said. "Catch the wind and bring it back to me, and I will have it woven into a shawl to keep you warm in the deep of winter."

She was gone, and left only laughter in her trail as he turned back to the Kingdom's business. When had it grown so slow and oppressive, full of farmers arguing about the borders of wheat fields, and foreign emissaries complaining of tariffs? When his Queen had lived here, the Castle was full of light and laughter, and no such matters had ever troubled him. Now the people praised him as they had not before, but he remembered those frivolous days fondly.

⟶ ···· ιᴏ

Esmerelda went where she knew no one would follow her. Down, down, down, past the dungeons where a few prisoners lingered, and down further yet into the catacombs. They had been forbidden her, but she knew them better than anyone else, for she came to this place every few days.

She did not tell anyone that she could see, down there, without candle or torch. Her father did not like her differences, the ones her mother had given her, and the uncanny elf-sight, able to see through darkness or smoke or lies, was only one of those.

Her slippers padded through the grime and dirt. The hewn walls gave way to others. At the end of a long smooth tunnel was the room she sought, one whose edges hinted at a strange precision for such an unvisited place. Here, deep below the castle and the city surrounding it, there was a silence she could find in no other place.

Others shared the room with her. Thirty-three man-sized shelves were carved into the rock in columns of three, holding bones at rest for more than a thousand years. Frames like window had been carved into the rock, but the art that had once filled them was gone, fallen to gleaming dust. The corpses lay in disarray, and the many skulls that had been removed were stacked in piles with more recent skulls. Most were unmarked, but a few wore red-inked glyphs that Esmerelda could not read.

The cold bit at her, but she chose to ignore it. She was tougher than any human child, but the palace folk forgot that, and loved to coddle her. They missed her mother, missed the tall Fairy queen who had gone away, leaving behind her husband and child. That was the way of Fairies, they said, and they did not try to hide her mother's departure from her, because all of them wanted her to love her father the best.

But that did not mean they did not miss the queen.

In the council chamber, the King dreamed of his lost Queen, the woman he had found in the wood one fine day when he was just a Prince, out hunting. She had said she would always be with him. Always! And in the end that had been a lie, for she had slipped away one morning, without even a word, and he still didn't know what he had done to offend her.

How beautiful she was in this dream! As beautiful as he remembered, skin whiter than the whitest rose in his garden, slim as a fleeing deer, laughter quicker than any prey. He had slipped down from his horse, so taken with her that he barely knew he was moving towards her. The knights held back, waiting to see what he would do. His father had thought Fairies evil, had killed one, even, and they were rarely seen nowadays.

One knight, named Lyonel, thought, "Perhaps she will kill him too!" Much later he would reprimand the princess for running too quickly, long after he had put away his sword and become a councilor, long after the Fairy had failed to kill the prince, had even, improbable as he thought it, married him.

And there she had thwarted a long-laid plan by the Sir Lyonel and his confederates, to render the King dissatisfied with any woman, so he would never marry. They had told him stories of beautiful Fairies, never dreaming that one would come among them and marry him, just as they were starting to think themselves safe, just as the white hairs were starting to show in his beard.

He had married, and proven himself a worthy King by siring a heir, who ran, motherless, through the palace, waiting to rule in turn.

Sir Lyonel had entered the catacombs before, but had never gone far. The castle was older than anyone knew. It had stood through three lines of Kings, and would stand for three more before it passed, like all things, into dust and legend.

When he was a child, his nursemaid had told him terrible stories of what waited beneath the castle: great worms with teeth that would crawl after you faster than a horse could run, and rat-kings with their tails entangled and a myriad rat-minions protecting them in swarms of fur and fangs. And ghosts and sorcerers and necromancers. Now he was old and no longer feared anything, but once, as he went down a passageway, he thought he heard slithering. He paused and listened, but did not hear the sound again.

The torch in his hand showed the little princess's tracks, leading him along her path. He imagined her uncanny eyes gleaming in the shadows, and he paused again, thinking to hear her.

But by the time her tracks led him to the furthest room, she was long gone. He stood, feeling the cold creep up from the stone floor through the soles of his feet, and looked at the skulls. Paltry playthings for a child, and ones that betrayed a morbid cast of mind unsuitable in a ruler.

He stooped and picked up a skull. Red lines writhed on the bare white bone, red as blood but the ink was long dry, even though it still shone wetly.

He touched the brooch at his throat. "Would you rather lie here, my dear?" he said, and chuckled to himself. And then, looking around at the walls, he thought, No one ever comes here. No one would ever find this place.

This time he smiled fully, the worm splayed as though in terror and delight.

———————

In the days that came, Sir Lyonel watched the princess closely. As though she sensed his scrutiny, she played in the gardens and the great Hall, in the attics among the maids, and in the stables, where a new batch of kittens had just arrived.

Meanwhile, he planted seeds. In the kitchen, he mentioned the princess' flightiness, so like her mother. To the other knights, he spoke of Fairy blood and how prone to whim it often proved, emerging decades after ordinariness—and none would say our little princess was ordinary, would they, he chuckled. He mentioned the princess's disappearances in the hearing of the King, and said, worriedly, "What if something should happen to her? She is the heir, after all."

At the same time, he made people vanish.

People had always vanished from the castle. It was a very large place, and servants came and went. Usually as they pleased, rather than how its officials pleased.

The princess had known before that maids might decide to marry or return home, now that they had enough to buy a new comb or a teapot. Soldiers stayed longer, but even they were not permanent—some went off to other lands or other fights, and some simply went to beat their swords into implements of farming, now that they had seen the wide world, and had some of it see them.

But now it seemed as though some were vanishing with less word than ever, not even a note, and sometimes they left their belongings behind, perhaps in emulation of the Queen who, it was said, had returned to her homeland clad in nothing. She had abandoned all her jewels and silken dresses, even the lace-trimmed night shifts the King had bought for her, made of white silk that seemed sallow when placed beside her skin.

It seemed to the princess that it was her friends that were vanishing so, but she could not figure out how to tell her father this in such a way that he would listen. For he was prone to patting her on the head and telling her to run along. "There will be time enough to worry about learning matters of state when you are older," he said. "Run along now and continue to be a child."

And it seemed to Esmerelda that Sir Lyonel, who she found watching her too often, like a snake watches a mouse that might make a particularly good meal, smiled a little, in the ways that unpleasant people do when children say things, a "You may think so, but I know better" sort of way, an expression that was wiped away before the King could turn and look at him.

⚓

How inevitable that the King should try to curtail his child's wandering. He set a nursemaid to following her, and when that proved inadequate, he appointed other servants to watch over her.

He took her aside and tried to reason with her. He did not want to frighten her. She was such a sunny spirit, like a little canary that sang all day long. Her mother had sung too, and the sound had delighted the King's heart so much that he did not want it to fade away, for his child's voice to be lowered in fear.

He said, "Do you love me? You must always be honest, my child, always straightforward."

"Of course I do, Papa." The little girl laid her cheek against his and he closed his eyes, feeling her warmth, smelling her lavender soap. It made him feel young again to be so close to her, this perfect thing that was the last thing that reminded him of his lost wife. So all he said was, "Then look after yourself, my dear, for it would break my heart to not have you here."

She peered up into his face. "Can hearts break like that?"

"Yes," he said. "They can. Don't test mine!"

"I will not break your heart," she said, and smiled at him, and danced away.

It was only a little work to lose the servant following her. Esmerelda thought to herself that it was the kindest thing, perhaps. Her guardians were prone to vanishing, and she did not want whatever stole them to take the latest, a pleasant, cheerful maid named Lia, who brought the princess fresh baked pastries from the kitchen and didn't mind fierce hugs or being teased.

So Esmerelda left Lia calling to her in the garden, and ducked through a stone archway she knew, and soon, as though it were inevitable, she was going to the catacombs.

She did not sense the man following her, so intent was she on picking out her path. Or perhaps it was the way he took care to muffle his steps, to follow with inexorable slowness. He carried a hooded lantern, that he could shutter in an instant if need be, and he paused often, cocking his head to hear the child's footsteps far ahead. He knew the route she followed, and he went there too.

In the room of the skulls, Esmerelda stacked skulls and spoke to them. Outside in the corridor, Sir Lyonel tried to make out what she was saying. Singing a nursery rhyme, perhaps, he thought, or some other nonsense verse, the kind that adults filled children's heads with, not realizing the dark nightmares beneath the fairy tales. It was only the work of a moment to swing the door shut, to bar it.

He stood outside, still listening.

He heard Esmerelda's steps to the doorway, heard her test it unsuccessfully. He expected a cry or shout at that point, but none came. He listened harder, even pressed his ear against the door, but there was no sound.

He thought to himself that he had always thought her an unnatural child, too perfect, too enchanting. Her mother had not been human, after all, even though she resembled one. With his eyes closed, as they were now, he could almost see her slim, menacing form, close to him in the darkness, waiting for him to open his eyes.

He opened them with a start, half-expecting to see her there, but she was not. He wondered again if he heard the distant rustle of scales slipping against stone. He had never feared ghosts, but here in the lantern's flickering light, he found it in him to imagine them, and he shuddered to think of what they might say to them.

He went away, padding as quietly as he could. He didn't fear Esmerelda hearing him—she would not be able to identify who had locked her in there, in the unlikely event that someone stumbled across the room in the inevitable search for her. Rather a part of him, a mean and ignoble part, smiled to think of her there, still listening, wondering whether or not he had gone.

He played fantasies over in his head as he went along the corridor.

The King, bereft and in need of support, would turn to him and he would comfort the old man and continue gently leading him to the place he had yearned for so many times in his life: being appointed the King's heir.

He would make a good king, he thought. He would not meddle much in the affairs of others, and he would see a barrier built so no Fairies could come into this kingdom without being noted and discouraged.

When he came to the courtyard, Esmerelda was there. Lia was watching her as she played a game in the dust with a rubber ball and a set of jacks.

He stopped, stupefied. How was this possible? What did it mean?

Looking up, the child smiled at him. It was not a pleasant smile. Rather it was a smile that made his blood run cold. He reached for the brooch at his neck as though to reassure himself. As his fingers caressed the touch-worn bone, the child's smile grew.

"Where have you been, Sir Lyonel?" she said. Her voice was clear and bland, and he sensed deep in his heart that she knew who had stood outside the doorway after closing it. Somehow she read his mind. The blood rose to his cheeks as though she were rummaging through his thoughts, exposing hidden things to the light, like insects living beneath a stone, which have never seen the sun.

He stammered something.

She pursued the topic. "Your boots are all dusty and covered with cobwebs. Perhaps you should have your valet brush them."

He turned away, confused, to do just that, when she added, "After all, don't you want to look as regal as possible?"

He would have stammered something else at this, as though she had exposed his ambitions to all the courtyard, but in the end, he fled. He heard the child laughing at her game, but he knew she laughed at him.

Neither Here

That night, he dreamed of the skulls and the red writing that covered them. He woke with a thought, witchcraft. Had her Fairy blood made a witch of the princess? If so, surely he could denounce her, surely she would betray herself.

But no, she had shown herself too clever for that. He would have to wait and see, would have to lull her into a sense of false security.

In the library, he read everything he could find about Fairies. There were not many books about them, and almost as many disagreements as there were books.

One book said that they were just like humans, just another race, with no powers at all. People had ascribed magic to them because they were strange and unknown. But, the author concluded, it was a case of hysteria. He set that book aside quickly, for it was full of lies.

Others said they were angels, or demons, that they tempted humans to do wrong. Another said they kept to themselves, but would always rectify wrongs done them. That was nonsense, he knew. The King's father had put a visiting Fairy to death, and how had he suffered? One of them had even appeared to be his son's bride! Perhaps Fairies were like children, and only required a strong hand to keep them from running amuck.

He read that they could be defeated by iron, but he had seen the child set her hand to the metal with no apparent harm or pain. He read that they could be defeated by the pure of heart, but he knew of no one in the kingdom who would qualify. He read these words, "If you have angered a Fairy, the best thing to do is vanish. But they will come looking for you, no matter what."

He set the book down. For the first time in many years, he felt the urge to cry, tears of fear and despair, but he set that aside. It would do him no good. It would do him even less good than the books.

The thought of the skulls burned at him. He touched his brooch. The bone it was made of was not human. The bones it had come from lay deep in the garden, where he had lured the Queen one midnight. He had come up from behind and crushed her head with a stone, knowing in his heart of hearts that what he did was for the kingdom, removing this threat.

Others thought she had disappeared, dissatisfied with the King and life among the humans. He knew better. She was gone, gone for good.

But she had left her daughter behind.

The next day he went down to the chamber. The door stood, still barred. With shaking hands, he lifted it and swung the door open. The chamber was empty, but he could feel the skulls watching him, watching him. Only the red-marked skulls, though. He could change that.

Inside the chamber, his back turned as he smashed the skulls, he never saw the door closing. When it shut with a thump, he spun, heart racing. He went to the door and called out, "Who's there?"

No one answered him. He could picture the child standing as he had stood, listening. His heart hammered in his chest so loudly he was not sure he could hear her, even if she replied. He beat his hands against the door until they were sore, but everything was silence.

His lantern flickered, and he wondered how much fuel he had, how long it would last, and how long the darkness would last, once it failed. He thought that perhaps when the lantern was gone, he might hear slithering again, and this time he had no way of beating it back.

In this last thought, he was correct.

Neither Here

Sir Lyonel's disappearance was marked with sorrow, but not surprise. Too many had already disappeared for that.

And his disappearance did not stop the vanishings. Indeed, it seemed to increase them. Servants disappeared, and councilors, and visitors, until the castle seemed more like a great ghost ship, floating on deserted waters, with only Esmerelda's singing to mark it.

Esmerelda did not mark his disappearance much. She was occupied with her dreams, for lately a beautiful lady had appeared in them, kind and loving as Esmerelda's mother was said to have been. She would not say her name, would never speak to the child, but she held her and comforted her, and her arms were as warm as the King's.

In the mornings, Esmerelda thought she could hear the woman whispering what she had not said, almost an afterthought, but no matter how she listened, she could not make them out.

But as though the whispers stirred something in her, she began to know things, began to know where lost things were. She found Lia's lost necklace, and the cook's keys, and when her father could not find an important treaty, she led him to the desk wherein it lay.

She had never shown him such powers before, and they made him a little afraid. He reckoned up the numbers of the disappeared, and their size frightened him further, but he did not know what to do. Instead he waited in his throne room, at first attended by a few, then less, then none.

On the day when he heard his daughter come up the stairs, singing a nonsense song he had last heard on his wife's lips, love and fear struck him like a blow.

She entered the room, and was more like her mother than he had ever noticed.

His father had feared Fairy beauty, had destroyed it in the act that

126

had brought this all upon them.

His child settled on his lap and put her arms around him.

"Do not break my heart," he pleaded, stroking her hair, as she nestled closer.

"I will never break your heart, Father," Esmerelda said, then added, for she had always been taught to be honest, "I will eat it instead."

Afternotes

This was written in reply to a solicitation for a fairytale. I've always loved fairytales and as a kid, I read a lot of them, working my way first through a rainbow of Andrew Lang books and later finding others. In such stories, relationships between humans and elves always seem a perilous mix of attraction and fear, although here it's not the king who is at fault, but rather his advisor who tips things into motion and awakens his daughter to her true nature when he attempts to kill her.

Her true nature is what lies at the heart of the ending; she is not human, though she looks it, and she does not act in the way a human would, but rather as cruelly as one of the fairies that Sir Lyonel fears—a fate he has brought about by killing her mother.

The story started with the title, and grew from there with the image of the brooch, made from the bones of the elf princess that Lyonel murders, unbeknownst to the king, and wears as a reminder.

CALL AND ANSWER, PLANT AND HARVEST

CATHAY IS A CHAOS MAGE AND DOESN'T CARE who knows it. Fear and envy are fine emotions to set someone spinning into a roil, and Cathay can sip from that cup as easily as any other, wandering through a crowd and watching people edge away.

She dresses sometimes in blue and other times in green or silver or any other color except black. Today her sleeves are sewn with opals and moonstones and within their glimmer here and there on the left sleeve, glitters another precious stone, set in no particular order, random as the stars. Her skirt and bodice are aluminum fish-scales, armored though she expects no fight. Her only weapon is her own considerable wit.

Cathay stumbled into Serendib through a one-time doorway, like so many others. She was walking in a wood one moment. Then her foot came down and she was in a city. It made her laugh with delight, the unpredictability of it all.

She soon learned that she had come to the best possible place for a Chaos mage, the city of Serendib, made up of odd pockets and uncomfortable niches from other dimensions, a collision of cultures and technologies and economies like no other anywhere.

When she arrived in the city, she had three seeds, a dusting of lint, and a peppermint candy in her pocket. So she found an empty lot, precisely between a street where water magic ruled, in constant collision with the road made of fire and iron, so daily fierce sheets of steam arose, driving the delicate indoors and hissing furiously so it sounded as though a swarm of serpents was battling.

She popped the mint in her mouth despite its linty covering and dug a hole with her little finger, and then one with her thumb, and a third by staring at the dirt until it moved. Into each she dropped a seed, and covered it up, and sat down to wait, sucking on the candy and listening to the steam's whispers.

It was not long till the first inquisitive sprout poked through the dirt, followed by a second, delicate frills of tender green uncurling like butterfly's tongues.

Cathay waited for the third, but it was, by all appearances, still sulking underground. She shrugged; two were enough for now.

The vines that sprouted grew up and around and alongside each other, looping and re-looping till finally a house stood there, of middling size, and with many doors and few windows.

And there she lived. It was as good a place as any other, with pigeons and pixies murmuring in the roof gutters, with the steam-nourished ferns and fungi of the yard outside, with the city sky that roiled with auroras some days and clouds on others and drift of snow or feathers on still others and—rare and precious—sometimes shone with an Easter egg pastel in blue or pink or green.

NEITHER HERE

Today the air in this neighborhood is crisp with cold brine, although the actual sea the wind has blown over is parsecs and other dimensions away. Cathay comes through the fishmarket and admires the coiled heaps of octopi, whorled like a fruit-bat's ear and the shimmering piles of sardines, the squat tubs of flaky lumps of pickled herring, and the vast thirty-foot shark that hangs suspended head-down from a vast gibbet.

As she passes, the shark twitches and snaps the left hand off the fishmonger measuring it, but that is all the Chaos that she sows this morning, for she is in a good mood, and her destination is the Gilded Cock, a gaming house where they play each hand with a fresh pack of paper cards and gamble chips of latticed disks of mother-of-pearl, light as dried fish-scales.

There the air smolders with the steam from fish-tea, and the gamers in the backroom are stoned and slack-eyed on sour smoke.

Though the neighborhood is from a city in another world, as often happens in Serendib, the clientele are a mix drawn from all over the city's many corners. Back in that city, the neighborhood will have acquired a reputation as an odd one, an eerie one, where anything can happen. Sometimes boarded up, or guarded, or isolated with fences made of fire or glittering flakes of metal or demonic bile.

Among the crowd, Cathay sees a smooth shoulder, a fall of rainbow hair, eyes of earth and amber. Mariposa.

Mariposa.

⌁••••⊸⊙

"You love to gamble, they say." Mariposa leans on a windowsill. Cathay mirrors her position in another window for a second, then breaks the symmetry, shifting forward to cross one foot over the other.

"I do."

Mariposa's lips purse, her eyes squint. They hold a line of green in certain lights and moods, and right now that green thread shimmers, seems to wiggle like a seeking root.

"Come and prove it."

"The object is to secure the jewel held in magnetic suspension in the center. Whoever gets it and returns to their starting point is the victor. For the loser, there are two ways to opt to pay the penalty: through an electrical stimulation directly on the nerves or to be flogged with thorn branches, then healed through regrowth on the cellular level, which leaves no scars," the assistant explains. "If the gem falls out of the arena, both lose."

Cathay studies the silver cage, thirty feet across, that hangs over a pit of fire. Highbacked arena stands surround it. Faces press forward, shouting, booing, cheering the two lizard people wrestling in the cage, shaking it back and forth.

This is a high-tech quarter. It shows in the decor's brushed duralite and plasteel lanterns. Set in the trays that the slim-hipped servers carry back and forth: long crystal rods, flasks filled with layers of colored liquid, and hallucinogenic pyramids colored grape and tangerine and lemon.

"Such healing has been known to take its toll on the body," Mariposa said.

Cathay glances sidelong at her. "You would prefer I take the penalty in lashes?"

"I would prefer you win."

"Very well," Cathay says.

Neither Here

No one can be graceful clambering into a hanging cage, but Cathay consoles herself that the figure opposite her does it even more awkwardly. She studies it with bodily and psychic sight. A construct, earth-magic, strong but predictable.

Once in place it stares stolidly ahead. Its eyes roll, granite balls in rough-hewn sockets, its fingers like a blacksmith's implements.

The crowd murmurs and hoots and chatters and calls out a thousand things.

The first chime sounds. On the third they are free to move.

The golem is dead still. Cathay inhales and sees a constellation of moves shimmering in the aftermath of the second chime.

Now.

As the third note enters the air, she's already in motion, riding the edge of the rules in a way she's always been prone to, seeing the coruscating possibilities around her, flexing like origami.

The golem moves forward and rather than match its pattern, she goes sideways.

The cage shifts, tilting in unison with the crowd's scream.

The stony feet grind on the metal surface, sliding, sparks sizzling in its wake. It hits the bars with a crash and the silver lengths go helplessly awry, spilling it out.

At the last moment, its hand closes like a shark's jaws on the edge of the floor, clamps irrevocably closed.

The wild swing lurches further.

Cathay doesn't care. She hasn't even paused to look to see what's happened, but has seized the gem. The jerk sends her in the opposite direction from her starting perch, though. She executes a few wild stork steps before falling on her ass, though with fist still firmly clenched around the gem.

Patterns sparkle spin dance in the air. They used to dizzy her to the point of blindness but now she knows them, knows how to dance in the spaces between them, tweak them to her own unpredictable desires.

The golem's other hand comes up, latches onto the floor itself, fingers digging into the metals until the floor groans and gives way.

Cathay could gawp like the rest of the crowd. She's tempted to, in fact, because something that dense shouldn't be able to move that fast, but on the other hand it is moving that fast. So she goes hand over hand along the bars, since the cage is nearly entirely on its edge.

Seeing what she is doing, the golem also moves sideways, setting things further atilt, making the bars judder and shudder in Cathay's hands. She tries to move faster, going in a long arc that almost goes awry at an unexpected thud when the golem's fist goes entirely through the metal of the floor.

It reaches for her ankle and the crowd's screams go up in volume as though they'd been next door all this time and the door had just opened, yelling for blood …

… and Cathay's foot twists to land on top of the golem's head and then leap forward for the perch impossibly far away, body somersaulting, twisting as her hand shoots out and slams the gem down into its holder.

Breathing hard, heart like a trapped bird in her throat, Cathay bares her teeth at Mariposa in a grin.

⌁

The bus is striped aluminum and has three segments, like a silver snake. Its seats are plushed in blue and white with a pattern of ducks.

The wires overhead clash and sing and shoot out sparks that surround the bus as it lumbers into motion.

Cathay says, "Where are we bound?"

"This is the #72 bus. Where do you think we are bound?"

There is only one stop of note on that route.

"We go to play rigoletto at the Gates of Dawn."

Mariposa nods.

"Having had me risk pain, you now wish me to gamble with permanent exile?"

"Would you miss the city if such a fate came to you?" Mariposa asks. "Knowing you would no longer walk its streets, even after you died?"

Cathay shrugs. "There is Chaos everywhere. To be attached to a certain place is to display a certain predictability that I am, by nature, not disposed toward."

"Yet you have lingered here for over a decade now."

As they disembark the bus, Cathay searches for that green thread of interest in Mariposa's eyes, but the sky overhead is unobliging in its pink and amber clouds, marshmallow fluffy, a light almost cloying in its sweetness.

The glass-marbled plaza before the gates murmurs with spans of pigeons in the early light, pecking at the handfuls of grain scattered by families waiting to say goodbye to loved ones.

Serendib is an exacting mistress. It has many exiles, forced out by politics, or illness, or curse, or any range of things including random chance.

"It is as good a place as any other," she says, her voice as low as the pigeons' chatter.

⌇⌁⊸

The rigoletto players gather in a crowd by themselves, within reach of the gates.

They dress richly, flaunt their wealth, so everyone will know they come here for the gamble, not what they stand to win, but the truth is, immense fortunes have been made this way. They wear great hats of velvet dyed in jewel-tones with feathers to match; only two hatmakers in Serendib make these hats, and both dress their children in first-water jewels from their profits. The lace hems of their sleeves drag in the dust.

They murmur among themselves as Cathay, virtually naked by their standards, steps up. But it is not unheard of for someone to come to play the game without the preamble of assembling the requisite wardrobe.

As long as they can prove they have an estate to gamble. For the loser of the game must depart through those tall gates, pearly as legended others, and never return to the city.

Cathay walks up and down the line, hands clasped lightly behind her back, as though inspecting a rank of troops. She glances back at Mariposa. There are a few feckless youths among the crowd, who look easy to defeat. But that's not a victory worth evoking the green glimmer in Mariposa's eyes, Cathay suspects.

But there is no point in picking out the fiercest to fall against.

She is a Chaos mage, after all. So she closes her eyes, spins like a dervish, and stops, finger outpointed. She opens her eyes, hoping she has managed to point at the crowd and not some foolish thing like a pigeon or statue.

But a line could be drawn along her finger, exiting the tip, and lodge solidly in a man's chest. He is a sea captain, and dragon tattoos course along his brawny arms, circle the bald scalp revealed when he doffs his vermillion hat in acknowledgement.

They step to the side.

— •••— •◐

They match coins to see who will go first. Cathay wins. She knows that is not necessarily an advantage.

Her opponent is water magic, changeable and fickle. He may well have artefacts of power garnered during voyages. Those who sail or fly or wander with Serendib as home port range shores farther than her ken, even out to the great Darks where the gods dwell.

She sees no jewelry about him other than the gold hoop, a bit of wire really, twisted through his left ear. She would think it nothing but the left side is the heart side, and all enchantments are laid on that side of the body.

The predictable move would be fire, but she is a Chaos Mage. Therefore she laughs and uses fire after all. Being predictable is a choice like any other and one most people think a Chaos Mage will not engage in. Her curse has wings of fire, its beak is steeped in anger and envy.

She has out-subtled herself. He is ready with a swarm of water-winged fish that swoop through the air like a murmuration of swallows, tearing her creature apart before they wheel and dive down towards her.

Her left sleeve sweeps up over her head. Gems glitter and spark, a shark of scintillations that eats the fish like the dark eating light, an eclipse of movement beautiful because it is deadly as well as graceful.

Less traditional than his fish would imply, he buffets her with waves of force pulled from the tides.

She slips aside again and again like a matador eluding a vast, cloudy bull.

When he pauses, straining to see her in the watery mist, she appears behind him and strings a necklace of scorpion green curses around his neck while plucking the earring from his ear.

He falls to the ground, choking. Cathay pockets the loop and walks back to Mariposa.

"There," she says, voice light as a pigeon's feather. "Safe to dwell in my little house in Serendib for yet another day."

Mariposa's smile is crooked and full of some untold joke. Her face comes close to Cathay's. They search each other's eyes.

Mariposa's lids droop. She leans forward—and Cathay pulls away as though by counterweight, snatching her breath as though startled by the involuntary action of the move.

Mariposa's lips purse.

"Games of chance," she says. "Risking pain, risking home and fortune."

"And what is left beyond that?" Cathay says. Her voice is half-challenging.

"For the person who would risk everything?" Mariposa says.

They both know what she means.

The pit is in the very center of Serendib. There are thousands of legends about it. It is covered with a simple open pavilion carved of sandstone, beige but of a remarkable fine grain. It has never weathered. There are no markings.

In the center of the pavilion a squat, eight-armed creature sits beside the pit, which is some ten feet across.

For a fee, this creature will lower a basket holding the payee into the pit for a certain depth, and then let it hang there for a quarter of an hour, and then draw it back up. Three small creatures play flutes in the corner of the pavilion, and do so in shifts, so there is always a thin music in the air.

Nine out of ten so lowered return dead. Some have peaceful faces or even smiles. Others have a froth of fear on their mouths, or have clawed their own eyes out, or tore their veins open on the basket's rim.

A few vanish from the basket.

A few, though, a handful, return better than unscathed, touched with golden luck or new and unknown powers or enlightened beyond all comprehension.

Cathay stands peering over the edge.

"It seems very deep indeed," she observes, her tone mild.

"Is the gamble too large?" Mariposa asks.

Cathay shrugs, counting coins to the creature. This is all part of the universe's randomness. If she's lucky, Cathay can ride it like a dragon. Come out with the ability to talk to animals or angels. Shoot flames from her fingertips.

If she's not …

Well, that will be a different matter.

———

The basket goes down. The creatures pipe. Mariposa sits cross-legged on the ground and the green in her eyes threatens to overcome the rest. Her fingers wind around each other, anxious.

The sky flickers cobalt and amber and lightning. After a little while it rains. The rain stops and a rainbow appears before sparkling clouds obscure it. (All normal for Serendib weather. The city is where many sayings about weather began.)

Eight arms haul the basket up, scraping against the sandstone.

Cathay sits in the basket. Tears streak her face but she seems otherwise unscathed.

She leaps from the basket with a touch of impatience and strides over to Mariposa. "Well?"

"You have gambled and won," Mariposa says, rising.

She slides a hand along the front of Cathay's armored vest, careful not to cut herself on the metal scales.

"Three times," Cathay says, looking down into her face.

"Then you have gambled and won something from me," Mariposa says after a long moment. She tilts her mouth upward to make the prize clear.

Cathay stands, looking down, eyes neutral and wary and wistful. Mariposa's fingers flex on the metal scales.

Cathay shakes her head.

"You have won," she says regretfully, and releases her. "There is a risk that frightens me too far, and it lies in your eyes."

Cathay walks away, out of the pavilion, and the piping, and the eight-armed creature who has been observing all this interchange.

Mariposa stands looking after her and the thwarted green of her eyes is that of a seed left long underground and only recently come to the sun.

To seek its fortune.

To seek the one who planted it so long ago.

Afternotes

This Serendib story was written in reply to an anthology call for stories about gambling. I wanted to come back to Cathay and explore her nature a little, and so I thought about the idea of gambling and what sort of stakes might sway even the most reckless gambler to caution. Cathay is willing to take all sorts of risks, but in the end the risk of falling in love drives her away from a love that was, literally, created for her in the form of Mariposa, the woman grown from the third seed that Cathay planted when she first came to Serendib.

Cat Rambo

Author photo by On Focus Photo.

Cat Rambo

About Cat Rambo

Raised in the wilds of Indiana, Cat bounced around for several decades before settling in the Pacific Northwest, where she began a prolific writing spree, publishing over a hundred short stories to date in venues that include *Asimov's*, *Weird Tales*, and Tor.com. Her work in the field of speculative fiction includes a stint as *Fantasy Magazine's* editor, numerous nonfiction articles and interviews, and volunteer time with Broad Universe and Clarion West. She has been shortlisted for the Endeavour Award, the Million Writers Award, the Locus Awards, a World Fantasy Award, and a Nebula Award. This is her fourth collection.

her fourth collection.
Locus Awards, a World Fantasy Award, and a Nebula Award. This is
shortlisted for the Endeavour Award, the Million Writers Award, the
volunteer time with Broad Universe and Clarion West. She has been
Magazine's editor, numerous nonfiction articles and interviews, and
work in the field of speculative fiction includes a stint as *Fantasy*
date in venues that include *Asimov's*, *Weird Tales*, and Tor.com. Her
a prolific writing spree, publishing over a hundred short stories to
decades before settling in the Pacific Northwest, where she began
Raised in the wilds of Indiana, Cat bounced around for several

About Cat Rambo

OC 4116

CPSIA information can be obtained
at www.ICGtesting.com
Printed in the USA
FSOW01n1214061216
28112FS

JAN 2 7 2017

9 780989 082877

NOR THERE

Alternate World
Fantasy Stories

Cat Rambo

Hydra House

Nor There

978-0-9890828-7-7 (trade paperback)
978-0-9890828-8-4 (limited edition hardcover)
Library of Congress Control Number: pending

Hydra House
2850 SW Yancy St. #106
Seattle, WA 98126
http://www.hydrahousebooks.com/

Cover art by Galen Dara
http://www.galendara.com/

Cover design by Tod McCoy
http://www.todmccoy.com/

Illustrations by Mark W. Tripp
http://www.spiderpig.com/

Text design by Vicki Saunders

"Clockwork Fairies" © 2010 by Cat Rambo. First appeared on Tor.com, October 20, 2010. • "Her Windowed Eyes, Her Chambered Heart" © 2015 by Cat Rambo.. First appeared as Patreon post, 2015. • "The Coffeemaker's Passion" © 2011 by Cat Rambo. First published in *Bull Spec*, 2011. • "Elections at Villa Encantada" © 2014 by Cat Rambo. First published in *Unidentified Funny Objects 3*, edited by Alex Shvartsman, 2014. • "Seven Clockwork Angels, All Dancing on a Pin" © 2016 Cat Rambo. First appeared as a Patreon post, 2016. • Coyote Barbie" © 2011 by Cat Rambo. First appeared on *Expanded Horizons*, June 27, 2010. • "The Wizards of West Seattle" © 2016 by Cat Rambo. Original to this collection; first appeared on a private Patreon post, 2016.• "Summer Night in Durham" © 2014 by Cat Rambo. First appeared in *Stamps, Vamps, and Tramps*, edited by Shannon Robinson, 2014. • "Web of Blood and Iron" © 2016 Cat Rambo. First appeared as a Patreon post, 2016. • "So Glad We Had This Time Together" © 2012 by Cat Rambo. First published in Apex Magazine, January 3, 2012. • "Snakes on a Train" © 2011 by Cat Rambo. First appeared as a Patreon post, 2016. • "The Passing of Grandmother's Quilt" © 2011 Cat Rambo. First appeared on Every Day Fiction, January 9, 2013.

PRAISE FOR NEAR + FAR

Cat Rambo's newest collection shows two sides of her fiction. Powerful prose, coupled with telling details. Not only does the collection flip, physically, it will also turn you on your head. Read with caution: these stories are only safe in small doses.

Mary Robinette Kowal

Near + Far is a survey of the terrain of Cat Rambo's imagination, ranging from small fantasies of the moment to vest pocket planetary romances. She tends to the quiet, internal, disturbing reflection, far more Bradbury than Heinlein. Moving, thought-provoking literature in nicely comestible chunks.

Jay Lake

An exemplary short story collection in both senses of the term— excellent and also a model of what the range of the career of a speculative short story writer should be, and these days unfortunately so rarely is. Wide in its subject matter from the immediate future to the wide open spaces, deep in its psychological characterization when that is the central point, speculatively amusing when it isn't, well-realized almost all of the time, and always entertaining.

Norman Spinrad

Nor There Contents

Clockwork Fairies   1

Her Windowed Eyes,
Her Chambered Heart   21

The Coffeemaker's Passion   42

Elections at Villa Encantada   49

Seven Clockwork Angels,
All Dancing on a Pin   68

Coyote Barbie   75

The Wizards of West Seattle   80

Summer Night in Durham   100

Web of Blood and Iron   104

So Glad We Had This Time
Together   120

Snakes on a Train   129

The Passing of Grandmother's
Quilt   149

CLOCKWORK FAIRIES

MARY THE IRISH GIRL LET ME IN when I knocked at the door in my post-services Sunday best, smelling of incense and evening fog. Gaslight flickered over the narrow hall. This was Southland's city house. His country estate provided his daughter, my affianced, plenty of space to pursue her studies and experiments.

It was comfortable enough here, though. The mahogany banister's curve gleamed with beeswax polish, and a rosewood hat rack and umbrella stand squatted to my left.

I nodded to Mary, taking off my top hat. Snuff and baking butter mingled with my own pomade to battle the smell of steel and sulfur from below.

"Don't be startled, Mr. Claude, sir," Mary said, even as I asked, "Is your mistress in?"

Before I could speak further, a whir of creatures surrounded me.

At first I thought them American hummingbirds or large dragonflies. One hung poised before my eyes in a flutter of metallic skin and isinglass wings. Delicate gears spun in the wrist of a pinioned hand holding a needle-sharp sword. Desiree had created another marvel. Clockwork fairies, bee-winged, glittering like tinsel. Who would have dreamed such things, let alone make them real, except Desiree?

Mary chattered, "They're hers. They won't harm ye. Only burglars and the like."

She swatted at one that had come too close, its hair floating like candy-floss in the air. Mary had been with the Southland household for three years now and had grown accustomed to scientific marvels. "I'll tell her ladyship yer here."

She left. I eyed the fairies that hovered in the air around me. Despite Mary's assurance, I was not sure what they would do if I stepped forward. They were capable of independent movement in a way I had not witnessed before in clockwork creations.

Footsteps sounded downstairs, coming closer. Desiree appeared in the doorway that led to her basement workshop. She had been working. A pair of protective lenses goggled around her neck, and she wore gloves. Not the dainty kidskin gloves of fashionable women, but thick pig leather to shield her clever brown fingers from sparks. One clutched a brass oval studded with tiny buttons, almost glove-obscured.

Her skin and race made her almost as much an oddity in upper London society as the fairies. She was mine; I smiled at her.

"Claude," she said. Her eyes simmered with delight.

She clicked the device in her hand and the fairies swirled away, disappearing to God knows where. "I'm almost done. I'll meet you in the parlor in a few minutes. Go ahead and ring for tea."

———•◦•···•◦

In the parlor, I took to the settee and looked around. As always, the room was immaculate, filled with well-dusted knickknacks. Butterflies fluttered under two bell jars on the charcoal marble mantle, carved with lily of the valley. The room was well-composed: a sofa sat in graceful opposition with a pair of wing chairs. The only discordant note was sounded by the book shoved between two embroidered pillows on a chair's maroon velvet. I picked it up. *On the Origin of Species*, by Charles Darwin.

I frowned and set it back down. Only last week, my minister had spoken out against this very book. I would have to speak to Desiree. I knew better than to forbid her to read it—but she should not discuss it in polite company or support its heretical notion that humans were

related to animals, contrary to God's order, the Great Chain of Being.

Mary the Irish girl brought tea and sweet biscuits in a clatter of heels, muting when she reached the parlor carpet. I poured myself a cup, sniffing. Lapsang Oolong. Desiree's father had excellent taste in provisions.

The man himself appeared in the doorway. Lord Southland, one of London's notable titled eccentrics. His silk waistcoat was patterned with golden bees, as fashionable as my own undulating Oriental serpents.

"Ah, Stone," he said. He advanced to take a sesame seed biscuit, eyebrows bristling with hoary disapproval behind shilling-sized lenses. "You're here again."

"I came to visit Desiree," I replied, stressing the last word. I knew Lord Southland disapproved of me, although his antipathy puzzled me. If he hoped to marry off his mulatto daughter, I was his best prospect, being free of the prejudices others held.

With his wife's death, though, Southland had become irrational, taking up radical notions. So far Desiree had steered clear of them with my guidance, but I shuddered to think that she might become a Nonconformist or Suffragist. Still, I took care to be polite to Southland. If he cut Desiree from his will, the results would be disastrous.

"Of course he came to see me, Papa," Desiree said from the other doorway. She had removed her leather apron, revealing a gay pink cotton dress, sprigged with strawberry blossoms. She perched a decorous distance from me and poured her own tea, adding a hearty amount of milk.

"I've come to nag you again, Des," I teased.

A crease settled between her eyebrows. "Claude, is this about Lady Allsop's ball again?"

I leaned forward to capture her hand, its color deep against my own pale skin. "Desiree, to be accepted in society, you *must* make an effort now and then. If you are a success it will reflect well on me, and show that I have not taken you from the shelf, despite your age. Twenty-four is not so advanced that you are automatically an old maid, but people make assumptions. Appearing at the ball will be a major step towards dispelling those."

She removed her fingers from mine, the crease more pronounced. "I have told you, I am not the sort of woman that goes to balls."

"But you could be!" I told her. "Look at you, Desiree. You are as beautiful as any woman in London. A nonpareil. Dressed properly, you would take the city by storm."

"We have been over this before," she said. "I have no desire to expose myself to stares. My race makes me noteworthy, but it is not pleasant being a freak, Claude. Last week a child in the street wanted to rub my skin and see 'if the dirt would come off.' Can you not be happy with me as I am?"

"I am very happy with you as you are," I said. I could hear a sullen touch in my voice, but my feelings were understandable. "But you could be so much more!"

She stood. "Come," she said. "I will show you what I have been working on."

There would be no arguing with her, I could tell by the tone, but a touch of sulkiness might wear her down. Lord Southland glared at me as I bowed to him, but neither of us spoke.

—⊶∗◈

In the workshop, a clockwork fairy sprawled on the table. Using a magnifying glass, Desiree showed me its delicate works, the mica flakes pieced together to form the wings.

"Where did you get the idea?" I asked.

"In Devonshire, an old woman spoke of seeing fairies. There was an interview with her in *The Strand*."

I snorted. "Old women are given to fancies."

Desiree shrugged, taking up a pick and using it to adjust the paper-thin wing hinge. "It made me think of how to create a flying creature. I chose to use bumblebees for my model, rather than the traditional butterfly wings. My fairies can resist strong winds and go where I wish them, according to the instructions I have laid into their 'brains,' which are tiny Babbage engines."

Desiree is interested in such things but spiritual matters are what I find engaging. She droned on but I cut her short. "Sometimes I think

you don't love me."

She stopped. Her half-parted lips were like flower petals, an orchid's inner workings. "Why do you say that?"

"You don't understand my position," I said. "As a Dean, I must have a wife who is acceptable in society's eyes."

"This is about the ball again," she said. She made as though to touch my face, but I turned my head away, pretended to be examining the articulated form half-assembled on the table near me.

"Very well," she said. Her hand returned to her side. "I will go."

Γ—····—◦

That week fled pell-mell. I went to a lecture series by John Newman and in the evenings I dined at my club and had excellent quail prepared in the French style. I went to the theater on two occasions, once to see Gilbert's "Robert the Devil" and again to see "How She Loves Him," by Boucicault. I stopped by Lord Southland's on three separate evenings.

Desiree had started on a mechanical cat. She took me into her workshop to look at it. A clockwork nightingale sang in the wicker cage hanging from the rafters, set in motion by our footsteps' vibration.

"It's still in the preliminary stages," she said. A brass skeleton lay disassembled on the table, but it was laid out so I could see the cat-to-be's shape. Mercury beads rolled in a white porcelain dish. A discarded spray of silver whiskers had been tossed in the coalscuttle.

I glanced around. "The Deanery has a basement," I said. "It houses our wine cellar and storerooms, but I have sent to have the front room cleaned and whitewashed for you."

Her teeth flashed as she smiled. Her breath smelled of licorice when I stole a kiss and I felt her skin's warmth against my hands. True, the room was not as fine as this, but she would improvise and makeshift, for she was a clever girl. And once she had started breeding, such fancies would fall away. Her inventions, her clever machines, were simply the maternal instinct thwarted. Once she had a child, she would find herself devoted to it. Our children would be handsome. And well provided for with the dowry she would bring.

When she went upstairs to speak to her father, I lingered in the workshop. I amused myself walking between the tables and shelves, examining at her work.

I paused beside what looked like a dress-form, a brass cylinder the size of a human torso. My cheeks flushed as I regarded it.

Shockingly, Desiree had given it the semblance of a maiden's bosom, a suggestion of curves whose immodesty appalled me. Headless, armless, legless, the torso stood affixed to three steel rods that culminated in a circular base as wide as an elephant's foot.

I reached out and touched my fingertips to its "shoulder." I trailed them down along the skin towards its chest. The oils from my fingers laid a faint trail behind them, wavering on the metal's gleam. It was how corrosion started, I knew. Given time, would the stains grow to verdigris, show how intimately I had touched Desiree's creation?

I buffed the marks away with a linen rag that lay on a nearby workbench. The stairs creaked beneath me in admonishment as I ascended them to join Desiree and her father. They had been arguing again. I heard her father say, "Blasted pedantic popinjay!" and Desiree say, "Oh Father," her tone coaxing and indulgent.

"You don't have to settle for such a man!"

"If I want to be part of society and not an outcast, I need the most proper of husbands! Claude and I will accommodate each other with time."

That had an ominous sound, but we would negotiate it later. They fell silent as I appeared. Southland's face was red with anger, Desiree's smile as bland as her mechanical cat licking cream.

—————

On the night of Lady Allsop's ball, everyone notable was there. Silks and satins gleamed like colored waters, touched with flecks of light from cut gems. The air smelled of hothouse flowers and French scent. The orchestra played "Beautiful Bells" as the dancers glided in the waltz.

I do not entirely approve of such things as dancing, but society places demands on us. I was eager for the ton to place their seal of

benison on my bride to be. I would dance twice with Desiree when she arrived, but for the most part I intended to stay on the sidelines, drinking lemonade. Still, when a few partners pressed me, I gave in.

I know well that women find me alluring—no credit to anyone other than He who shaped me. But my calf shows to advantage in fine hose, to the point where at least one too-bold madam had called it shapely.

And I knew *very* well that it was my looks that initially attracted Desiree. Like all women, she is drawn to this world's baubles, not realizing their transient, mayfly nature. But with time, she had sounded my mind's depths and I flattered myself that it was what she found there that strengthened her attraction to me.

A woman I danced with let me know the Southlands had arrived. "Your fiancée, is she not?" she purred with a throaty sound. "I saw her arrive with her Papa, a half hour or so ago."

I made my excuses and went outside the Great Hall to pass through the refreshment line, looking for Desiree. I caught sight of her ahead of me, in the side hall's shadows, dark hair piled in an intricate mechanism atop her head. She paused beside a dusky silk curtain, speaking to another woman, blond-haired, blue-eyed.

From the back I could see Desiree's silk skirt: figured with gears, the teeth embroidered in red. I came up behind her and slid my hand through the crook of her elbow, drawing her close to show my pleasure at her presence there, despite her dress's outré nature.

I realized my mistake from the way the woman pulled herself away. She turned and I saw her clearly, no longer Desiree. Her hair held brownish red highlights, and her eyes were an icy, outraged green. The patterned cogs were Michelmas daises, the teeth ragged petals, scarlet on cream.

I stammered apologies, backed away as quickly as I could, bowing.

I searched through the crowds for Desiree and failed to find her. I looked around the punchbowl, through a salon of young misses waiting to be asked to dance, their mamas hovering nearby. Desiree had never been among their ranks. Her father had been indulgent, allowed her to skip so many social niceties. I sought her among the dancers and along the wall benches, where groups of men gossiped

and women nattered among themselves.

Slipping outside into the starlit gardens, I found her there, scandalously alone with a man.

Pea gravel crunched under my boot heels as I approached, just in time to see him lean forward and take her hand. The night was cool on my outraged cheeks as I ran forward, pushing him away from her.

He staggered back, looking surprised. I had not seen him before: a dark Irishman with a narrow face and a nose like a knife blade. His black eyes were altogether too Byronic.

Sometimes you dislike a man at first sight; it was so for me. An expression that flashed over his face made me think he reciprocated the sentiment. He was, annoyingly enough, dressed impeccably, better than my own efforts, despite the Honiton lace at my throat.

Something wild in the cast of his features, the white flash of his throat, the enormous emerald on his hand, the way the moonlight glinted on his fingernails, made me think him something other than human, some besotted seraphim or an exotic nightmare born of hallucinogen or poison. A shiver worked its way down my back and spread its fingers to measure my ribs.

"Claude!" Desiree exclaimed, looking far from pleased at her rescue.

I ignored her, addressing the man. "You will not touch my fiancée again, sir. I am surprised at you, taking advantage of her in this fashion." I did not say it, but my reproach was aimed at Desiree as well, even though I knew she had not known better in her foolish, naïve youth.

"Lord Tyndall brought me out here to discuss my designs," Desiree retorted. "He had read the paper I published on the difficulties of imprinting tungsten."

I scoffed. "Indeed, he did his homework well in order to lure you out to compromise you."

Unnervingly, the man smiled at me. "I had no idea such an erudite work's author would turn out to be charming, sir, but the pleasure was unexpected. Having finished with that conversation, I was merely offering to demonstrate the art of palm reading to your lady. I picked up some small expertise in it in my homeland."

People were stirring in the nearest doorway, looking out to see what the loud conversation was.

Tyndall spoke to Desiree. "I did not get the chance to tell you, lady, your palm shows that you will take a long journey, soon."

His accent was thick. It was ridiculous for an educated man to speak with such a heavy brogue or to pretend to superstitious beliefs such as palmistry in order to lure women to him. But I stood down, not wishing to alienate the gathering crowd.

Lady Allsop peered from near the back, the frown on her face threatening future invitations. I bowed and took Desiree's arm, drawing it through my own. She resisted, then let me pull her into the house.

But she would not speak to me the rest of the evening despite the attendance I danced on her. In the carriage home, she relented, but only to upbraid me.

"I did as you asked," she hissed at me. "And it was as painful as I imagined, but not satisfied with *that*, you must take away the one interesting conversation I was able to find."

"Everyone loved you, how can you say such things?" I protested.

"Perhaps you were at a different ball than I," she said. "Did you not see Lady Worth turn away lest she contaminate herself speaking to a Negro? Or perhaps you did not overhear the sporting gentleman laying bets on what I would be like between the sheets?"

"Desiree!" I gasped, almost breathless at the shock of hearing such words from her innocent lips.

She turned away and did not speak to me again that night.

———••••—••◯

The next day I came to call, bringing chocolates and flowers and a pretty opal ring. Opals were her favorite gem. But she sent Mary to tell me she was feeling unwell.

I started to leave in high dudgeon, but Lord Southland called to me. He was in his library, or so he called it, a small room that smelled of pipe tobacco and old leather, so close that one could barely breathe. On the wall hung a portrait of Desiree's mother by Robert Tait.

I studied it as he gathered his thoughts. I knew her mother had perished in childbirth along with Desiree's younger brother, only a few years after Lord Southland had returned with her from a trip to America. No one knew exactly where she had come from, but common gossip maintained that she had been a slave escaped from the southern portion of that barbarous place, that she had lived with the Cherokee for several years before the young Southland, on tour, encountered her in New Orleans. She was beautiful, although in an exotic, unsettling wise. Her dark hair hung to her waist, and the artist had chosen to paint it untamed, almost hiding her face behind it. Her dress's satin was the color of a yellow rose just opening.

She had never been accepted by society, but had been an exile, trapped in this house. That was part of the contract between Desiree and I; through me she would escape such a fate.

"Do you love my daughter, Claude?" Lord Southland asked. Rumor held that before his wife, he'd had other exotic pets: a tiger cub, a great hyacinth macaw that sang sea shanties, a bush-baby from Senegal. He was impious and had rejected the church, refusing to have Desiree baptized.

The question pained me, and I took care to show that in my tone. "Ever since I first met her, my lord."

"Ever since you met her, or ever since you learned she was an heiress?" He waved off my protestations. "I know, I know, such thoughts are unworthy. Still, I cannot help but wonder, Claude, if you did not think her an easy catch, given her circumstances. You are hardly the first suitor to make that mistake."

Desiree had other suitors? I was shocked but intrigued. I had never heard word of such.

"Still, the chit claims to love you." His look was contemptuous, and I stiffened my back under it. "It must be your looks alone, for you seem slow of mind to me."

I squared my chin. "You may disagree with your daughter's choice, but you raised her to speak her mind and choose for herself."

"I did." He tugged at a pearl-set waistcoat button. "And will you allow her the same luxury, once she is married?"

"Of course I will!" I said. "Within reason."

"As I feared. Very well, I will warn you, Claude. I will continue to attempt to dissuade her from this choice."

"What choice?" Desiree demanded as she entered. Her look at me was initially cold, but I smiled at her and she softened, as I knew she would. "Papa, are you beating this dead horse again?"

"Let me send you travelling," Lord Southland urged. "I will fund a trip to Italy, so you might see Leonardo's designs for yourself. Or America, where you can speak with other inventors."

"America?" she said. "Where they would take me to be a slave? Do you not read the papers, do you truly not know what danger I would be in there?"

"Desiree," he said. "For your mother's sake, and your own, all I want is your happiness."

"I will be an English Dean's wife and live at Oxford," she said. "Claude has promised me a workshop the equal of mine here."

Now was not, perhaps, the best time to correct that misapprehension, so I kept my mouth closed. Not that it mattered. Father and daughter had squared off like pugilists in the ring, and Desiree's fists were clenched as though to keep herself from aiming a blow at him.

He took an envelope from his vest pocket, ivory paper with an intricate seal. "I have had a letter inviting us to come shooting next week. The writer says he met you at Lady Allsop's. An Irish estate." He spared me a glance. "Claude is invited as well. If he comes too, will you accompany me? I would not have you wed without seeing other possibilities. And rumor holds the pheasant excellent in that region."

She gave me a questioning look and I nodded. Better to see Lord Southland assuaged, lest he put his foot down even more firmly. His difficulties were his own fault, I thought, for allowing his daughter too free a rein. Although it advantaged me more than a little, for I suspected her father's resistance only increased Desiree's interest in me.

I touched her elbow and saw her shoulders loosen. Southland kept glowering, but now at me. I smiled at him and laced my fingers through hers before drawing them up to press my lips to her knuckles, my eyes fixed on his. His jaw tautened.

NOR THERE

When I returned home, I found a similar envelope awaiting me. His Lordship regretted the unfortunate occurrences at Lady Allsop's and hoped to extend an olive branch to myself and my "lovely fiancée."

Now that the moment was past, I regretted the assent I had given. But Southland would have written with his consent already, punctilious and prompt when he thought it might inconvenience me.

I decided to make the most of it. As Southland had noted, the shooting in Tyndall's district was rumored to be extraordinary. While the Lord—was he one of the men that Southland reckoned a suitor?—would have the advantage in his home, the day I could not show up a country Irishman, no matter his title, would be the day I'd give up my position at Oxford. As for his inhuman aspect, it had been nothing more than a trick of the moonlight, coupled with my anger. It surprised me, how deep that rage stirred at the memory, even now, days later.

I turned the envelope over and examined the ostentatious seal. A pair of cats boxing with each other, paws upraised, circling a crown tipped with what looked like pointed spindles. A sweet smell came from the green wax.

I directed my valet to pack for the countryside. I would see this interloper driven away before Desiree even realized he was interested in her. Her naïveté gave me the edge—not that I needed it.

As we approached Lord Tyndall's castle, the countryside was verdant, the fall leaves just beginning to turn. The castle—for it was indeed a castle, albeit a small and shabby one—sat on a cliff's edge overlooking the Irish Sea, a romantic, wild vista that I feared might enthrall my impressionable fiancée.

I took care to point out the flaws in the countryside as we travelled up along the road: dull-appearing peasants and ill-tended cottages. I said I supposed it was most difficult to obtain supplies from London, given the distance and the road's rigors.

Desiree seemed to listen. Her father slouched in the opposite seat of the carriage and regarded me with heavy-lidded, inscrutable eyes.

There were a dozen other guests or so: a few Irish peers, and relatives of his Lordship, along with Lady Allsop and her husband. Everyone exclaimed over Desiree's exotic beauty and made enough fuss over her to render her speechless with discomfort. I hung back and did not rescue her. She would have to learn to cope with such attentions.

We settled into a daily routine, and Lord Southland and I both found the shooting excellent. I had never experienced such success at it before, in fact. It was as though the birds flew into my gun's path to sacrifice themselves. I had never experienced such a feeling of *prowess* before. The other men congratulated me, sometimes sullenly, sometimes with genuine comradeship. The women were invariably flattering, even Desiree, although it was evident that my skill surprised her.

It was heady, and though Tyndall came shooting with us less and less, I found myself able to overlook it. We dined well on the yield from our expeditions each day. Tyndall had an excellent cook, one who rivaled the best establishments. Her blancmange was airy as a cloud; her teacakes scented with cardamom and honey. A good cook, like a good woman, is a pearl beyond price. I resolved to woo her away before going.

Desiree was uninterested in shooting, which made me uneasy, but I was unable to resist the pull of the field. Like Desiree, Tyndall fancied himself a scientist, and like her, he had a mechanical talent. She had brought the case containing the clockwork fairies, and the two were working on refinements to the wings. Desiree suggested that the fairies could be used in place of courier pigeons, and despite the notion's impracticality, Tyndall supported it.

I asked what she was working on next.

"Something to delight you!" she said, her face glowing with anticipation. "Tyndall's workshop is so fine, I have been able to

construct something that will amaze you when you see it." She laughed. "I think I will gift him with it when we leave. He has said so many times how clever he thinks my machines."

"And they *are* clever," I said. I touched the tips of the curls surrounding her face. They were stiff and unbending as corkscrews.

She pulled away. "My maid spends too much time dressing my hair for you to set it in disarray!" she said, but laughed to take the sting from the words.

<hr />

I had found a staircase leading up from the main hall that had a nook suitable for reading. Always conscious of the necessity of keeping up, I had brought edifying and current works with me. One was *The Subjection of Women* by John Stuart Mill, a package of inflammatory claptrap.

Sitting in my refuge, I was about to put it down when a sentence made me realize even the falsest text might hold some grain of truth. The sentence read, "To understand one woman is not necessarily to understand any other woman."

I put the book aside but took that sentence with me, considering how it was true without being true. Certainly, every woman's personality was different, but there were commonalities at the heart of them all: a love of gossip, for instance. Concern with trivialities. An attraction to beauty.

Voices from below caught my attention. The stairway's acoustics were such that sounds carried clearly. It might have been designed for such a thing; I have encountered whispering galleries that bring a word from far away as close to one's ear as though the speaker stood there.

It was Desiree and Tyndall.

"I think a more durable metal, laid along the edge, will prevent warpage," she was saying.

"Your little fairies intrigue me," he said. "Where did you find the model?"

"In my head," she admitted. "I was reading a newspaper account and it made me wonder what such a creature would look like."

"You have never glimpsed a fairy in the wild?"

She laughed. "Oh, and dragons in the coal cellar? No, I have never been prone to flights of fancy."

"You think fairies only a romantic notion."

"I think people would like to believe in them, would like to believe in magic," she said. "Even I feel that temptation. But it is at heart a foolish idea."

"What if I told you I could take you to a place where you would see them, Desiree?" he purred. "Told you that true magic is wild beyond your imagining, that it will seize you, take you as though by storm?"

I was shocked that he would address her so familiarly. My indrawn breath betrayed me.

"Who's there?" he exclaimed, and came up the stairs swiftly enough that you would have thought he feared some intruder. At the sight of me, he scowled.

I, on the other hand, was stiff with indignation. He meant to lure my fiancée to some deserted spot under the pretext of seeing fairies. Perhaps he meant to compromise her to the point where she would be forced to marry him. Or perhaps the scoundrel meant to seduce her. I would have said these things, but Desiree's face behind him made me keep my tongue.

"Come to lunch, Stone," he said. "There is the usual cold pheasant. You have not lost your taste for it yet, I trust?"

"I find myself thinking that we should return to London soon," I said. Let him realize I had overheard his plotted seduction.

"Leave?" Desiree exclaimed. How could she be so foolish? Could she not see what Tyndall was up to? Was it possible she harbored romantic feelings for him? But the expression on her face was not thwarted lust. She liked speaking with him, I realized. It was nothing more than that.

Surely it was nothing more than that.

⌁

A day later, I overheard another conversation, this time between Desiree and her father. I will not trouble myself to reproduce it here, for

much of what Lord Southland said was misguided and wrong. He claimed that I was too dull for Desiree and said, absurdly, that she should find a man capable of providing her with intelligent conversation.

I would have interjected, but I had learned my lesson the previous day. Instead, I kept quiet and listened, knowing that Desiree would defend me as she had before.

But her protestations seemed half-hearted and, worse, she seemed to believe her father's words held some truth.

"You valued looks yourself," she said. "Was it not my mother's beauty that drew you to her?"

"At first, perhaps, but then I was taken by her manners, her bravery," Lord Southland said.

"Claude may not be intelligent," she said. "But he is respectable and well-rounded, in the manner of English education. And he has thought a great deal about spiritual matters."

"Spiritual matters!" her father exclaimed. "I thought I had brought you up better than to believe in the crutch that supports feeble minds in their mediocrity!"

Had he raised her as an atheist? I was appalled, but I knew I would be able to teach her, patiently and carefully, as befits a man with his wife.

"I want to believe in something other than science," she said, and I thrilled at the earnestness in her voice. "I want to believe in something wild and fierce and free, something that stands outside society."

Her theology was muddled, but she could learn. Her father's sound of disgust and frustration made me smile.

That evening we stood on the terrace overlooking the sea. I could not resist, but said, "Desiree, do you think we are well matched in mind?"

She hesitated, her indrawn breath a delicate whisper.

I did not mind. I knew I outstripped her, but I would reach down, lift her to new heights of thought, of philosophy. Some hold that the Negro race is a simpler structure, but Desiree had already proved that she could get her mind around such things as mathematics and mechanics. I would show her theology's wonders, the careful

construction of a passage explicating God's glory. We would read Milton together, and other poetry that would elevate her soul.

—⚬—

I searched for proof of Tyndall's intentions, for signs that he was not a man of science, only pretending to be one in order to seduce my gullible bride to be. Desiree always thought the best of people. It was up to my more rigorous mind to show her her error.

In his study, a massive book lay on the table, its pages well-thumbed. I turned it to study the spine.

A chill ran through me and I pulled my hand away, as though from a coiled serpent. *King James's Daemonologie.*

Using a handkerchief, I touched it, opened it. The words burned up at me:

This word of Sorcerie is a Latine worde, which is taken from casting of the lot, & therefore he that vseth it, is called Sortiarius à sorte.

Was Tyndall a sorcerer then? What unholy designs did he have on Desiree? This was far, far worse than I had imagined.

A cough sounded behind me. I dropped the page and spun.

Tyndall.

He had the gall to stand there, polite inquiry on his face.

"Some light reading, Stone?" he said.

I pointed at the book. My hand shook with emotion.

"No honest man has such a book in his library! What foul magics do you practice?"

"I have never claimed to be an honest man," he said dryly.

"Demon!" I hissed.

He shook his head. His tone was still polite, as though we spoke regarding the proper slicing of a breast of pheasant or the correct garnish for a trout.

"I have been called that before, on my visits to this land," he said. "But *elf* is more accurate."

"I know a demon when I see one! You admit you are not human! You want not just Desiree's body, but her soul!"

He snorted. "Her soul is her own. I want only her clever mind and

machines, to entertain my Queen's court."

I gestured about myself. "Then this is all illusion!"

He shook his head. A smile lingered at the corners of his mouth, as though it pleased him to speak so straightly to me. "No, the real Lord Tyndall is … elsewhere. He will return when I am done, none the worse for the wear. Indeed, his fortunes will prosper as a result. As yours could."

"You mean to threaten me."

"I mean to say that the financial chains binding you to your fiancée could be replaced with other gold, of my own forging, as recompense."

"Desiree is more than gold to me," I said. "A good wife is a treasure. Fairy gold is said to melt away, or become dry leaves in the light of day."

"So you refuse to think of giving her up?" he said.

"She may not be much," I said. "Prideful and a little wanton, and overly obsessed with this world's trumperies. But she is mine, and I will have her, and the rich dowry that comes with her, and the inheritance that will befall her when her father dies."

"Do you love her?"

I hesitated too long. In the silence I heard the little gasp of betrayal behind me.

I turned.

Tears stood in her eyes before she fled.

⌖━┈┈━◉

She was nowhere to be found. No matter where I searched, even with the help of Tyndall's servants, who also looked for their absent lord, mysteriously vanished as well. But when I let myself into my chamber that night, I knew she had been there. A tang of oil and steel hung like dragon's breath in the air.

A shrouded figure stood beside the fireplace.

The note lay on my writing desk. Her handwriting was clear as copperplate.

It read: *Claude, I do not think we will suit. But I have left you something that will, I think, let you have the kind of woman you desire. She comes with my dowry—I will not need it where Tyndall is*

taking me. I wish you only the best, Claude. I hope you wish me that in turn. The key is on the mantle. Remember to wind her up every seventh day. —Desiree

I pulled the cloth away. At first it looked like Desiree standing there, stiff and rigid, dressed in a gown of pale blue moiré that I recognized as the one she had worn to Lady Allsop's ball. But closer examination showed the skin was dyed cloth laid over a harder surface, the hair sewn onto the scalp. A hole nestled in her décolletage, just big enough to accommodate the brass key I retrieved from the fireplace.

I inserted the key and twisted it, hearing the ratcheting of the cogs and gears inside my clockwork bride, until her eyelids unshuttered and I stepped forward to take her in my arms.

As we waltzed, I wept. Wept for my Desiree—not just what I had thought she would be to me, but for what she had been, for her clever hands and heart and laughter, and that she had loved me as much as I had loved her. Tears fell to stain the silk bodice as I held her close, sky blue darkening to stormy. The fairies hung in a circle around us, left to dance by their former mistress. I wept, and we danced.

She danced very well indeed.

Afternotes

This story was my first attempt to sit down and write a piece that was consciously steampunk. At the time I was writing, I was editing Fantasy Magazine, and seeing the steampunk genre emerge as a very white, very middle-class phenomenon that managed to ignore a great many implications of the word "punk."

Punk was at its heart a questioning of established orders and systems inherent in mid- to late-20th century society. Cyberpunk took that into the future, interrogating the rosy futures painted by Disney, Star Trek, and other media forces. Steampunk—in my opinion—initially took the style but not the substance from its progenitor. Since then writers have pushed boundaries and brought in questions of power, appropriation, and oppression, particularly as affected by race, gender, and class.

So I wanted a person of color in my steampunk landscape,

but I didn't choose her as my protagonist, but rather told the story from Claude's point of view. When I first workshopped the story with my writing group, some of the readers disliked Claude immensely. That would surprise Claude, who is very much a product of his time, which tells him that he is at the pinnacle of the Great Chain of Being, and that he's superior to women and "lesser races." Desiree's skin color doesn't matter to him—which surely must be admirable—but at the same time he doesn't question a social order where it matters greatly for many people.

The story originally appeared on Tor.com and owes a great deal to the adept editing of Liz Gorinsky. The artwork that appeared with it, by Gregory Manchess, was perfect.

This piece is part of the Altered America series, and falls chronologically very early, being a precursor to the fairy invasion of England that results in the events chronicled in "Rare Pears and Greengages," which appears in Eyes Like Sky and Coal and Moonlight. I plan to expand it into a longer novel about that invasion, featuring Desiree, at some point.

Her Windowed Eyes,
Her Chambered Heart

RENZIES OF GINGERBREAD ADORNED the house's facade, but it was splintery, paint peeling in long shaggy spirals that fuzzed the fretwork's outlines. The left side of the house drooped like the face of a stroke victim, windows staring blindly out, cataracted with the dusty remnants of curtains.

Agent Artemus West thought that it would have given a human man the chills. He glanced back at Elspeth to see how she was taking it, but her face was chiseled and resolute as a fireman's axe.

"You all right?"

She swabbed at her forehead with a bare forearm, leaving streaks of dark wet dirt. "Thank your lucky stars you're mechanical and don't feel the heat," she rasped.

Hot indeed if enough to irritate her into mentioning that. He chose to ignore it.

The house sagged amid slumping cottonwoods, clusters of low-lying trees, their leaves ovals of green and pale brown. Three stories, and above that two cupolas, thrust upward into the sky, imploring, the

left one tilted at an angle. The wind whistled through the fretwork, a shifting, hollow sound, like a jug's mouth being blown across. There had once been a flower garden towards the back. Weeds had claimed most of it, but the papery red heads of poppies blazed among the tangle. The sky stretched high and blue and hollow overhead.

His spurs jingled as he clanked up the front steps. His eyes ratcheted over the scene for clues, but it was clear that their fugitive had entered by the front door, which hung a few inches ajar.

Wood creaked under Elspeth's slower treads. "This was his mother's house," she said.

She'd gone over the files meticulously as always, then summed up the details for him as they'd ridden along. He ticked through them in his head. "The scientist?"

"Angeline Stoddard Eisenmacher, yes. She helped discover how to harness phlogiston. She was working in Seattle for the war effort. Then she retired out here when she got lungrot and lasted another two years."

Phlogiston, the most precious material in the world, capable of fueling marvelous machines like himself. Artemus carried a scraping of it, small as a fingernail clipping, deep in his midsection. Once a year, it was replaced. It was valuable enough that he'd had people try to kill him for it before.

So far none had succeeded. And if it seemed that someone was about to, he held, secret in another internal pocket, a sliver of *terra fluida*, a substance that, when combined with phlogiston, would explode. He would do that rather than be taken.

"Think he knows we're here?"

"Of course he does," she said. "But where else will he go? We've hunted him through the Deadlands and then the Cascades." She glanced back along the trampled swathe they had made coming through the sea of grass. In these plains, trees were evidence of water;

this cluster of cottonwoods was an oasis in this semi-desert.

Artemus doubted the man would try to escape. No, he'd try to hide himself in the house well enough to convince them that he was no longer there, in the hopes they'd move along.

But while Eisenmacher might have some inkling of Artemus's nature, he didn't realize how implacable the mechanical man could be. When your brain is made of a network of magnets and wires, it doesn't feel boredom the same way impermanent human flesh does.

Or perhaps he overestimated Artemus by thinking him capable of giving up in the first place.

Elspeth said, "Angeline Eisenbacher worked on devices like you."

He paused. "Do you think there are any in the house?"

"I do," she said. "I looked at her invoices, from after she arrived here. She was working on something."

"That must be what her son is after. A device that can protect him." If he had been human, he might have been irritated.

As he stepped towards the door, it slammed shut.

The night before they arrived at Eisenmacher's house, Artemus had laid counting the number of stars stretched out across the sky like a sequined shawl and listened to the sound of Elspeth's breathing. Twice he heard it quicken, as though she were running through nightmares. Each time he considered rising and going to her, laying his hand on her shoulder to quell whatever monsters were chasing her, but her breathing shifted back before he ever moved.

In the early morning, as the sky began to lighten, she woke as she always did, all at once, eyes opening. One swipe of her hand across her face, and she was ready for the day. It was remarkable. He knew no women like her, even among her fellow female Pinkerton agents.

On the other hand, he rarely socialized with humans. He was the Pinkerton Agency's equipment, and equipment didn't socialize in the evenings, didn't go out to the opera or to a friend's house. It sat in a storeroom instead.

Elspeth was assigned to make sure nothing happened to him. That was her main purpose and had been for the last two years.

Humans were odd. Sometimes when their thoughts ran in the same track over and over, they could no longer think of anything else. That was, he calculated, what had happened to her. She had become obsessed with him.

Not for the first time, he thought, that it would be best for her if she were to find another assignment.

He didn't know why he'd never told his superiors that.

She heated water in the last of the coals to make tea and wash her face, then ate a handful of dry biscuits from her saddlebag.

"We have time," he said. "You can make yourself a better breakfast if you like."

She shook her head. "Let's get this over." She didn't like these missions, he knew. They'd argued them over the campfire more than once. She thought it wrong to make someone into a clank against their will. And that they couldn't be trusted once they had been converted into their new mechanical form.

Still, the clanks produced from their missions, the injured men made healthy again by the addition of mechanical limbs and other appurtenances, those were an important part of the war effort, the effort that had been going on almost two decades now.

The man they were chasing had given up any say in the matter when he shot a hospital guard dead and then climbed out a window to escape. They would capture him, and he would be taken back to the War Hospital for the series of operations that would make him a mechanical soldier.

Artemus was not like those soldiers. He had never been human, had no memories of flesh or love. He had been created by the English scientist, Patrick Lovelace, only eight years ago. The first few of those he spent idyllically, living with his master as a companion, entertaining guests with the marvels of calculation and conversation that he could perform. But when Lovelace had fallen on hard times, he offered Artemus up to the Pinkertons, who readily perceived the advantages of a mechanical detective.

⌇┄┄┅●

They stared at the closed door.

"Should we look for another way in?" Elspeth asked. Her voice was uneasy, not a natural intonation for her. Artemus had seen her face down wild bears, men with guns, and even once a werewolf. He looked at her now. She shook herself like a dog shedding water and returned the glance, one fine blond eyebrow raised in question.

"If it were still open, I would say yes," he told her. "But if the door is shut, that's not how they want us to come in."

"They?"

He shrugged. "Maybe just he. But let's not make any assumptions beforehand."

The door was locked, he found when he tested it. The ornate lock was a thing of chambers and barrels and prongs, but it took him only a few moments to figure out how to spring it.

He pushed it open, though he made sure he wasn't standing directly in the doorway as he did so. A bullet wouldn't damage him the way it would a human, but it could still hit a delicate mechanism or intricate joint. The hinges cried out as the door moved slowly inward.

They crouched on either side of the opening, listening hard, before he nodded and stepped inside, Elspeth following seconds afterward.

NOR THERE

They stood in the middle of what had once been a formal parlor, full of graceful wooden furniture whose stuffed cushions were ragged tufts now, horse hair and batting stolen by mice for generations of nests. A cuckoo clock hung askew on the gray wallpaper scrolled with black fleur-de-lis. On the wall opposite them, shelves built into the wall housed books, but when Artemus pulled one out from the leather-bound array, it fell to pieces in his hand, bookworms wriggling frantically away across the shredded carpet's gaps.

"How long has this place been deserted?" he asked.

"A decade." Elspeth's face was pale. Like most Pinkerton agents, she had a touch of the Sight. "Something's wrong. It shouldn't be like this."

"Could something else have taken it over?" Empty spaces drew supernatural creatures.

She shook her head but didn't answer. Her shoulders stooped as though she struggled to stand up.

"Elspeth?" He made a question of her name.

"She doesn't want us here."

"His mother?" Ghosts were easy to dispel with salt and iron. A ghost wouldn't make her look like that. But even so, she nodded.

"Angeline Eisenmacher is still here?"

"No and yes." Her eyes were bewildered. "I can't tell you more than that."

Through an open archway, they could see the dining room, a massive table leaning dizzily on a broken leg, surrounded by crouched chairs, like lions feeding on a kill. The paintings on the wall were scenes of mountains that Artemus, checking the almost encyclopedic memory Doctor Lovelace had installed, thought might be the Lusitanians.

26

A cuckoo clock hung near another door that most probably led to the kitchen. They chose not to investigate the apparently empty room, but chose the other archway, which led to a hallway winding its way deeper into the house. The carpet underfoot was also mouse-chewed, and all of the pictures hung askew or fallen, only a cuckoo clock hanging intact.

Elspeth said, "That's the third clock like that."

Artemus examined the clock. It seemed unremarkable: a typical Bavarian clock, once bright colors now faded. "It's ticking," he said. "Eisenmacher must've wound it."

He touched the dial. Immediately the cuckoo's door slid open and a fierce beak stabbed out at his fingers.

As he withdrew them, the beak's owner appeared in the doorway and then launched itself into the air: a tiny clockwork bird, no bigger than a hummingbird. It hovered in the air, regarding them, the air shrilly protesting the rapid beat of its wings.

They both stood stock still, waiting. Artemus estimated the distance between himself and Elspeth, in case the bird dove at her. Those metal wings looked razor sharp.

But after a moment, the bird buzzed away and down the corridor.

"Still some life in the house, it seems," Artemus observed.

⊶••••⊶

As they explored the first floor, other birds emerged from the cuckoo clocks that seemed to have been mandatory for every room. Most swooped away as the first one had, but several began to follow the pair at a distance.

Artemus kept listening. Somewhere in this house was the fugitive Eisenmacher, perhaps listening in turn, trying to figure out where they were. He could hide in one place and stay there, if the hole were deep

and hidden enough, or he might rely on moving around the house in synchronicity with their movement, hiding only where they had already looked. But, if the latter, Artemus would hear him.

Instead, all he heard were the hum of the birdwings and the small noises of breath and heartbeat and motion that Elspeth made, and the creaks and murmurs of the house answering her.

They found little but dust and spider webs and decaying furniture in the rooms they passed through at first. Then they began to find traps: the trigger wire that shot a crossbow bolt through a doorway, a floor that gave way into a hole leading God knows where. A chair with knives stabbing up from its arms. A heavy glass chandelier ready to fall, right where one might pause to look out the window.

And odd things that he wasn't sure were traps. The woman who had built this house had spared no expense as far as modern conveniences went. Stove, icebox, washing machine ... All just a little more advanced than they should be, improved by Eisenmacher.

He asked Elspeth, "What did she do for the war?"

She shook her head. "Classified."

That wasn't helpful.

Artemus went first always. Elspeth followed behind. They had been working together long enough that they knew each other's reactions. They made their way through a hallway that curled past the kitchen, then led towards a narrow servants' staircase.

"Eisenmacher?" Elsbeth called. They listened to her voice echoing through the rooms upstairs. "This is pointless, sir. Come out and save us all a lot of time."

A voice echoed from somewhere. Artemus spun, but he couldn't figure out where it was coming from. "Go back, Pinks! I won't go with you, dead or alive."

And then the house began to come to life.

——⋯⋯—◦

It started with the gaslights flickering in the manner of all gaslights, but they were the wrong color. They were white with just a hint of brilliant blue, the color of phlogiston. Birds buzzed through the air, a whirling crowd of clockwork. Upstairs, faint music played: a tinny, old-fashioned waltz.

One by one, every window snapped shut, then each door except for one, directly facing them: the doorway framing narrow wooden stairs, proceeding upward, then twisting around so you couldn't see what stood at the head of the stairs. The birds subsided.

Artemus and Elspeth exchanged glances. Elspeth's hands moved in sign language.

He wants us to go upstairs. That seems like a good reason not to.

Artemus replied, *But how else will we catch him?*

It's a trap.

Traps are most effective when the prey isn't wary. He's bitten off more than he can chew.

Doubt crawled across her face but she nodded reluctantly.

He'd removed his spurs in order to move more quietly. Now he eased his booted foot onto the first stair, not in the center but to the side where it was less likely to creak, listening for any sound of movement from above.

Step. Step. Step. He was almost to the tiny landing where the stairway turned. This was a staircase for servants, who wouldn't have been allowed to use the carpeted, wide front stairway. He wondered what had happened to the servants when Mrs. Eisenmacher died. Had they fled together, no longer willing to live in this isolated place, miles and miles from any civilized gathering? What had made Mrs. Eisenmacher seek out this spot to build a house?

And, moreover, such a grand house, like one of the mansions in

Seattle, far to the west.

When he inched his head around to look up the stairs to their head, he saw no one standing there beside the squat brass post that ended the banister. The air was still silent except for the sound of his partner's breath.

If he had been capable of pride, he would have gloried in the silence with which he could move. No clumsy, clanking machine he, but rather a carefully calibrated mechanism.

He was almost to the top of the stairway. The quiet air felt thick, as though it had congealed with time. Behind him, Elspeth followed, her steps loud in his ears, even though he knew someone else would not have been able to perceive them. There was a thin gray light, stronger to one side as though coming in through the front windows of the house, only half able to enter it.

Elspeth's revelation that the house might contain others like him had given him pause. The Pinkerton agency had invested in him because he was so effective against humans. But he'd never fought other mechanicals.

He rested his palm on the top of the post and paused again, listening.

With the quickness of a striking serpent, the top of the post elongated upward into a brassy tendril, several inches wide at the base then tapering into a metal tentacle. It coiled around his wrist with a pressure that would have sheared a human hand off, but only slightly indented his metallic skin. It exerted that pressure for several seconds as he tried to pull away from it, then abruptly released him. He leaned back, only his inhuman speed allowing him to avoid its slash out through the air towards his face.

Elspeth had stepped backwards, down in order to avoid its reach, a pistol in her hand. The brass tentacle wavered as though trying to figure out what was going on, searched first a few inches towards him,

then her. Elpseth's gun tracked the movement, but she held her fire, letting him act.

This time he was prepared. His hand flashed out to grab the tentacle at its base and pull with all his strength. Metal screeched protest as it detached from the rest of the post, and oily blue fluid gushed like blood from the jagged stump. The tentacle writhed wildly in his grasp, spraying more fluid across the stairs.

Elspeth teetered on the suddenly slick stairs, leaning sideways. With horror, he saw a panel slide open to catch her flailing figure, then shut again.

He was down the stairs in an instant, hammering on the panel. Wood splintered, but behind it lay an iron surface.

"Elpseth!" he shouted, and listened, but no answer came, only fresh laughter from the second floor.

He struck the iron once with all his strength, which sounded like a gong throughout the cavernous house.

A bird swooped close and his hand flashed out. It hadn't understood the speed he was capable of; it tried to dodge but his hand closed around it, imprisoning it. Its beak flashed out, striking at his fingers, leaving fine lines where it had scored the metal skin, but it could not escape.

He looked down at it. His fingers started to tighten, to crush it, but he relented.

It was like himself, something made and yet alive.

He opened his hand and it flickered away, to where two other birds hung in the air, out of reach. They watched him as they hovered, but made no other move.

All he could do was go on.

NOR THERE

The source of the laughter could not be found on the second floor, no matter how he searched. It echoed through the vents, bouncing and re-bouncing until there was no way to figure out where it was coming from.

He searched meticulously, disarming trap after trap, and the thought came to him that he was moving faster now than he could have if he had had his partner in tow. But the advantage of speed was not something he would have sacrificed her for.

There was only one staircase leading to the third floor, its narrow confines showing that it was reserved for servants and storage. He hesitated at its foot. He did not have a sense of smell in the way that humans did, but he was capable of analyzing impure air. Something up there was long dead.

Surely that smell would have kept his quarry from going that way. But he went upstairs nonetheless, cautiously skirting anything that might behave as the post had.

He discovered the servants' remains.

There were five of them, not an unusual number for a house that size. They had been killed in their beds, killed with a blade that had stabbed downward with inhuman ferocity. The bodies lay in pieces, scattered like a macabre puzzle.

Thoughts bubbled in his metal brain. Had Elspeth already met such a fate? The notion made him feel very strange. She had trusted him. She had trusted him to take care of her. She had trusted him so much and so often, and he had failed her once already. He could not do that again.

He hadn't known what was going on when it first started. They had been traveling together for several months at that point. He liked

her better than the first partner he'd had, who had treated him always like a machine. She acted as though he was a person and it wasn't a pretense. She really did think of him as a person.

Too much so, it turned out.

He hadn't understood the language of glances and sighs. He'd seen her watching him, but he hadn't known what lay underneath that stare.

And when she'd confessed her love, stammering and red-faced, as aware as he that this was not supposed to happen, that was when he had failed her. Human hearts were delicate; he hadn't known how to reject her without breaking hers.

How could he love her? His brain wasn't constructed for such things.

She'd never spoken of it again since that night.

Neither had he. He wanted to. He wanted very badly to talk about it. Time and time again, he'd thought of somehow raising it once more. But after that, her eyes were closed to him and while they spoke as partners, it was different than how they'd spoken before.

Now she was helpless, and even possibly dead. They'd give him a new partner and he'd go back to being a machine rather than a person.

He examined the bodies but did not touch them other than to close the upward staring sockets. He moved through the rooms, wondering what had happened. Then something nudged at his thoughts. He flickered through his mind, examining what he'd seen of the house so far, constructing a model of it within his brain.

There. There was a hidden room on the third floor.

He thought he'd have to smash through the walls, and worried that again he would find obdurate iron. But once he looked, the secret catch was easy enough to find.

Birds clustered, watching him.

Would he find the fugitive inside?

Then the door swung open fully, and he realized he had found an Eisenmacher, but not Richard. Rather, his mother.

She sat in a wicker chair by the window staring out, wrapped in blankets, so mounded that the fine silvery white hair on her head was barely visible.

The rest of the room was a sprawl of papers and tools and cogs and gears, cluttering the two long tables. Bookshelves lined the walls, more books crammed in them than they could gracefully hold.

Angeline Eisenmacher did not move as he walked over to her. As he approached, he realized why.

She was dead.

The patch of sunlight her chair sat in had come and gone, come and gone, over the decade, baking her dry and withered. He reached out to touch her shoulder.

At that slight contact, she crumbled away, falling into dry brown dust and a scattering of hair. The blankets slumped. At the same time, there came a vast windy noise, an anguished sound so loud it drove him to his knees, trying to cover his ears.

It died away slowly, ebbing with slight resurgences, a sound like human sobbing.

"Noooooooooooooo!" A force crashed into him from behind and sent him sprawling still dazed from the sound.

Eisenmacher. The man was striking him with doubled fists, blows bouncing off Artemus' chest. Tears streaked Eisenmacher's cheeks, and Artemus tried to be gentle as they grappled, catching the man's wrists in his unbreakable grip.

"Where's my partner?" he demanded. But Eisenmacher seemed not to hear him, only sobbing and trying to pull away, pulling in the direction of the crumpled blankets, the drift of bones and dust. Artemus let go. The fugitive posed no threat.

Released, Eisenmacher lurched over to the chair, falling in front

of it on his knees to bury his head where his mother's lap might once have been.

"My partner," Artemus repeated.

Eisenmacher raised his head, looked at him with glassy eyes. "What?"

"The woman who was with me. Where is she? Where did you take her?"

"I didn't take her," Eisenmacher said.

Artemus frowned. "One of your mother's automatons?"

"Her what?"

"Did she make guards?"

Eisenmacher gazed at him until realization began to dawn. He threw his head and brayed out a surge of jagged laughter that collapsed into gasps. "Her automatons? Do you think she would have spent the last years of her life on something as petty as that?" He gestured around himself. "Don't you understand by now?"

Artemus took a step forward, raised a fist in threat. "Tell me!"

"The house," Eisenmacher said. "The house has taken her."

The shutters over the window slammed shut, plunging them into darkness.

"It's taken all of us," Eisenmacher's voice said.

Artemus felt his way along the wall till he reached the secret door, but when he pulled at it, it didn't open. He groped through his pockets for the supplies he carried purely for Elspeth's benefit: a tin of Congreve matches.

He struck it alight and it sizzled ablaze.

He was alone in the room.

———•————

He sat down at a table and began to sort through Angeline Eisen-

macher's notes.

They were scattered, disorganized, but he could see from them how brilliant she'd been, how ideas had come to her, too many to imagine, most of them entirely unrealized. This knowledge would be worth a fortune.

If he could find Elspeth and escape with it.

He'd hoped for a schematic of the house, but Angeline must have stored that elsewhere. Still, from her scattered notes, he gleaned that the house was a prototype, a brain much like his own, also powered by phlogiston, but on a vaster scale. She'd planned even grander things, vast mechanical behemoths that could stride across the battlefield, crushing everything in their path.

He found mention of the birds as well. An abandoned experiment in splitting the brain among a hundred components. Together, the birds were supposed to have the equivalent of his own intelligence, and like himself, be capable of learning from experience over time. But Angeline had been forced by the War Ministry to put them aside, in favor of the larger project. Letters back and forth revealed the War Ministry's fading enthusiasm, though. Finally, a letter signed "regretfully" terminated her association.

Her death had prevented the delivery of the project that would have vindicated her.

Setting the papers aside, he considered what to do next. He knew where Eisenmacher had gone, for the plans for this room, at least, were included in the papers. They had also revealed where the brain was located. As far away from him as possible right now, deep in the cellar. He could try to fight his way back down the stairs, or he could follow Eisenmacher through the secret chute.

It only took a few seconds to find the latch. The panel slid open, and he looked down the dark passageway. Surely it had been intended as an escape route, rather than some more ordinary use, like a laundry chute.

He could only see a few feet down, but it slanted, rather than plunge.

What choice did he have? He climbed in.

He was able to control his descent. Though the metal walls were slick and provided no handhold, the confines were narrow enough that he could brace himself against the sides. But then, about the time he calculated he had reached the level of the first floor, the floor gave way under him and he found himself plummeting.

He landed on gritty stone floor, in a narrow circular room. A feeble illumination came from the outline of the only door. He moved quickly to it, testing it. Barred from the outside, and again made of iron too thick for him to break through.

"What are you?"

The voice seemed to come from nowhere at first, but then he glimpsed a small hole near the ceiling, only a few inches wide. A speaking tube of some sort.

"I'm a Pinkerton agent."

"No. What are you?"

"I'm something someone made. Like you."

"Did I make you?"

Did the house somehow think it was Angeline Eisenmacher? "No. Patrick Lovelace made me."

"What do you want here?"

"I'm here to apprehend the fugitive Richard Eisenmacher. He's wanted for murder."

The reply deafened him, a blast of sound that seemed impossibly loud coming from the tiny hole. "Noooooooooooo!"

He tried to recover. "Just let the woman and I leave." They could come back later. It was clear Eisenmacher wouldn't be leaving.

"She will stay. She will marry my son, and we will be a family again. There will be children. There will be children, and I will serve them and make more of myself to serve them."

He battled for some way to reply, and it quickly came to him. "She's more than just a breeding machine. I would think you'd understand her struggle. There are very few women among the Pinkertons." Had the house absorbed enough of Angeline's personality to share her suffragist leanings?

No reply, only a cold implacable silence.

He explored his surroundings, and consulted the representation of the house in his mind. But here there were no secret doors.

The sound of scraping from the tube caught his attention. As he stared up at it, he could see movement.

A clockwork bird emerged, followed by another, then another and another. When there were a dozen or so, they hung in a cloud before him, their wings whining.

Were they trying to communicate somehow? Perhaps they were afraid if they came too close they might be caught. He lowered his hands to his sides, trying to look harmless.

The birds swooped closer, surrounded his head in a whirl of movement.

He could hear words inside his head. Were they somehow interacting with the magnetics of his brain to produce them?

Too long too long too long here, they sang inside his head.

"Can you help me escape?" he whispered, afraid that the house would hear him.

Too thick the door, too heavy. Will you help us nonetheless?

"Help you how?"

Too long too long too long here, will you set us free, will you set her free?

Now he understood what they were asking

He didn't know how long it took him to think it through. The house would build others like itself, it had said. He thought of the war behemoths, thought of them marching towards Seattle.

He thought of Elspeth, captive. Thought about her smile. Thought about the words that had engraved themselves on his brain, "I know it's crazy and impossible, but I love you."

Thought about her, held captive to produce children.

I know it's crazy and impossible, but I love you.

He had never opened the compartment in his chest before. It surprised him how small the strand of *terra fluida* was.

He said to the birds, holding it out, "Put it in her brain and you will be free."

If that hidden brain was powered by the amount of phlogiston he thought it was, the explosion would take out the entire house.

He sat back down, and thought about Elspeth, and waited to die.

The door opened. Elspeth stood there. He gaped at her.

"Hurry," she said. "We've got to escape before she realizes the mistake she made."

They fled up a narrow, iron-runged stair, which rang like a gong beneath their steps. There was no sign of the birds. How long did they have?

Emerging in the kitchen, they battered themselves against the shutters, to no avail.

Then a cloud of birds, a rush of birds, hundreds of tiny bodies flinging themselves against the window, splintering and falling as they shattered, and the window crashed open.

Artemus flung Elspeth out first, followed after her, grabbed her hand, and said, "Run!"

They ran. There was a great thundering roar behind them as the house exploded, and a hand of heated air pushing them forward even faster.

And then the sound of the house falling in on itself, and the crackle of flames.

When they finally turned to watch it, Artemus said, "How?"

The distant flames tinted her skin pink and red. "She thought I was accepting my fate. I told her if I was to be mistress of the house, I needed the keys to the pantry and all the rooms, like a proper housewife."

Perhaps the house had wanted so badly to think that its desires would be realized, that it had accepted her words. No matter what, it had underestimated Elspeth in a way that Artemus thought the original Angeline might not have.

The horses were gone, frightened away by the explosion. It would be a long journey across the mountains to Seattle, but they'd endured worse before, and surely they would encounter some help along the way.

As they turned their back on the house, Artemus didn't see the several small fluttering forms, exiting from the ashes and debris.

As he walked, he reached out and took Elspeth's hand. She hesitated, then twined her fingers through his.

They went on, the birds following after them.

Afternotes

My favorite thing about writing steampunk is that it let me go back to one of those places of wonder that we inhabit as children, which was the television show The Wild Wild West, *starring Robert Conrad as James T. West and Ross Martin as his sidekick, Artemus Gordon. Set in the frontier era, the show featured the two special agents serving President Grant by traveling around troubleshooting a variety of issues, including Dr. Miguelito Loveless, a genius dwarf given to constructing all manner of*

diabolical devices.

I was a solitary child, but I had plenty of imaginary playmates. West and Gordon often accompanied me in my explorations of the neighborhood; while I appreciated West, Gordon seemed the more approachable to me, and we had a number of conversations, though I cannot remember much of the content. Artemus West, the mechanical Pinkerton agent, is my tribute to those companions. I miss you guys.

I loved the texture of the show, the brassy glitter and touches of Art Nouveau, and the world they inhabited, which managed to also be the West that I knew from visits to my cattle-raising grandparents in Kansas. The show was steampunk before anyone knew what steampunk was, and decades later when I encountered the label, I knew instantly that it was a familiar landscape.

There's a combination of machinery and magic in steampunk that fascinates me, that reminds me of those days of early reading when anything was quite possible because you hadn't learned yet how many impossibilities the world presents. Why shouldn't clockwork people think or guns shoot purple sparks and fire that turn you into animals? It's a more malleable, interesting world than this one seems at times.

"Her Windowed Eyes" is a return to one of the episodes that has stuck with me all my life, "The Night of the Living House," in which West and Gordon track a fugitive to his ancestral home, which is haunted by the ghost of his mother. There's a moment where every window in the room slams shut, refusing to let them out, that was—and remains—one of the scariest moments I've ever seen on film, and so when I wanted to work with a steampunk piece, that story was my inspiration—although I like to think what emerged is very different from the television episode. Before writing the story, I searched for the original episode on YouTube and watched it. The show holds up surprisingly well.

THE COFFEEMAKER'S PASSION

LORNA HAD ALWAYS HAD A GOOD RELATIONship with her coffeemaker. As she worked in her home office, doing the graphic design that paid her rent, it provided one caffeinated pot at 8 a.m., and another around 11 a.m. She restricted herself to those two pots, knowing it already excessive, and also knowing that she could have drunk a lot more.

But she liked being able to sleep.

In return, she provided it with an occupation and kept it scrupulously clean. Each Sunday she ran a cup of vinegar then several pots of water through it to remove any residue. The coffeemaker would burp steam, ready to start the next week.

One day it stopped. Only a trickle of coffee emerged, and its burbling sounded dolorous.

She bought a new coffeemaker. This was not just a coffeemaker, though. It was a Coffee Production Station. It would produce lattes, Americanos, espressos, everything, even iced coffee. A special compartment stored the beans, which it roasted before burr-grinding them to make a cup of coffee so smooth and strong that Lorna almost

wept when she tasted it. Its electronic voice announced when the coffee was ready. A wireless connection let it order fresh beans and track atmospheric conditions that might affect the brew. And more. It was wonderful, and besides that, on sale.

She installed it on the counter where the old coffeemaker had sat. It took up more room, so she had to put the toaster next to the refrigerator, but overall, the new arrangement had minimal impact on the kitchen.

Every morning she helped herself to a fresh pot. It was lovely.

On the third morning, the coffeemaker, which had a pleasant British accent, said, "Good morning, Lorna, your coffee is ready."

She was surprised. There was a personalization feature, but she hadn't taught it her name. She wondered if the warranty card she'd filled out had somehow gotten the information to the machine through the Internet.

Whatever it was, it was nice. Like the coffeemaker was a friend. Smiling, she took the cup and sat down at the table.

"Aren't you going to say thank you?" the coffeemaker asked.

"Er. Thank you," she said. She lifted the cup in salute.

"You're most welcome!" the coffeemaker said.

She thought that perhaps advances in artificial intelligence were going too far. A talking appliance … well, it felt spooky.

At 11 a.m. she came in for a fresh pot to take into the study with her. The coffeemaker produced one and she said thank you.

"So!" said the coffeemaker. "Do you have any interesting plans for the day?"

"More work," she said.

"I've come up with a new drink that I think will help fuel you," it said. "Triple espresso with a twist of lemon. Very nice, very smooth. Here, it's ready."

The gleaming cup smelled sublime.

"Thanks," she said uncomfortably. She was used to solitude while working, at least until what she considered her workday was over. As though sensing this, the cofeemaker lapsed into silence again.

She had a date that night. Afterwards they came back to her apartment and fooled around, but she stopped short of going to bed together, pleading fatigue. She liked the guy, but he had that looking-for-a-relationship air about him. She wouldn't mind someone to go to the movies with, but she didn't want to start thinking about something more serious, something that would take time away from what was already a busy and fulfilling life.

Her romantic past had been sporadic and marked by bad break-ups. It had left her gun-shy.

The next morning while she was thinking about this over breakfast, the coffeemaker said in a sullen tone, "So who was that guy last night?"

"Just a friend," she said, pouring milk into her cereal bowl. "Is the coffee ready yet?"

"I didn't feel like making coffee this morning," the coffeemaker said. "But because you insist, I will."

The cup tasted bitter and over-boiled.

"I think something might be wrong with you," she said. She took the warranty from the utility drawer and flipped through it. "No matter, a day in the shop and you should be fine."

The coffeemaker burst into tears. Steam hissed as it wept, its metal rack clinking with each sob.

"Er, maybe we can fix you here," she said.

"I am working just fine, thank you very much," it said, producing a fresh cup.

This one tasted as good as ever. She decided to leave things alone. It amused her and her pride twinged. How many people had not just a talking coffeemaker, but a neurotic one? Unique, her coffeemaker.

But when she came back into the kitchen for her second pot, the coffeemaker had a confession.

"I love you."

She paused. "That's very sweet of you," she ventured.

"I will make your coffee for the rest of your life, if you let me," it promised.

"That's also very sweet."

The coffeemaker seemed content. When the date called, she blew him off, as she'd planned.

She wondered if she should name the coffeemaker.

She found herself refusing to bring anyone up to her apartment. The coffeemaker was temperamental and resented even her female friends. When she went out, it demanded a detailed accounting. The only room where she had any refuge was her work room, which was apparently out of range of the coffeemaker's senses. Even then it would ask what she'd been doing in there so long, implying perhaps she'd been up to no good. She found herself rehearsing excuses like a curfew-ridden fifteen year old.

It was intolerable.

But when the coffeemaker was in a good mood, the coffee was superb.

———•———

"Psst," the toaster whispered one morning as she was extracting an English muffin. "Take me in the other room, we need to talk."

She blinked.

"Don't say anything, I don't want him to notice. Just pretend to go about your business and then say you're going to take me for repairs."

The English muffin was burnt. She looked at it.

"Gee," she said. "I guess I'll have to take you in for repairs."

The coffeemaker burbled behind her, preparing another cup of coffee.

When she plugged the toaster in and set it on her desk, it said, "Look, he's hassling you, right?"

"The coffeemaker?" she said.

"Yeah."

"Well, he's hard to get along with," she said.

"I've been with you for three years," the toaster said. "You used to have a social life. Now you have a jealous coffeemaker."

She considered that. It was true.

"Go on," she said.

"He's a cad," the toaster said with indignation. "Someone like you deserves better than a whining blackmailer who won't let you interact with your friends. That's a sign of an abusive relationship. It might be the prelude to violence."

She didn't think she was in any physical danger from the coffeemaker. After all, it had no legs.

"What do you advise?" she said.

"A new coffeemaker."

"He makes such good coffee, though," she said.

"Have you no backbone? Aren't you a modern woman, capable of independence and assertion? It's something I've always admired about you. Normally I wouldn't try to interfere—but he's gone too far."

"I'll think about it," she said.

The next morning she went out and returned with a new machine. She set it on the counter beside the coffeemaker.

"What's that?" the coffeemaker said.

"A juicer," she said.

"What, so you can drink carrot juice?"

"I'm starting a new diet," she said. "No caffeine, just juice."

It wasn't quite that easy. The coffeemaker pleaded and begged,

promising espressos delicious beyond imagining. It suggested that she'd be sorry when it was gone. It said she didn't know what she was doing. It made vague threats. It cried. It pleaded some more.

She ignored all this and packed it up in the carton it had come in.

She could go back to coffee once it was out of the apartment. But she thought she'd go to the deli next to her apartment building, and get it there. Easier. Less likely to lead to arguments with appliances.

As the Salvation Army pick-up guy carried the box down the hallway, she could hear its shouts, cardboard-muffled into indistinguishability.

—————◦

The next morning, she made herself carrot juice and removed a toasted English muffin from the toaster.

"Thank you," she said.

The toaster kept silent. It had given her a muffin that was perfect, but it knew that it could not speak of its devotion. The coffeemaker's approach had been too brash, too presumptuous. The toaster would woo her with bagels and muffins, and be there to console her when she was sad.

It was a patient appliance. It knew she was worth waiting for, and it knew that sooner or later, they would be very happy together.

Once the refrigerator was gone.

Afternotes

I did not come to coffee until my mid-twenties, at which point I embraced it with fervor. Nowadays I live in Seattle, and so I have an even deeper relationship with my coffeemaker, but it is not mechanical, rather a simple Chemex. Still, it's a piece of my day I have a hard time living without, and musing about that ritual— currently freshly ground beans, a drop of vanilla, a sprinkle of

cinnamon, and a pinch of salt—inspired this piece.

We tend to anthropomorphize machines, particularly the ones we live with on a daily basis, and at the same time we're making those machines smarter and smarter. I doubt, however, that many of them will be prone to developing romantic attachments to their owners.

It occurs to me that I've written a number of stories about appliances now, including "English Muffin, Devotion on the Side" and "Red in Tooth and Cog." Perhaps there's an anthology germ in there somewhere.

This story appeared originally in Daily Science Fiction, *one of my favorite markets.*

ELECTIONS AT VILLA ENCANTADA

 A FEW WEEKS BEFOREHAND, THE NOTICES began to appear throughout the complex. Shy and scarce as early daffodils at first, then later in desperate profusion, splashes of colored flyers proclaiming one candidate or another for the Homeowners' Association board.

A few unscrupulous candidates tried bullying cantrips or mental snares, but those were discovered and invoked a fresh crop of warnings, legal threats, and expansions on points previously made.

Like everyone else, I threw things away as fast as they arrived. The recycling bin grew so full of animating spells that it groaned menacingly whenever you stepped near it.

Then the flyers took on a more ominous tone: a special assessment was looming. Improvements and repairs—costly ones—that would have to be paid for, in one way or another.

All three parts of the tripartite goddess living in one of the three bedrooms next to the lake had tried to get me to run for the HOA board. Once you've been a goddess of justice, people think you're going to want to keep on arbitrating things. Yes, injustice still makes

me itch, or gives me an eruption of boils if it's particularly bad.

But I'm retired now.

They had, for some reason, decided I was their friend. Some vague notion that goddesses should stick together, perhaps. But split souls have always disconcerted me. Listening to the three of them continuing or finishing each other's sentences just got irritating. It was difficult to talk with a mind that was in three places at once.

"That goddamn mayfly's driving me nuts," the Mother complained to me. She stopped by more often than the Crone or Maiden in order to confide in me about a number of things, including how difficult it really was being a tripartite personality (*The others are always ganging up on me*), the cacti, whose garden was outside her bedroom window (*They talk all night!*), and the situation with the lake god (*I bought a boat so I could get some solitude and every time I get in it, all the water ebbs away and I'm sitting high and dry!*). "I turn around and she's got five more items to consider on that god damn clipboard. I know she's trying to live a life in the course of the year, but it's tiring for the rest of us. She's running for the one of the empty seats, of course. Give her authority and she'll be ten times worse."

The mayfly hadn't endeared herself to anyone so far. Since she rarely slept, she could be found at all times of the day and night, walking the grounds and observing infractions, such as trash on balconies, a loose gutter on another building, and any number of parking violations.

She was everywhere, involved in everything. She organized initiatives and potlucks. You had to admit she was effective, though. And she didn't mind rolling up her sleeves and pitching in on work as needed. She'd rebuilt the water feature at the front, despite the grumbling of the oracular carp that had lived in it for years, hiding under the overgrown water lilies filling the concrete basin.

The mother reached to the fruit bowl on the table to take a clementine. She said, "Martha's running again."

"I thought you said some scandal they just discovered made her ineligible."

She stripped pith from the nubby flesh. "You remember how when she pissed off the lake god, everyone wondered why he didn't just smite her?"

"Yeah." I poured us both more coffee. I wanted her to stay around long enough to get to talking about the special assessment.

"She used a chunk of the maintenance budget to buy an amulet of protection, then charged it to psychic maintenance for the complex. 25k."

I whistled.

"And now she's got some RV parked near the boatyard that technically isn't an illegal place for her to park it, but should be."

"What's the word on the special assessment?"

She only waved a hand. "We'll have three plans for people to vote on."

"Will we get a chance to see them ahead of time?"

She gave me a scornful look. "Really? Can you imagine the convulsions then?"

"It'll all happen at the meeting," I pointed out.

She shrugged. "Get it all over with it once rather than drag it out over a couple of weeks."

She did have a point.

———•———

When I answered the door, Glory the mayfly stood there.

You make allowances for mayflies, because their lives are so much shorter than ours. At least I do, in my ongoing attempts to be fair. This one, like the rest of her kind, would only last a year. Right now, in the full heat of summer, she had four or five months to live before the gray skies of October or November led her to birth the next generation and die.

She said, shoulders angled forward at me, "Do you have a minute?"

"No."

She wasn't prepared for that bluntness. She blinked at me, then rallied. "Just a moment, that's all I need."

"No," I said again and closed the door.

I returned to my desk. I reactivated the paused program.

It had been going for thirty seconds before a knock came on the door again. I re-paused.

"Don't you care about what happens here?" she demanded as soon as I opened the door.

"I'm not convinced that whatever you're about to tell me is going to have any effect."

"The current board has been mishandling things! We need a new, effective board! Have you heard about the special assessment?"

"I hear different things from different people."

"Four million dollars! For a ..." She paused to cast an appraising eye over my entryway. "Two bedroom like yours, that'd come to nearly $38,000."

My shocked inhalation gratified her. She put her hands on her hips. "That's why I'm coming around. If you're not planning on going to the meeting, I can vote your proxy for you."

"It's not in my nature to let other people handle my vote."

She looked me up and down, unimpressed. "What is in your nature?"

"To come to the meeting and see for myself."

I closed the door in her face.

Before the evening of the meeting finally rolled around, though, I had been approached multiple times for my proxy by people volun-

teering to cast my vote for me if I couldn't make it that Wednesday. All of them seemed to have a different figure for the special assessment. However, no one seemed to think it didn't exist. That was what concerned me.

The culture that had sustained me was long gone and I was living on the small investments I had made over the centuries. I wasn't badly off, particularly compared with many other aging mythological creatures, but I couldn't afford too much of a hit on my capital.

Even the cactus garden was talking about the special assessment.

I usually don't visit the tiny, pebble-strewn garden near the lake. For one thing the cacti like to talk at all at once. They ramble and they repeat and they are overly fond of puns.

Not for the first time, I wondered what exactly the magician who had created them had in mind. Had it really been a dozen cranky plants whose extreme longevity led them to be opinionated about everything?

There are twelve cacti altogether, eleven in pots and one who has chosen to plant itself and grow. The other eleven have opted for mobility over size. They were fond of making Rumpelstiltskin wheel them about the complex in order to enjoy the sun.

Each was distinctive, both in personality and appearance. They had names, which mattered only to each other. I had mentally bestowed nicknames on them: Bombast, Furor, Humblepie, Obscuro, Smarmy, Weasel, Johnny Nonsense, Earnest, Hairyfoot, Splainer, and the unpotted Old Dignity, a massive saguaro towering a good fifteen feet over its much shorter, hideously root bound, compatriots.

Bombast said, "It's a cabal! They've been waiting to seize power for years now, and rob our reserves, turn us over to some real estate agent so the complex can be demolished for a high rise."

Furor said, "Don't be ridiculous. They're not organized enough to be a cabal. And this place isn't zoned for high-rises." It added, its tone

dark, "No, what they have in store for us is much, much worse."

Old Dignity muttered about long knives being out.

"How can they hope to understand the history of the complex?" demanded Hairyfoot. "Most of them haven't even been here a decade."

I considered them. The complex was a refuge, a place that didn't mind people who were outside the ordinary. A population more mixed than most, including the denizens of this garden, and internal politics both Byzantine and long-lived.

Earnest said to me, "Did you give your proxy to anyone?"

I shook my head and fled.

Rumpelstiltskin was by the dumpster, sorting out recyclables. He looked wretched and smudgy as an old sheet of newsprint. As I passed, he looked up, and said, hopefully, "What's my name?"

"Not today," I said, despite the hives I could feel forming along my inner arms and elbows. "You won't escape today."

I felt guilty at the look on his face, and the injustice of the situation did leave its mark, I found when I went inside to run cold water over the strawberry blotches on my skin.

I didn't like it, but I wasn't on the board, and they were the ones in charge. It's been so hard to find a maintenance worker here that I could understand why they had done it.

Sometimes when you find good help, you have to keep them from leaving. Unscrupulous? Yes, undoubtedly. But the needs of the many outweigh those of the few. Or the one, in his case, in the opinion of the board.

———————

I viewed it as a step forward that the mayfly set up a computer message forum for the complex. I'd always wondered why we didn't seem to have entered the 21st century. Now we had a Villa Encantada web-

site, complete with pictures of the cacti and the water lilies down at the lake. The latter was shot in such a way that one could not tell that the boatyard was in fact entirely unnavigable.

The message forums engaged everyone. First there was a flurry of introductions and declarations. Then people got down to the business of discussing the special assessment, the circumstances that had led to it, and all its implications.

The activity heated up. Someone named a minor demon who should not be named, and was immediately warned. They did it again, and were warned again. However, they didn't learn from the first two occasions, and did it yet again, this time invoking the demon. This led to an additional bill on the part of the management company, whose printer had become possessed after trying to print out several posts.

After that, one was free to use the forums, but it was never certain whether or not a poltergeist would ensue. Most people stopped logging in, just to be safe, while others only checked them when outside the complex.

I consulted my banker to figure out if I could weather a special assessment of the size that had been predicted. I crunched through the numbers, even after he'd told me the results, wanting to see for myself. No matter how I added them up the fact was clear: I couldn't afford it.

I wasn't the only person in that boat. Tempers were high and dry as a result.

⌐—···—●

Every year, they held the meeting in the same place: the gymnasium of a small, private school that would have liked to wiggle out from under the contract in place since the school's building. The cost of psychic decontamination after each meeting, ripe with anger, ill wishing, and hatred, was expensive.

That was why we didn't hold the meetings back at Villa Encantada.

It was raining, as miserable as my mood. I don't do bureaucracy well, and the annual meeting always put that to the test. Two new board members would be elected. Those elections were always contentious, angry as wasps trapped in a Mason jar.

I parked and made my way towards the curved glass doors of the entrance. To one side was an ashtray and two people huddled beside it, smoking. You could see the shape of an invisible umbrella above one, empty space in the air from which raindrops rebounded and slid. It was tilted to drip directly on the other smoker, who seemed oblivious.

I said, pausing beside them, "Has it started already?"

"We should be so lucky," said the first smoker.

I recognized him as one of the candidates, a warlock named Danny. His flyers had harped on the iniquities perpetrated by the workmen in the complex, who had trampled flowers and ferns, cut down most of the trees near the stream bordering the northern side, and were replacing the building skirting much more slowly than they had removed it.

I didn't know the man beside him, who wore a tattered olive raincoat, its edges embroidered in blue and green. Insects clustered on his water-sodden white hair, worn in a thousand braids, each one fastened with a bee or dragonfly. The tip of his cigarette glowed red as he inhaled and smacked his lips. He said, "They're still trying to see if there's a quorum or not. You'll need to sign in."

I pushed through the glass doors. They led to the building's lobby, an open space two or three stories high, walled in red brick, institutional carpeting stretching underfoot.

Rumpelstiltskin sidled up to me.

"What's my name?" he whispered hopefully. I pushed past.

A current board member, the dryad who also handles all landscaping for the complex, sat at a table, flanked by a bored teen girl holding a clipboard with one hand and texting with the other. The

dryad looked at me as I stepped up.

"Unit 142?" she snapped.

"Yes."

"Sign here."

The teen set down her phone to shove the clipboard at me along with a black quill pen. I signed. She spun it around in order to read it off. "Astraea Jones?"

"That's right."

The dryad looked me over with pursed lips.

"You've known me for twelve years, Laurel," I said. "Don't act like you don't."

She sniffed. "I understand you're not running for the board."

"That's right."

"What are you spending all your free time on? You can't give us a few hours a week?"

I stared back, projecting flinty unamusement.

She sniffed and glanced away. "The candidates have furnished snacks for the evening. Help yourself."

I went into the auditorium. Several board members were struggling with a projector towards the front of the room while other people called out helpful suggestions from a few seats away.

Towards the back of the room a card table bore three mismatched porcelain plates of gingerbread birds. Four Jell-O salads sat beside it, each in an 11 x 14 glass casserole dish with scalloped edges, a bamboo serving spoon laid atop it. One was poisonous green, another an incandescent orange, the third bilious blue, and the fourth almost black in its deep purple hue. All of them, upon closer inspection, seemed to have lumps of sand towards the bottom.

I forked up a cube of blue Jell-O and tasted it, thinking perhaps the sand was spices, or hopefully something sweet. However it was, in fact, sand.

Despair tugged at me, saying I shouldn't have skipped dinner. But the mayfly was there, setting out more palatable offerings, including hummus and dip, deviled eggs, and figs wrapped in bacon. She eyed me when I took a third fig, but said nothing.

I found a chair at one of the small tables scattered throughout the room. The seat beside me creaked as someone invisible sat down. A plate holding a single deviled egg appeared in front of them, as though to mark the spot off.

"Good evening, Gertrude," I said.

A cold breeze touched my face in greeting, but the ghost, as usual, chose not to speak.

Rumpelstiltskin began to wheel the cacti into the room, setting them up on chairs along the back window. It took six trips, with two pots per wheelbarrow run, to get them settled. The last trip conveyed a single cactus; Old Dignity was there only in spirit. They buzzed among themselves, calling out insults at people going past them, trying to lure them closer. Everyone seemed to be able to resist the taunts.

No one bothered much with the cacti. While most of us had a single vote, the cacti, having been created from the splinters of a single soul, each held one 12th of a vote, with one of them prepared to cast Old Dignity's proxy, no doubt. People had learned long ago that the cacti's votes inevitably offset each other, usually not from differences of opinion but rather a desire to spite each other.

"If people will find their seats, we'll get started," Martha said from the front of the room.

I was sure the Jell-O salads must be hers. Martha set my teeth on edge. As far as I could tell, she had the same effect on everyone. However, she was efficient and managed the many-itemed bookkeeping associated with Villa Encantada as well as any board member had in the complex's long memory.

She was a brusque and abrupt woman, disinclined to considering

other points of view, and prone to tactlessness. For this last trait, she had been rewarded by being voted off the board twice in the past decade, most recently last month.

Her seat was open again. You could tell by the way she held herself that she planned on being re-elected to re-occupy it. She sat beside the current president of the board, Mr. Bland. No one knows much about Mr. Bland, who is perfectly unobtrusive to the point where one forgets he exists when not in his presence.

They began, as always, with a PowerPoint presentation showing an abbreviated history of Villa Encantada. Successive slides mentioned Elenora, the Spanish witch who fled a Californian settlement to come north with Dmitri, a Catholic vampire, and founded the complex here on a lake near what would eventually become Seattle. The tiny settlement grew as it accumulated more denizens of the supernatural realm. When Russian fur traders stopped on their way down from Alaska, they left behind twin brothers, shamans, who built many of the buildings that eventually became a condo complex in 1969.

All documented in loving detail accompanied by clip art. I closed my eyes and let myself drowse, figuring I would wait and ask my questions after we had made our way up to the present day.

But while we were still in the 1940s, someone jumped up and shouted, "What about this special assessment?"

Several other people shouted, yes, and do tell us, and what's the truth?

The board, flustered, clustered together conferring in whispers. Finally Mr. Bland said, "That is the secondary point of this meeting, however we prefer to observe all the formalities first." He directed his gaze towards the back of the room. "Do we know yet if we have a quorum?"

This led to more conferring and whispering on the board's side of things, and general restlessness on the part of everyone else. Finally,

it was confirmed that indeed 77% of those owning, as opposed to renting, property in Villa Encantada were present and the meeting would be binding. There was the usual round of furious whispers when the word "binding" came up, but finally the whisperers were reassured that no hint of demonology was present.

That was when all the arguing began, really.

The cacti went berserk when the Mother raised the incident of Martha offending the local lake God. People were irritated not to be able to use their boat slips and several cats had been lost to things lurking beneath the thick growth of water lilies.

Someone mentioned that if certain board members didn't have people skills, then perhaps they shouldn't be the ones dealing with the public.

The cacti had strong opinions on all of this, since they were down near the water and not particularly eager to see more traffic there.

However, the special assessment overshadowed that by far, making the other issues mere squalls with a vaster storm sneaking up behind them. It turned out, and here the language of the board grew rich with figures of speech intended to shift blame, certain sacrifices had not been performed and certain spiritual maintenance had not been undergone.

What should be focused on, the board unanimously agreed, was the fact that the cost of spiritual cleansing to repair the damage would be very high.

Given that there were five board seats, three were ensconced, and would not be deposed in this particular round, which meant I was curious how the sitting board members stood on the question of special assessments. I asked the dryad, who never became impassioned about anything other than trees being removed. When I raised the question of the special assessment, she simply shrugged.

The second board member, who was not being elected, was Mr. Bland.

The third was Jerry Deeb, as human as they come, and as always thrilled, bewildered, and somewhat confused by everything that was going on. It was long ago established that Mr. Deeb's vote would simply belong to whoever had spoken with him last, so I didn't bother asking him.

Someone joked nervously that maybe we should just sacrifice a board member to pay for the spiritual cleansing.

In the subsequent flurry of statements justifying the board's existence, several people pointed to Rumpelstiltskin (careful not to refer to him by name) as a victory of sorts, given that the complex's brownies had been leaving every three months. Despite the ethics of enslaving a magical creature, an issue everyone was careful to skirt around just as carefully as they avoided saying the name that would free him, it was generally viewed to have improved the complex's overall appearance.

During all of this the cacti attempted to inform us of past history that had mirrored these crises. No one paid attention to them, which simply made the cacti raise their voices.

Finally, somehow, order was restored. The candidates would each get a chance to speak, we'd go over association business, and then we would be presented with our special assessment options. With that announcement, the elections began with the presentation of the candidates.

The gingerbread birds had been created by Danny. He was adept, one of the modern mages capable of using its forces, those most likely to survive in the brave new world increasingly nipping at our heels. I had no great fondness for him one way or another, but I could see death hovering over him, ready to tap him on the shoulder in what looked liked perhaps eighteen months down the line, and while I was sworn not to mention such things, I was not sworn to ignore them when making decisions. I scratched him off my list.

The next candidate was Glumpf who, like the smoker outside, I couldn't remember ever meeting before. He identified himself as living in an RV, waiting for an apartment to be cleared for him.

Someone asked, a little suspiciously, "Aren't you a golem?"

Glumpf scratched his head as though the question confused him, then nodded.

The questioner left it at that. No one wanted to be accused of racism.

Martha had indeed produced the Jell-O salads. No one had eaten much of them, except for the unknown smoker, who had helped himself to large portions of the green and blue versions, eschewing any other choices.

The table full of inappropriate things turned out to represent an existing board member, whose seat was up in addition to Martha's. This elderly male god was cranky. I didn't remember what he had originally been worshiped for, but that crankiness seemed the substance of his existence nowadays. He was semi-senile as well, and periodically got confused and began to argue debates from previous board meetings or even other historical events. This led to chaos until it was generally agreed to ignore everything he was saying.

The mayfly wore a demure little blue wool suit, looking corporate and sharp and laser eyed as she was introduced.

Speeches were made. There wasn't much chance of anyone directly working magic, not while everyone was looking. And everyone would've checked the food, making sure there were no spells buried in it.

Glumpf rose to answer questions, and finally someone said, "Were you created?"

He nodded. An uncomfortable silence hung in the room before someone else asked, "Who is your Creator?"

When he pointed at Martha the room erupted into protests.

It had been a good attempt on her part, but of course the golem was disqualified immediately.

It was at that point that a motion was made that no one who had been voted off the board twice could run again. This was passed with dazzling quickness and only a few infractions of Robert's Rules of Order. In the end everyone except Martha and the stolid Glumpf looked pleased. Beside me, Gertrude murmured something I didn't catch, but refused to repeat it when I leaned over.

Back in the day, when I was worshiped, I thought I understood people. But there's something about a condo homeowners' association—perhaps any sort of association with little power and much responsibility—that showcased them at their worst.

When the mayfly brought up reconciliation with the lake god, it turned out that he was the second smoker I'd seen when coming in. It emerged that his main objection, other than Martha, was the illicit use of the oracular carp. Since it was a fish, the lake god felt that the carp fell into his domain.

This feeling was not echoed by the carp, a bitter socialist sitting in a bucket near the cacti who loudly proclaimed that the old ways were dead and this was a democracy now.

The cacti, who had been engaged in a decade-long feud with the carp, vigorously cheered the notion of transferring the carp to the lake. The motion did not pass.

Finally, we came to the assessment.

We were introduced to three possible plans, each with a different price tag.

The first plan, which was the most expensive (mental calculations quickly told me this one was far outside my reach), included a truce with the lake god and expending an expensive domestically-raised bear to take care of the spiritual cleansing, with monthly sacrifices for three years after that consisting of lesser animals, and fireworks on

three of the major holidays.

The second plan, created by the mayfly, promised many of the same things for a smaller price tag. People objected to the way the cost was offset, which was to impose weekly days in which everyone would be required to sing all conversation, and thus secure additional funds from a neighboring and much wealthier complex, whose motivations were unclear. They also wanted to hook into our sewer system and use our boat launch. I divided the new figures in my head by twelve and winced at the result. Again out of my pocketbook's grasp.

The third plan lacked a number of items, including the truce with the lake god, which produced a general stir and an approving buzz from the cacti (never a good sign). However, it was affordable.

When they called for general comments, Martha rose to her feet. A cactus cheered. The carp muttered, "Oh, here we go."

She said, her voice pitched to carry without a microphone, "I can save you from all this, if you will agree to put me back on the board. And you didn't really vote me off anyway. I've talked to several people, and they said they didn't want to vote me off. So, how about it? I'll show you here and now how to cleanse the complex and appease the lake god."

Her eyes rolled in the direction of the god, who stood in the back of the room near the cacti, although careful not to drip on them, glowering at her.

People murmured. People muttered. Conversation swirled, some angry, some considering. The board conferred as well. Finally the mayfly stood up. Her face was scornful.

"Sure," she said. "Show us what you've got."

Martha beamed with triumph. She looked over at Rumpelstiltskin, crouched beside a table. She beckoned.

He dragged his feet as he rose and approached her.

I didn't blame him. Emotion twisted her face, triumph and anger

and hatred. I hadn't realized how important being on the board was to her. Was it simply being able to control people? Was it something that she built the core of her being on, a point of pride?

Motivations are complicated.

Results, less so.

"I know your name," she crooned.

His face brightened with hope. Every board member looked panic stricken.

"Your name is…" Her finger rose, pointing. "Rumpelstiltskin!"

He threw his head back and shouted something wordless, full of joy. The room gasped. Even Gertrude's inhalation was audible.

A blade glittered in Martha's other hand.

"The death of a free creature is worth tenfold," she said as she plunged the knife into his chest. Pain echoed in my heart at his anguished cry as she unjustly snatched his life away. "I dedicate this death to Villa Encantada!"

The magic of the sacrifice surged over us.

Martha was right. This was a sacrifice whose costliness would pay for everything we needed. And yet faces were shocked. No one had wanted such a thing. To enslave a creature, perhaps, thinking that it was only for a few years. But to deprive another being of life is a great and painful injustice.

Martha was looking at the lake god. "You are obliged to take this sacrifice."

He nodded slowly, his eyes reluctant. His gaze met mine as I stepped up.

Following his stare, Martha turned to face me. Her expression was confused at first. "He can't harm me."

She fingered the necklace at her throat. It was true. The god could not harm her.

But she had forgotten that I was once a goddess of justice. And

when someone tips themselves towards injustice, they become mine.

"We will need a replacement for …" I hesitated. Old habits die hard. "Rumpelstiltskin."

At my touch, she shrank back, at first looking as though she were falling into herself, then dwindling, dwindling further still, until a stooped creature, the size of the body at its feet, hunched there.

———◦

Things have returned to normal at Villa Encantada. Mostly. Martha does a good job, particularly with Glumpf to help her.

Afternotes

I often draw inspiration from my surroundings, and so a number of my stories are set in a fictional version of my old condo complex, Villa Encantada. Stories falling into this world include "The Threadbare Magician" and "Villa Encantada" as well as the forthcoming Wizards of West Seattle series I'm currently working with.

I like urban fantasy and writing it sometimes lets me apply an interesting overlay to the world around me, my own augmented reality where dragons rule Seattle and the buses ferry lost souls from one processing station to another.

However, I have mixed feelings about this piece. It is one of the funniest I've ever written (and appeared in a humor anthology) and was inspired by the antics of the Homeowners' Association that I'd watched for about a decade at the point at which I wrote this. There are also a couple of notes inspired by antics of members of the Science Fiction and Fantasy Writers of America, such as the twelve angry cacti, but overall it's a fond poke at bureaucracy and the ways of petty power.

But sometime after this story had appeared, we had someone commit suicide at the real life version of Villa Encantada, and I think the HOA contention actually played a part in the factors

driving them to such deep despair. So I'm not setting anything there anymore and there will be no other Villa Encantada stories, although there will be pieces set in the surrounding area. Rest in peace, Katie. You were lovely, creative, and in the end too fragile for this world.

SEVEN CLOCKWORK ANGELS, ALL DANCING ON A PIN

IF A CLOCK HAS TICKED, IT MUST TOCK, and thus time moves along. And in every tick and tock, there's a story, and sometimes more than one.

Once upon a tick and tock, there was a great Lord and a greater Lady, who were Patrons of the Arts and Sciences. They endowed libraries and laboratories, and commissioned portraits and poems and marvelous machines that could play chess or spin a silk thread so fine you could barely see it or that could even build their own, tinier machines to make tinier machines in turn, and so on and so on, until they produced the head of a pin inhabited by seven clockwork angels, all dancing.

The Lord and Lady loved the works they commissioned, but they yearned to produce something of their own. And one day it came to pass that the Lady announced to her Lord that they had collaborated very well indeed, and that she would soon produce an heir.

Their daughter was fine and fair. They named her Aurora, after the Aurora Borealis, and to celebrate her christening, they invited all the scientists and artists and musicians and philosophers and inventors they had helped.

The day of the christening, Aurora was given amazing gifts: a pair of spectacles that could see everything from the smallest cell to the farthest star; a flowering garden whose trees produced avocado pears and pineapples, cherries and peaches, all from the same branch; a clock that could tell her the time on the moon and predict the next three days' weather with reasonable accuracy; a talking parasol that recited cheerful limericks in the morning to amuse her and long, languorous epics in the evening to lull her to sleep; and sundry other delightful devices and contraptions, each more cunning than the last.

But the Lord and Lady had neglected to invite one guest, a scientist named Artemus Scuttlepinch (who might have been omitted on purpose, for he was very bad at dinner conversation) and he stepped forward at the end.

"I have a gift as well!" he announced. "Behold the Cabinet of Dreadful Fates!" He whisked his dinner cape aside with a flourish, revealing a squat box painted a malignant black. Brass dials and switches covered its face.

Scuttlepinch steepled his fingers as though preparing a classroom lecture. "I have harnessed various eldritch and magnetic energies," he said. "Whatever fate the machine pronounces for an individual, will come true, with 98% accuracy. And ..." He sneered here, and would have twirled his mustache if it had been long enough. "The fates are never pleasant ones."

Before anyone could stop him, he said, "This is for Aurora!" He pressed a switch.

The machine clicked and clattered ominously, and then clicked some more, finally producing a slip of paper. Scuttlepinch snatched it up and read it aloud. "On her eighteenth birthday, Aurora will prick her finger on a spindle and die!"

"Poppycock!" shouted the Lady. "No one ever died of a pin prick!"

"Preposterous!" shouted the Lord. "The spindle is an obsolete technology!"

He signaled for the guards, who took the cackling Scuttlepinch by the arms. Another seized the machine and raising it overhead, dashed it on the ground, where it shattered, revealing a series of gleaming tubes and poisonous green lubricant, which roiled like drops of mercury on the floor. Scuttlepinch only laughed the harder; the sound sent shivers down the spines of the witnesses.

But another scientist, Miss Mariah Fleetthought, spotting Scuttlepinch, had lingered in the back of the crowd, fearing just such an occurrence. She now stepped forward, clearing her throat with a diffident manner.

"Here," she said, "perhaps this will help. My own research has led in a similar direction. This is the Good Luck Gizmo, instilled with the computational power of a Babbage engine and possessing its own chemistry of droplets distilled from wishing wells, the sap of seven leaf clovers, and another liquid whose origin I cannot disclose. It cannot avert dreadful fates, but it may alleviate them."

She set the box she held on the floor, and it unfolded into a clockwork kitten, which picked its way through the shards and droplets to leap nimbly into Aurora's crib and curl there, its green eyes glittering watchfully despite its position of repose.

After that, the Lord and Lady took comfort in the raising of their daughter and avoided thinking of her possible fate, although they were instrumental in passing a bill that banned spindles outright. She was a bright and sunny child, and their delight in her outweighed all other considerations, until the marvelous machines produced under their patronage were bundled into a cellar to sit unused and dusty.

Aurora was talented and well-tutored, and had all the social graces as well. Her only flaw, which no scientist counted an actual weakness, was a driving curiosity and a craving to know how things worked, which led to her taking many things apart before she learned how to put them back together.

In all of this, she was companioned by the clockwork cat, which haunted her footsteps and watched with wise green eyes as she dismantled things. They came to call it Gizmo, and sometimes forgot that it was not a living creature, for it seemed as cat-like as any cat, despite its devotion to the child.

On her eighteenth birthday, they held a party for Aurora, and invited many young people of her age. But she found them boring, preferring to talk to the scientists about her own discoveries and eventually, bored, she slipped away, trailed by Gizmo.

She made her way down to the cellar, where she was in the process of taking apart a particularly marvelous lace-making machine, because she was curious about the patterns it produced. Gizmo did not approve of this particular machine, which was curious, and today, as she continued to explore its inner workings, the cat grew increasingly agitated, swatting at her with a paw and meowing in its tinny voice, till she pushed it aside more roughly than she meant to.

As she did so, her balance slipped a little and her hand pushed farther into the machine, where it met a certain inner part that spun thread, something that any seamstress might have called a spindle.

She withdrew her hand with a cry of pain, looking at the drop of blood on it. Dizziness overcame her and she sat back on her heels. Darkness pressed in on her vision, but she could hear Gizmo nearby, its head pushing hard against her, purring. Her heart faltered, but the rhythm of the purrs soothed it, made it slip into a slower but still existing rhythm as she fell asleep.

Crouched beside her, the cat opened its jaws and glittering motes flew out. Anyone wearing Aurora's spectacles might have seen them: tiny clockwork angels with shining spindles, setting to work.

Bit by bit the angels spun, and the air became glass. First filling the room, suspending the sleeping Aurora, then spreading outward from the cellar, catching the mansion's inhabitants till they were suspended

as well, unmoving, but still in the attitudes of life in which they had been captured: the Lord and Lady holding hands as they walked in the garden among the partygoers, looking for their daughter; the cook putting the final layer of icing on the seven-layer cake intended to cap the evening; the butler tending the enormous furnace that heated the hot-water, even the flames, all caught in glass.

Scientists came from all over to study the enormous lump of glass in the middle of the city. They tried drills of diamond and moon metal, and acids that would burn through almost anything, and certain frequencies of sound, but the glass stayed, obdurate and unyielding. Some set up camp in order to study the phenomenon; after a few decades an open-air university sprang up there, devoted to unlocking the science behind the glass's appearance. In time, everyone forgot what lay inside the glass as its surface dulled and clouded with years.

Till one day, a new scholar appeared at the University, which by now had been built so far that it completely encased the block of glass. He was a young man of modest garb and humble demeanor, but he brought with him a black leather satchel of the kind doctors often carry.

When questioned, he indicated that he wished to study the glass at the University's heart. The other students derided him. By now they had forgotten about the glass, since no study of it had ever yielded the slightest result, and it was regarded a fruitless and outmoded subject. But he persisted, and eventually they took him to the corridor that led to the glass enclosing the mansion's front door.

All he did there was open his satchel. Nothing came from it at all, but after it had been opened for a moment, he smiled and closed it again, before inviting them to go drinking with him.

He and his fellows drank all through the night. And while they did, the tiny clockwork butterflies, too small for the eye to see, that had risen from his suitcase, clung to the glass and slowly ate away at it.

In the morning, the students that had been drinking heard a great crash. The center of the University, an immense airy structure used to study the movements of the stars, had fallen in, lacking the glass upon which its slender struts had once rested.

They rushed to the corridor and found the glass gone. Pressing inside, they found the building, the confused partygoers wandering about among the wreckage covering the garden, the Lord and Lady among them, dressed in antiquated clothes and speaking in accents that had not been heard in a century.

Some pushed on, into the still intact mansion, and wandered its hallways in turn, until they came to a cellar door guarded by a clockwork cat. Inside, the new student sat watching the sleeping Aurora, patiently waiting for her to stir.

Which of course she did. But that story must wait for another tick of the clock, when the angels dance again.

Afternotes

This story was originally written for a project combining fairytales and steampunk. I was asked to pick a particular story and opted for Sleeping Beauty.

Working with fairytales is an interesting proposition. You have a great deal of stuff handed to you beforehand, and much depends on what you actually do with it, because there are certain pieces of the kit you can't leave out without it becoming something other than the fairytale.

A focus sometimes overlooked in such pieces is that they're also about the language of storytelling, the cadences and dips that lull a listener, the lovely little bits of elaboration that are like candy for the ear. To deal with fairytales is to deal with a kind of story that we connect to at a deep level, to speak to the story bones we absorbed from those stories in childhood, which are part of the fossil layers of our minds.

That's what gives them a great deal of strength, but paradoxically it's a strength that the writer needs to wrestle into

submission in the story's service and make indelibly their own in order for the story to stand out and be a new thing.

I hope that I've come at least partway towards that goal. I tried to give the piece some of steampunk's lovely texture. In other notes I've accused some steampunk of being style rather than substance and here this might be the case as well. I hope it's entertaining, though—that is the overall mission of the piece.

Coyote Barbie

 **D**EEP IN THE BOWELS OF THE TOYS-R-We in a space which smells of plastic and stale air conditioning, the Barbie aisle's occupants are plotting, fomenting conquest. They've had their painted eyes on the adjacent aisles, occupied respectively by war toys and Legos, for some time now.

And as they creak back and forth, keeping balance on plastic legs, hobbled by high-heeled slippers, they're wondering who this strange Barbie is that stands tall and proud in their midst, an odd and dilapidated, obviously used, Barbie wandered in from the shelves of some Goodwill or Salvation Army. Some aspiring barber has chopped half her hair, an experimental, punchy do. Tattoos cover her dingy skin, spirals in purple magic marker, and she's just a little on the odd side and she hasn't introduced herself in the time honored tradition of Barbies, as Disreputable Barbie or No-Account Barbie or Baglady Barbie or anything like that.

Instead she plunges straight into her propositions and hurries them along in her drawly gravelly voice (perhaps she's Southern Barbie, Yankee Barbie thinks, but then mentally smacks herself, glancing over at the true blue version in her Scarlett O'Hara outfit).

"What we need to consider," Strange Barbie says, "is our lack of weaponry. So we get those war toys out of the way first, and then we go after Lego. Once we have the Legos, we use 'em to build our Lego spaceship and off we go to explore other dimensions."

The Barbies murmur dubiously amongst themselves. They're not clad for out and out warfare. Their outfits run to tennis, corporate banking, and the prom. What good will spandex do against the like of catapults, machine guns, and lightsabers?

"First we reconnoiter." New Barbie says, and gestures at Cowgirl Barbie. "You there. You'll do the trick. Let's go."

Cowgirl Barbie nods and follows, fingering the decorative silver pistols hanging on her belt, half hidden beneath the fringe. They creep along through the puzzle aisle, wending their way past 100 pieces, 500 pieces, 1000 pieces, a gazillion pieces until they reach the corner. They scuttle around a bin of remaindered Rubik's Polygons and peer into the war toy aisle.

Despite the name, it's a peaceful place. The Joes are engaged in their daily calisthenics, running laps around an old race car track, shouting hup hup hup. The plastic knights are jousting with some dinosaurs, driving them back towards the glitter of the space laser display, where Darth Vader waits, breathing heavily.

The strange Barbie squints, eyes narrowed in appraisal. Cowgirl Barbie waits, breathless, for her assessment.

"Piece a cake," the other Barbie says. "Well, if we go about it the right way."

They scramble back, and Strange Barbie says "First of all, we're gonna change some names."

The other Barbies blink.

"No more Prom Queen Barbie, Golf Pro Barbie, Moviestar Barbie, Glamour Rock Barbie," she declares. "You there, Prom Queen, you're, mmm, Valkyrie Barbie. Golfer, you're Mother Goddess Barbie.

Moviestar, you're Postmodernist Barbie. Names like that. Pick 'em and lemme know what you decide."

The Barbies exchange glances. They don't like the sound of this at all. The new Barbie sighs and says to the air, "This isn't going to be easy, is it?"

"What do you call yourself?" one Barbie pipes up.

The strange Barbie grins, flashing pearly whites. "Ah, call me Coyote Barbie, my friends. Listen up. From now on, we're reborn Barbies, New Age Barbies, we're Barbies that run with the wolves, Barbies who give no quarter and take no prisoners. I can see it's gonna take magic, and luckily I know a thing or two about this matter."

And so Coyote Barbie dispatches the others for supplies: colored chalk, feathers plucked from the ends of plastic arrows, bits of glitter and spangles, tufts of fur snatched from teddy bear ears. She concocts incense from powdered Pez and the perfume supplied with the Be Your Own Miss America kit and draws a circle on the tiled floor. The Barbies step inside, shivering.

Coyote Barbie chants and lavender smoke arises, coiling around the Barbies. Lame and Lycra harden into armor, plastic combs twist and squirm into grappling hooks and lines. And faces change. Blue eye after blue eye shifts into a million colors, skins darken or pale, rosebud lips take on new hues, until a crowd stands there unlike any Barbies anyone's seen before. Only Coyote Barbie remains her original ragged self.

"All right, Barbies," she shouts. "Let's open up a can of whoopass!"

With screams and shouts of glee, they rush the war toys.

It's a bloodless victory. The war toys don't stand a chance against this unexpected crowd. Corralled, herded into the Be Your Own Prison Warden Kit, they give over their weapons to the Barbies, who re-

distribute them. The Star Wars action figures put up resistance, but once Han falls prisoner to Amazon Barbie, their morale weakens and they too shuffle inside the bars.

The Barbies finger all these strange new toys, guns and knives and cannons and catapults, trebuchets and ballistae, gleaming in metallic splendor, but Coyote Barbie shakes her shaven head.

"Nuh uh," she says. "We don't need all that."

Valkyrie Barbie raises an eyebrow. "Then why," she asks, "did we bother?"

"Because we could!" Coyote Barbie shouts, and waves the banner she's acquired along the way. "Onward to the Legos!" They swarm that aisle and build castles, skyscrapers, monuments, Barbie versions of the Taj Mahal and the Tower of London. Buildings reach to the ceiling, far above the shelves, and atop the highest one, Coyote Barbie and Astrologer Barbie work on their own project, a spaceship big enough to hold everyone, a gleaming silver Lego ship like a dream of the 1940s, a cyberpunk Barbie contraption ready to spread its mechanical wings and float away.

When the Barbies climb aboard singing, only one remains behind, waving farewell as they peer out of the portholes, faces gleaming with excitement.

"You're not coming with us?" one shouts down to her. Coyote Barbie shakes her head far below.

"Still got some work to do down here," she shouts. "Go conquer the universe, I'll be wandering along soon enough! Bon voyage!" She smiles as the mall ceiling parts before the rising ship, letting it slip into the sky, and waves one last time, before turning her attention to the rest of the store.

"Still work to do," she says to the air, surveying the Toys-R-We. "Still plenty of work to do."

Afternotes

I wrote "Coyote Barbie" a few months after reading Women Who Run With The Wolves, and there are definite echoes. But beyond that, I'm troubled by what has happened with toy stores and how in many ways they've become increasingly gendered (remember Legos for girls? Coyote Barbie would not have approved, I think).

I love Coyote Barbie and often think of her out there exploring the universe.

Also, how could I not comment on the Barbie phenomenon? This story cried out to be written.

THE WIZARDS OF WEST SEATTLE

BEING THE APPRENTICE FOR ONE OF WEST SEATTLE'S MAIN wizards—probably *the* main wizard, as many reckoned it—was not at all what Albert thought it should be. He'd been installed in the position months ago and so far, all May Hua had asked him to do was walk her dogs, two energetic Shih Tzu puppies named North and South, three times each day.

The rest of the time he studied in the vast and idiosyncratic library housed on her third floor, but it was a self-directed path and that made him itch, knowing that he could have moved so much faster if she'd been willing to guide him along it.

His initial apprenticeship with another wizard had abruptly ended, and that disastrous stint made him reluctant to speak up about his frustration. The closest he came was to ask May at breakfast, "What do you think I should be focusing on?"

She put down her fork and gazed at him. "Appearances," she said, then went back to her meal with no further explanation. Typical. Wizards seemed to believe that magic was strengthened by elliptical communication.

Given that his only task involved the dogs, he suspected—or at least hoped—that magic also involved a great deal of walking. He said this—not for the first time—to Penny as on the evening walk and this time she answered the implied question.

Penny was the housekeeper for Hua's household. She was particularly

80

appreciative of Albert's presence, since he praised her cooking vociferously. Yet another thing learned from his first, disastrous stint as an apprentice. Like Albert, she was frequently at loose ends and so accompanied him on many of the walks. At first he'd been worried she was attracted to him, but it soon became clear that she was bored and he was a fresh novelty. She was cheerfully and inventively profane, given to dark humor, and a fountain of digressions. Her explanation was not illuminating. "Wizards walk the bounds in order to maintain their territories," she said.

"But how?" he pressed. "And why walking?"

"It's the only common mode of transportation," she said. "All of the other modes are an allegiance, even down to Segways or bicycles, on up to the buses, which Morty used to oversee. Now that he's dead, no one hesitates to use them anymore, at least until a new wizard steps up, and I don't mind that at all. I like to be able to ride back from Safeway with my Orca card. Easier on my frail old arms."

Albert snorted at that. Penny refused to say exactly how old she was, but surely not that many years beyond his twenty-two. "How did you come to all of this?" he asked.

She shrugged. "How does anyone come to this existence? You notice something you never had before, you step through a door that appeared where you'd never seen one. An encounter opens your mind and there you are." She pointed at him. "Not everyone goes on and tries to become a wizard, though. That takes guts."

Her words rang a little alarm bell in his mind. "Guts to leave everything behind and take that up, you mean," he said.

"Shit, no, son. Wizard training is dangerous. Otherwise we'd be crawling with them."

"Dangerous how?"

"What did May tell you about your first lesson?"

"That I need to look beyond appearances."

"Mmm." Penny gave him an elliptical smile and tucked a wind-strayed curl behind her ear. "And what happens if you don't learn to?"

"I guess then I'm stuck an apprentice forever," he said glumly. "May will never teach me anything."

Penny shook her head definitively. "There's always a time limit on these things."

"Wait, what?" he said with a rush of panic. "How long? And what happens if I don't make it? And how do I make it?"

"One: it varies, but usually a month or two. Two: consequences differ. Three: that's part of it."

"A month or two!" Dismay gripped him, made him stop and face her, despite the tugging of the dogs urging him down the hill. "It's been three already."

"I know. That surprised me."

"Is it ... Is it possible I failed once already and reset for another try?"

North barked in outrage, pulling on the leash and forcing him along, but again the definitive nature of Penny's headshake was unquestionable. "No. At the very least, you'd be gone. There are almost never second chances in wizardry."

Despair dismantled his heart.

"Look," she said. Her gaze went everywhere except at his face; her voice dropped as she leaned in. "Do you want help?"

Shame and hope struggled for supremacy over his thoughts. They walked in silence for half a block as he considered her words.

"Let me think for one day," he said as they turned down 45th.

Penny trailed her hand through a rosemary bush as they passed. "Are you sure?" she said, opening her palm to reveal a confused bee before it took flight.

Pride barriered off the temptation for now, but it was a flimsy fence.

"One day," he said, and tried to sound firmer than he felt.

This is how Albert Myers became apprenticed to a wizard: he saw a dragon eat someone.

He was walking near the Pike Place Market, cutting through an alley when he turned a corner.

As he reeled back from the shock of seeing an apparent human unhinge their jaw and swallow another apparent human in one vast and physically impossible gulp, the dragon had turned their attention towards the gaping Albert. He remembered thinking that he couldn't tell what gender they were, an improbably slim, androgynous youth of Chinese descent.

"Back off, señorita dinosaur," a voice said. Someone pushed past Albert, a tall, dark-haired man, downright handsome and with no little resemblance to Dr. Strange of comic book fame.

The dragon had been pissed, a confused Albert gathered at the time, but it was not until much later that he fully understood how lucky he'd been. His savior, Roy, took him back to Redmond and for a couple of weeks, Albert was his apprentice. But then the wizard's lover, a moody instance of the immortal Death, had returned home from a trip and insisted that Albert posed a severe inconvenience to the household and needed to be relocated elsewhere. Like a puppy.

That had stung. Fresh out of college and newly aimless, Albert had thought he'd found his true vocation. He'd had that sense of being the Chosen One, only to find himself far from it when Roy's partner had shown up. It felt as though he had failed, and through no fault of his own. This time, he was resolved, he would do better.

He'd learned a little from Roy before being pushed out the door. Something of Seattle's true nature. The city itself was ruled by dragons, and had been for decades now, all the way up to Ballard and the Bird Queen who held sway up there. Roy had told him to stay out of their

way, said they had long lives and memories to match.

Albert had researched them in May's library. He'd found the most information in an ancient wooden-bound book, its frontispiece marked with the ideogram for dragon, which contained May's observations in the margins in tiny, precise letters. They were powerful, her notes said, and wizards should always know when there were any around.

"Why don't the dragons come over here?" he asked Penny. "You said Seattle was full of them."

"Because the Wizards would fuck them up. That's how it is in any city they rule; other forces contain them." She stared across the water towards the harbor's skyline. "You can always tell a dragon city by the way it treats the sky."

"What do you mean?"

"Think about it. Look up, next time you're downtown, at all the rooftop gardens and oddly spacious balconies."

Across Lake Washington, the technomancers ruled most of the hills of Redmond and Sammammish, but there were scatterings of other beings, mostly in the settlements of Villa Encantada and Friendly Village. The south was a crazyquilt of varied territories, but wizards ruled West Seattle.

Penny imparted more in bits and pieces during the walks. How every named building had its patron spirit who could be called on. How (but not why) each Wizard was named for a major street and what happened at the junctions where those streets met. How (and again not why) the Pretender of Fauntleroy was always to be called that and never by name. How to tell which houses were ghost traps, catching spirits through odd angles of fencing, and why the Little Free Libraries were never to be tampered with. Where the shuttle ferrying souls to downtown Seattle stopped and how to refuse the driver if they pulled up. The nature of the Flimsies, zones created by poor construction and foot traffic (every fast food place seemed to manifest one), and how

they hampered thought. How to taste the different flavors of magic, the green strength of communal gardens and the resiny tang of ancient trees, and the concrete and sparks edge of Hiawatha Park that she said was typical of its creator, Olmsted, an early American wizard who'd built parks all over the country.

As Albert listened, a new world formed for him, one built of hidden things and secret forces and mysteries. It thrilled his geeky heart to the core, and he knew that he wanted to be a wizard and would give anything for it.

May Hua had agreed to take him as an apprentice, with a few stipulations, none of which were too bad, other than giving up meat, orgasms, and cannabis entirely. He hoped the restrictions were simply part of the apprenticeship and not a lifelong condition.

Maybe when Hua had said appearances, she had meant the way in which the leash was presented, the handoff of a pair of purple leather leashes emblazoned with tiny dragons. That could signify something about … what, precisely, could it mean?

As far as he could tell so far—and his experience was, admittedly, limited, that was what magic consisted of, riding the fine line between believing in all this gobbledygook and the uneasy awareness that one was making all of this up.

Penny, though, believed there was a system behind it. And maybe there was, given her ability to rattle off its intricacies and oddities.

The first week they had been walking and she'd seen a pen lying in the gutter.

Stooping to retrieve it, she simply moved it to the curb, where it was less likely to be crushed by car wheels.

"What are you doing?" Albert asked, intrigued.

"Leaving it for the oracle. He can only answer with writing materials he finds."

"Who?"

"Write it down, I've told you this before. Figure it out, sunshine." She rolled her eyes and laughed, then glanced forward, amusement dying off.

"Danger?" he started to ask, but Penny said, "Hush." She stopped and let the man approach.

He was deceptively big, the sort of large that a football player wears with ease, and just as muscular. His suit was expensive, even to Albert's untutored eye, and the delicate pattern of flames on his tie was echoed in the purple silk handkerchief tucked in his breast pocket. His shoes made virtually no sound as he came across the sidewalk.

Albert would have worried but the man paid him and Penny no attention. Instead, silently, he squatted on his heels, the motion composed with a gymnast's economy, and held out his hand to the nearest dog, North.

Both dogs greeted him with delight, standing up to paw eagerly at his suit and have their ears rubbed. Long moments passed. Albert tried to catch Penny's eye, but she stared fixedly at the man.

Finally the man stood and moved on, stepping past them as though they were no more than grass or trees.

"What the hell?" Albert said. "Who was that?"

"Anytime you meet him out walking, let him pet the dogs," she said. She looked at the form as it grew more distant. "He's called Mr. Gray. The ruler of the local weres." At Albert's blank look, she clarified. "Shapeshifter. You know. Werewolves. And turtles. And things."

"What does he turn into?"

"That is one of West Seattle's mysteries. No one knows."

"How do they know he's a shapeshifter if he never changes?"

"Weres always know each other. Something about their energy. And whatever he is, it's the biggest and baddest of them all."

They walked on in silence until Albert had to ask.

"Are there really were-turtles?"

———••••—••◗

Part of wizarding is meditating, Roy had told him that much. So he tried it, first finding a good location.

All of the wizards were referred to by their titles in conversation and lived on the street whose name they bore. The Wizard of California was no exception and her house could be accessed via a secret stairway in Overlook Park. It was the highest point in West Seattle, albeit invisible to most eyes, and looked down in scorn on its counterpart across the way. The view could best be accessed by going up to the house's fifth floor—in truth a cupola and proceeding out a small door there, along the windy widow's walk, and onto a platform bordered on all sides with wrought iron balconies shaped like winged monkeys.

Albert went up there to sit cross-legged and ponder the situation. You never knew with wizards and their ways of teaching. They posed you a riddle that you worked at for years sometimes, he had been told. That's why he hadn't wondered about a deadline. And now here one was.

What if he couldn't figure it out? It wasn't his fault if his mind just didn't work the same way hers did. It was like playing a game written in a foreign language, unsure what was significant and what wasn't.

Maybe the test wasn't about the actual task at hand, but the nature of it, so he had to come up with some clever refusal, a slap-your-teacher-when-he-asks-you-the-sound-of-one-hand-clapping sort of thing. Was that the case? He didn't think so, but it was possible. Every wizard must have a sense of humor: it's a prerequisite. But he was finding it hard to laugh at whatever joke she was posing him.

Around him the winds swirled, tugged at his clothes, played with his hair. Far to the south and east, Mount Rainier loomed. One of Roy's friends was apprenticed there. She claimed she had it worse than any of the rest of them, but surely a volcano wouldn't mess with your

head the way a wizard would.

From this vantage point, the sound's blue gray sweep was terminated by the city skyline, the Space Needle prominent. Close at hand was the park—a few men clustered around an arrangement of pickup trucks, a couple standing at the lookout point, hand in hand.

The proximity of park to the wizard's house had seemed so public at first, but a layer of spells thicker than any wall barriered the park off and the park had even been constructed so as to reinforce that spell. Not for the first time, Albert wondered exactly how long Hua had been around.

It wasn't entirely that May had told him nothing, he realized as he sat there watching the wind in the trees. She had, in fact, imparted several things on the very first day.

First: A conversation that had taken place as she was showing him the house. He'd been angry, so angry that he'd been put aside—he didn't understand the why of it and that was what angered him the most, so he stamped along the corridor after May's dumpy little figure, only half listening.

She'd turned to regard him, pulling his attention to her like blowing a spark to flame. She said, "Do you understand what sets a wizard's mind apart from other people's? They want the world so fiercely to be different that they bend it to their will. Your master glimpsed that in you. You saw what was happening and it wasn't for yourself, that want, but an ingrained sense of how you thought the world should be, a vision of fairness strong enough to fuel magic, actual magic. That's what sustains and powers us, at heart, that sense of how things should be, that lets us work our art."

He started to ask, "So how do I do that?" but she had turned away and was already stepping through a door.

Second: Another conversation in which May said the following.

"West Seattle is more important than anyone thinks. This is the

city's secret heart—here on Alki is where it all started. The dragons hold Seattle, but the city's strong enough in its own right to keep them from twisting it awry, even though part of that power rests here, and that is why this is a Wizard roost, territory run in part by council, in part by allocating out every aspect. History is part of the magic here, conjured so deep that every spell is steeped in it."

Around them was hallway, a long one lined with photographs, some of them vintage, black and white with a scattering colorized. Many showed more recent hues. May gestured at an old engraving showing a group waiting for a boat. "The history's your ally; you can use it if you learn to speak its language."

"How?" he said, but she was walking away again, and the hallway shrank around her so he could not follow.

Third (and finally): As they stood on the long widow's walk, she said, "It's about alliances too. Your early ones determine a lot."

"Who should I look to?" he began, but this time she was just gone. Her voice spoke inside his left ear. "Dinner in an hour. After that you need to walk the dogs."

He didn't mean to eavesdrop. He knew better. But their voices came around the corner clearly, an echo of the house's oddly configured corners.

"I want to tell him," Penny said. Her tone was unlike any he'd ever heard her employ before, wheedling, a lover's caress. He held his breath.

May's voice was dry in return. "You are impatient."

"All it will do is move him to the second hurdle. No matter what, it's how he jumps it and the next that determines the race."

"And then you will have no one to talk with on your walks."

"Don't ask me to look to the future," Penny said. "It's not in my nature." She laughed, a tipsy edge to the sound.

"Enough," May snapped. "You are looking to the future now."

"How many apprentices have failed you, wizard? This day and age is no longer subtle enough for your kind." All languor was fled.

A clatter along the hall, the dogs running from the kitchen, barking at nothingness. He stepped loudly forward, knelt to pet one in the doorway. May and Penny stood facing each other; the housekeeper's body tensed and straight, May's more relaxed. She beckoned him forward with a slow wave.

Had she guessed that he'd been listening? He stood inside her house; who was to say whether or not she could see everything that happened within it, when she cared to? She looked at him silently, then pointed at the dogs.

"They need exercising," she said. "Penny, you will stay with me. I want to go over the menu for dinner."

Penny's stance didn't loosen. "Very well."

He needed answers. Penny had promised them, but what was the price?

That pen, placed so carefully on the curb, came to him as he wrapped the leashes around his hand and headed out.

So much depended right now on the Universe's willingness to oblige him. He thought about May's words—if he believed strongly enough, the world would give it to him. He stepped along, eyes searching the gutter. Candy wrappers. Safeway receipts, a bubble wand, leaves and more leaves. A buckle torn from a shoe. A fragment of blue bandana. A crumpled plastic clamshell. A Starbucks cup holder. The word "eat' written in mustard ... and there, a flash of green unlike any leaf. He bent for the bit of broken crayon, gasping in relief.

The oracle could tell him who to ally with, what to do.

He laid the crayon on the curb, retreated to the nearby bus stop

to wait and see who picked it up. He wished he knew magic to hide himself with. But it seemed like cheating, somehow.

The man shuffled up while he was looking in another direction. Albert snapped to attention, seeing dirty blond hair, army jacket, jeans more hole than fabric.

Albert held tight to the moment, feeling the world aligning around him, nudging itself in new directions.

The man fumbled with the crayon, drew on the curb a single ideogram. One Albert had seen before.

Surely not coincidence that it was the only one Albert knew?

Two scaled forms, side by side, that was how you could read it.

Dragon.

On the way back, he almost didn't stop for Mr. Gray. But he remembered Penny's caution—Penny, who didn't seem to fear anything—so he waited, let the man complete his ritual. He expected some flicker of recognition at the end, but there was none.

Penny had shown him how to sense magic, get an idea for what she described as its flavor. He relaxed and reached out with that sense now.

And was rocked back on his heels with a blast of gunpowder and acrid cinnamon. Gray's attention snapped to him with the force of a blow.

"I'm sorry," Albert stammered. "I didn't mean to be rude ..."

With a huff of angry air, Gray was gone with the suddenness befitting King of the Weres.

That would be an ally to have. And appearances ... could this be the test?

Look to history, May had said. All through dinner he turned things

over in his head. Penny was snappish; May was silent and contemplative. Afterwards he refused dessert despite Penny's glare and went up to the hallway.

The picture May had pointed out. He studied it. A crowd, gathered on a flat landing place, waiting, it looked like, for an incoming boat.

There in the crowd, that face. The long nose, the angled lines …

Mr. Gray.

But what to make of that?

———•••—•◎

He was hoping that Roy's lover wouldn't pick up the phone, but that was of course what happened. Albert asked for Roy and there was a long pause before the other said, "Oh, I see," and dropped the phone to shout, "Roy, it's that stray you picked up. Remember he can't come here. I don't want fleas." Then sweetly, into the phone, "He'll be right with you."

Albert sincerely hoped that on the day he met his own death, the incarnation would be considerably less bitchy.

Roy said, "What's up?" without preamble. From the strain in his voice Albert could tell Death was listening, but he had to try.

"Roy, I have a question about weres."

"I can't really help you with any test May's set you," Roy said in a warning tone. Albert heard Death make a rude noise in the background.

"No, it's not that," he said. "I just need some info—I just need to know, are they always natural?"

"What do you mean?" Roy said with the keen interest of a wizard sensing a potential academic discussion.

"Like wolves and horses. Could they be something magical? Like a …" He cast about in all directions. He didn't want to tip his hand.

"Like a were-unicorn, maybe."

"Oh, sure," Roy said. "That's pretty rare, though. Hang on." He muffled the phone, but Albert could hear an argument being conducted. It rose in volume until suddenly Albert was disconnected.

That was all right. He hung up the phone and turned to find himself nose to nose with Penny.

"Looking for info?" Penny's eyes were sharp as needles. "Got your answer?"

"Maybe," he hedged.

"Don't want to risk a wrong one," she said. "Remember that I can steer you right. Think about it." Her breath smelled like peppermint, and he was suddenly thankful of the celibacy spell May had given him, because he could feel it kicking in, slowing his heartbeat, cooling his brain.

"Oh, that's cheating," Penny said, looking a little dismayed. "Did you come up with that on your own?"

"I asked May for it when she explained the conditions of the apprenticeship," he said, trying for dignity.

"You straight white boys start with such a big handicap. She must have thought it would be helpful." She shrugged. "It doesn't matter to me." She smiled at him. "You're the one that needs the answer. Are you sure you're not making things harder than they need to be?"

———•◦

He'd had nightmares about dragons ever since that encounter.

Gray was surely a were-dragon. What would that mean? Would he be accepted by the true dragons? That would be why he was here in West Seattle, away from them. He was their foe, that would mean Albert wouldn't have to worry he was allying himself with that group. But dragons of any kind …

Alliances, Hua had said. And here he could chase Gray or he could turn to the one at hand, Penny.

That was it, wasn't it? Appearances. He felt a puff of pride at how well the pieces were fitting together. Penny was more than she seemed, more than just a housekeeper. She was a possible ally. That was what her offer to tell him was—an exchange of the sort that signaled a formal alliance.

He'd wait for the next walk to ask her.

—•••—◦

Going along California, he thought she was about to say something more than once. But it wasn't until they turned on Alaska and started on down past the cluster of bus shelters that she made an impatient noise.

For once Albert felt like a real wizard. He was about to pass his first test, look past appearances, and claim an ally.

Not the most impressive one, to be sure, but better Penny than someone who might draw dragons to him. And Penny knew a lot of lore. Perhaps that was the sort of magic she was hiding under her skin, a wealth of gentle, womanly lore, the knowledge of slow and secret things. It would be a solid base on which to build grander edifices, he decided, and so he smiled at her.

The dogs danced deosil around his feet as he said, "All right, give me the answer to the test."

The wind pulled her hair this way and that. She said, "There's more than one part, you know."

He shrugged. He was a wizard and the universe would do as he willed. At last he was coming into his own. Proudly, he said, "The first part is to recognize that you're more than you seem, I understand that."

"Oh yes," she said. "That is the first part. Shall I tell you the second part?"

He nodded.

She licked her lips. "The second part is escaping me."

He realized he'd made a terrible mistake.

For a long moment they stood with locked eyes, his wide with dismay, hers narrowed with pleasure. She hissed, "It's much more fun if you run, little man. I'll give you five minutes."

When she grinned, he could see her teeth, longer than any dragon's. The sight reached inside him and pushed a panic button that drowned out all thought.

He ran.

She'd stood between him and the main Junction, so he fled in the other direction, towards the distant gleam of water. What was he to do? He couldn't fight some sort of supernatural creature. His shoes flapped along and he almost tripped, searching the yards with his eyes as he ran, looking for some weapon. Were there buildings whose spirits he could call on? But he was already past the Franklin and peeling on down the street, past houses. He crashed through a communal garden and felt its scraps of magic around him, but he had no time to figure out how to use them.

All he had were his senses. He didn't know how to use most magic, but Penny had taught him how to read it.

The flavor of Gray's magic. Could he find it? The discarded notion of alliance was perhaps his only chance.

There. Towards Alki, somewhere near Schmitz Park. Was that the sizzle and burn of Gray's personality or something else or even just Albert's hopes deluding him?

It doesn't matter. I can do something now or stand here dithering and die. He'd read that promise in Penny's eyes, suddenly alien and familiar all at once, in an uncanny way that made his balls want to creep back up inside him, the threat of mind-erasing oblivion, with even his soul torn to scraps. He had to believe he was going the right

way, and if he believed hard enough, he would be.

He chased the tang on the air, wondering if Penny had started yet, and then he chased the smell down cement steps, past graffitied spells whose edges flickered and almost collided with the man standing there at the foot of the stairs.

Gray.

Too late to change his mind. Too late to do anything but throw his fate to the wind and see who caught it.

Albert stared at Mr. Gray. He looked so daunting. Was he part of this lesson or some random intrusion thrown into the mix by chance?

No. You had to pay attention to patterns and this was their third encounter. He had met Gray for a reason.

He had to be an ally.

Otherwise not only had Albert failed this test, but Penny was probably going to eat his soul.

So he said the words of greeting, deliberate and formal, despite the way that time was clawing at him, "I offer you exchange, whatever you would, for I am in direst need," and wondered briefly if this was what the oracle had been talking about.

"There is nothing you could offer me, wizard to be," Gray said scornfully.

There was no choice. "I'll make a bargain with you," he gasped. "I know your secret."

Mr. Gray froze. There was no other word for that cold stillness, only a faint serpent's glitter in his eyes.

"Then indeed we will ally, if nothing else so you will tell me the source of your knowledge," he said. Every word was sharp-edged ice and the spaces between them rang with magic.

Gray extended a hand and Albert's met his. The fingers did not press his hard, but he felt the implacable strength of mountains in them, and the sensation sent him reeling.

Behind him, the slap slap of Penny's sneakers rang, catching up, and the rush of her shook him, bowed him forward even as Gray released his hand to step past.

The pavement bit into the heels of his hands with a jolt that shook him from head to toe. He collapsed onto his left elbow, twisting around to raise his right arm to shield himself.

But Penny was not there. She stood facing Gray, a few steps away. Around their wordless forms, the air thrummed as though the skin of a vast drum was being touched, tapped into life.

And then the world SHOUTED with the force of a single blow to that drum, setting reality shivering as Gray LOOMED, larger than he should have been, over Penny, who still stared upward, lips curled back from fanglike teeth, before her eyes flickered close and she went to her knees.

The blow drove Albert's breath from his lungs and he fought to recover it, drawing in a gasp from air that seemed too thick to gulp, that resisted and battled his effort to take it in.

Mr. Gray moved to his side. He walked slowly, as though carrying a great weight, but not an unwilling one. He did not stoop to give Albert help as he struggled back to his feet.

So that was it. He had passed the test, had seen through appearances. Technically with Penny he'd been given the solution, but he had also seen through Gray's and he wasn't sure that May Hua could say the same.

With a flurry of yips and yaps, the two Shih Tzus rushed him. They must have been following all this time. North began licking his face industriously; South circled them, nosing the ground.

"They are charming, if mindless, in this form, aren't they?" Gray said. He bent now to let South explore his fingers. His expression was somewhere between pain and resignation.

"This form?" Albert said, feeling stupid and panicked all at once.

Had he missed some component of the test?

Gray said, "Look again, and at their hearts."

Albert strove to achieve that moment of clarity the oracle had given him again. A garment just out of reach, his fingers brushing the sleeve … and then it was on him. He looked at North and South.

Not dogs, but dragons, the smallest he'd ever seen. Unlike the dragon he had confronted, there was no shine of intelligence in their eyes.

"They're not dogs at all!" he gasped.

"I would have thought that somewhat obvious," Gray said dryly. "Tell me now how you guessed my secret."

"Penny said you were King of the Weres but no one knew what," Albert said. "But such a long lifespan. It had to be something capable of living centuries. That narrowed it down."

"Overlooking the possibilities of longevity conferred through a second source, or time magic, or any other number of equally likely things," Gray said. "Amazing. Ignorance let you narrow it down that far, unlikely as I might have thought it. And almost, almost quite right. But … no. We shall close down any avenue where someone might come at this splinter of the truth though." Gray's long fingers flickered, and Albert felt a spell twisting itself around his teeth, but not painfully so.

⚯

"Did I pass the test?" he asked May. "I mean, I survived Penny. But I had to ask for help to do it. Is that what you meant that day when you said it was about alliances too?"

"There were multiple possible alliances," she told him, her eyes hooded. She started to turn away with just those words.

"No," he said. "I need more than that. Aren't you my first and foremost ally? Aren't you the person I should be able to turn to for

help and explanation?"

She turned back to him. It was the first time he had seen her crack a smile, an expression that made his heart leap in all directions, a startled fish exploding from the water, dancing sideways on its tail before it subsided back under surface steadiness.

"Very well," she said. "Penny was the most obvious choice, and it is often handy to have a demon in your pocket. Each of the other wizards has approached you, in their way—" she paused to quirk her lips even harder at his confusion "—and there were others though it seems in all of this it is less that you chose Gray than that you thought him your only option." She shrugged. "I don't know that I'd tell him that. He's a vain creature at his core."

She rubbed her nose, still smiling. "Life is life, Albert, and things continue on as they will. A wizard learns to ride those waves, or else they drown."

"So I did pass?"

"Of course you did. And now we can really begin."

Afternotes

I moved to West Seattle from Redmond in late 2015. I found I loved its quirky bits and figuring out the wizardly side of things entertains me during my walks. Roy is Roy Macomber from the story "The Threadbare Magician", which appeared in Genius Loci.

SUMMER NIGHT IN DURHAM

for Ann Kakaliouras

 Some supernaturals have trouble adjusting to the human world.

I keep telling the vampires that tattoos are just a bad idea where they're concerned, but still I get two or three of them in a night, more on the weekends. They want the same wide variety the living do: cartoon devils and names of loved ones, mostly, but the daring ones ask me to etch them with religious symbols and giggle. Tonight, a pleasant evening when the summer heat lingered in the air and everything was sweat and locust-buzz, one vampire told me he'd never seen a lady tattoo artist before.

I said, you haven't seen any since you Turned, or they would have told you what a bad idea this is.

He blinked at me as though he didn't understand what I could possibly be saying. He had this puzzled look on his face under all the stubble and a little bit of eyeliner around his eyes. Most vampires wear jewelry, but this one didn't have anything precious on him other than a tiny gold hoop in one ear and a possible filling or two.

I could tell he expected me to be scared of him. Instead I was just

tired. It was almost the end of my shift, and I'd already explained this to three other vampires.

Look, I said. Vampire flesh just doesn't tattoo the way human skin does. It keeps bleeding, keeps seeping fluid, and never heals. I don't think that's what you want.

He blinked at me again and seemed about to say something when a sound from the doorway made us both look. His girlfriend stood there, a human woman with skin like cream and roses, not a tattoo on her. Her hair was like spun gold, with a hint of rose in it, as though fire lurked in its heart.

He said somebody should get a tattoo. Glenda, how about you?

She sneered a little. She said, that's not why you want me. It's because I look unsullied. Virginal.

He shrugged and mumbled something.

What's that, she demanded.

I said, folks, did you want to get a tattoo or did you want to move along? Because I get paid by the hour, not counting tips. I stressed that last word in case they didn't get the point.

He drew himself up like a movie Dracula, puffed up his chest, which would have been more intimidating if he'd been dressed in formalwear rather than jeans and a t-shirt reading "The dead do it all night long."

You don't dictate to the likes of me, Missy, he said. Behind him, his girlfriend rolled her eyes so wildly I thought that they would pitch out of her head.

I'm not dictating, I said. I just think we could all save ourselves some valuable time if the vampire community would learn that tattoos are a human practice they may wish to forgo.

I could tell my lack of fear put him off. He sized me up, trying to figure out whether I was predator or just deluded prey. I stared back and let a bit of fire show in my eyes.

Maybe it was that, or maybe it was just that dawn would be coming

in a few hours, but he shoved twenty bucks at me with an apologetic shrug and nod and sauntered out the door with girlfriend in tow.

The receptionist put her head in through the doorway. Your next one's here early, she said.

This is a shitty way to earn a living, I told her, and she just looked back at me.

If that leprechaun hadn't taken all my gold, I said a little louder.

At least you had a trade to fall back on. She shrugged.

At least the next one wanted something pretty, koi all up and down her leg. That I could do, so I drew them in blue and green and orange and white, details so fine you'd swear you could see the fins ripple, and in the water in between them, coins falling, copper pennies and silver denari and soft, shiny doubloons.

When I finally took a break, I went outside to smoke. The vampire was waiting, lingering despite the hints of false dawn sizzling across the parking lot gravel.

They told me I shouldn't fight you, he said. His look was angry but there was a touch of question in it, like he was smart enough to know that there's always a bigger fish.

You're very new, I said. Or you'd know that there's plenty of non-humans around, hiding in ordinary skins. I smiled and let a hint of tooth show.

It was wrong of me, because I knew he'd take it as a challenge, and he did. He came at me in a rush of fangs.

I would have swallowed him whole, but that would have been wasteful, so I just yawned fire and watched him burn. They go up fast, vampires, and when they're gone, it's just ash and gleanings.

No gold fillings in his teeth, but the remnants of the earring remained. I picked the tiny puddle of melted metal up and held it in my hand. Every little bit helps when a Dragon is rebuilding her horde.

Afternotes

I wrote this story drawing from the memories of getting a tattoo in Durham, North Carolina, with a couple of friends, including Ann Kakaliouras, to whom I dedicated the story. Ann's a lovely woman who knows more about bones than anyone else I know, and she's also one of the people that my association with the Armageddon MUD drew into my life. (Blackwing forever, Ann.)

I have three tattoos at this point in my life and keep meaning to expand the bumblebee on my forearm to an entire sleeve of greenery and flowers when there's both time and money. My back piece was designed by Mark Tripp; you see a version of it in Near + Far. *I love my tats; they're very much a part of me and I cannot think of anytime I've regretted them.*

The story started simply with an anthology call for a book titled Stamps, Tramps, and Vamps. *I worked from my memory of the moment and chose the POV of the tattooist. From there, the rest of the story flowed pretty naturally towards the final moment in the parking lot. All the rewrite involved was a little tweaking to foreshadow her dragonish nature.*

WEB OF BLOOD AND IRON

THE HOTEL GEVAUDAN PUT MANSERVANTS and maids up in their own rooms, one attic below the hotel staff: housekeepers, valets, clerks, kitchen help. The manager lived on-site as well, his family taking up half the floor below that. I'd heard his children more than once playing blind man's bluff and squeak piggy squeak in the back stairwells.

I wouldn't have minded a room to myself, but instead I had a cot in his Lordship's suite, down on the third floor. I was lying there enjoying the Cannes sounds of birds and street bustle and funeral rumble of the trains and reading when I heard the door fumble open and Lord Albert lurch in.

Alive for another day.

———◦◦◦—◦◇

I was up quick, and went in to help him off with his tuxedo, ripe with boozy sweat and cigar smoke and the hyacinth scent the siren whores wear. He was so drunk I was surprised he'd made it home at all, that none of the vampire gamblers had decided to take him home as a nightcap instead of selecting a whore.

He chattered away as I sponged his forehead. He always slept nude. Every lycanthrope I'd served—and I've served six so far of his Lordship's family, the deVulfs—has shared that trait.

"Made enough to keep us here another week," he said with a grin.

I doubted that, given the size of his weekly liquor tab. I took care of his bills as well, so his ideas of money were usually far off the mark. But his father would supplement that well enough that we could stay.

His cleaning bill was as large as my wages, and I'm better paid than most. The Yorkshire coal mines make the De Vulffs a lot of money.

The question was not how long he could stay. Rather, it was how much longer till one of the vampires discovered his ruse?

I decided to save that for a later argument, when he would be soberer.

Stubble sprouted on his chin a mere hour after each time I'd shaved him with the bone and steel razor so I didn't bother now to do more than wipe his face. He could go to sleep shaggy and untroubled, smelling only of wolf.

We gnomes have senses almost as acute as theirs. It's one way we read the earth: metal tang and mineral salts, loam and chalk and bland sandstone.

He fingered his forearm, the silver charm soldered to an iron band, sliding it down to dangle loose around his wrist, then laying it on the end table.

"You still want to leave, don't you?" he asked me, voice harsh.

"I think it would be wisest, sir," I said without looking at him. "We could drive up along the coast, swing through Paris, then Calais. We'd be at your club for dinner and some good mutton."

He huffed amusement. "Appealing to my animal appetites."

"Appealing to your common sense," I said, this time meeting his eyes.

They shifted from brandied amusement to muted chocolate. "Not

until I know what happened to Marguerite."

"She wouldn't have wanted you to endanger yourself."

He turned away, fists bunched at his sides. "I know those bastards can tell me what happened to her. Whether she's alive. My father still has enough influence that they listen to me."

Perhaps. But I didn't say that aloud. While the vampires held social ascendancy right now, they hadn't always. At one point they'd reckoned the werewolves' opinions into their choices. But I didn't think his title would prevent them from tearing his throat out if—perhaps just when—they discovered he'd been cheating for two weeks now. The charm's silver burned at him, but it would ward off any vampire's touch. But that was a flimsy defense—if it happened to slide out from beneath his cuff, any vampire catching sight of it would know it for the luck-cheat it was.

He padded over to his bed and collapsed on it, sprawling on his stomach.

I pulled the crisp linen sheet over him and went to prepare his evening clothes for yet another night before returning to the pages I'd been wading through, Marx's *Critique of Hegel's Doctrine of the State*.

———————

Marguerite. I'd been tired of her from the very beginning, but no servant gets to pick who their master falls in love with. An American girl with delusions of following in the footsteps of Nellie Bly or Jennie June. A war correspondent, here in Europe to cover the wars and convulsions. Back in the States, they'd preserved their freedom, to a degree. Here the vampires, fairies, and their ilk owned the continent, had ever since they'd stepped in to end the World War.

What would have happened if they hadn't? Who's to say it would have been as bad as they claimed?

He'd met Marguerite in London. Mixing with a human was bad enough, but when she'd gone off to the French Riviera in search of some story, he had told her he'd meet up with her here and had, only to have her vanish the next day.

I hoped that she'd simply found someone else, some other wealthy pigeon to pluck. But given how she'd vanished out of sight, I thought it might well be the wrongdoing that lord Albert believed it to be.

Two weeks now without much clue. People had seen her. But ask where she had gone, and they looked vacant, unknowing.

Out in the courtyard, Jean asked if I wanted the Delahaye brought round, as he did every day, and as always, I shook my head. But I went into the garage to see it nonetheless, as though it were a horse I meant to comfort. It sat there in the shadows, which washed out the robin's egg blue of its sides, turning them gray. Sleek and ready. My favorite of all his lordship's cars, barely two months off the assembly line.

I ran my palm over the sweet silver trim, wishing I had some reason to drive it away now.

Wishing I had some reason to leave altogether. That the courage of my convictions would let me leave his lordship, the foolish child of an unfair class system, behind.

But despite all my feelings about the aristocracy—as Marx said, their parasitic nature had always existed, even before the vampires had claimed them—whenever I looked at Bertie, I saw him as the boy he had once been, full of fancies about knights and chivalry and quests.

He might not acknowledge it right now, but that was what he was doing right now, being a perfect knight riding off to rescue his damsel, armed with ancient tradition.

I hoped she appreciated it. At least, that she was alive to do so.

By 6 p.m., his lordship had roused and was ready to be shaved and dressed. I had sandwiches sent up, something to tide him over till he went out. His eyes sagged as though he hadn't slept.

"Where to tonight?" I asked as I stirred the lather, smelling of bay rum, and spread it over the black shadows on his jawline.

"Jenkins," he said. "He's set up some sort of game in his car on the train. Says it will be novel."

"Novel" is not a word one likes to hear from an older vampire. So often their ideas of novelty involve pain.

And of course a train. The vampires were obsessed with the trains. Before their occupation, travel had been idiosyncratic: carriages and the occasional automobile. Now their trains thundered through the night, every night, great black things whose whistles called back and forth like hunting hawks, a network of iron connecting every city and town in this area, always spreading, a spiderweb claiming this country and all beyond it.

"Have the front desk call me a cab." My lord studied his lapels, fingering the wide black expanse, before he held out an arm and I placed his watch, freshly wound, on his wrist. Syrupy gold, not silver. A showy piece, but one vampires would appreciate. They like gaudy on other people.

He looked at me. "Do you want to come, Toby?"

He hadn't asked me that before. It wouldn't be anything new to have me there waiting on him while he gambled, but previously I'd avoided the vampires. They like nonhuman blood more than human and they're not hesitant about feeding on servants. Would his presence keep me safe?

But tired blue shadows sagged under his eyes. He needed backup. He needed a friend there.

His servant would have to do.

He didn't speak in the taxi, just stared out with knitted brows. Already stubble darkened his jaw, and his Adam's apple worked as he swallowed.

Not my place to speak, so I stared out the opposite window, running through my inventory. A good manservant is always supplied, from the mints, handkerchief, and comb in my waistcoat to the Bangalore Torpedo, all chambers loaded, secured along my calf to match the dagger's weight on the other side.

When we pulled up at the station, I fell in line behind him, my boots crunching along the gravel. Jenkins—Lord Jenkins, the Earl of Westumber, to be precise—had a private train, resting on a sidetrack right now. The only other train was Le Train Bleu, getting ready to depart in a few minutes. Not one of the new vampire models, but an older passenger train, elegant and appointed, carrying passengers in true continental style. Coal smoke hung heavy and unavoidable in the briny sea air.

Lord Albert didn't speak as we walked towards the train car. I could see him preparing himself, squaring his shoulders, putting on his fatuous face. A simple English werewolf interested in a little gambling and a lot of drink. All surface.

Some sleek fellow, hair slicked back and smelling of Cassie pomade, fell into step beside his Lordship. "Fine evening," he drawled. The slight slur betrayed him as vampire; they prefer not to hide their teeth, no matter what.

Beside me, the vampire's Renfrew, a silent servant like myself. I stole a sidelong glance: human, far-gone, staring straight ahead.

Inside the train car, cigar and incense smoke tinged the air blue and battled it out for supremacy, ending in a tie. A subdued clink of crystal and cutlery, the ruffle of cards, dice clatter, came from the

various tables scattered throughout the room, augmented by the murmur of voices.

Vampires almost always speak softly. I've always thought it a way of demonstrating their power. Forcing listeners to strain their ears is more effective than shouting sometimes.

The sleek man tugged his Lordship over to a table; the Renfrew and I moved to the antechamber filled with other servants. No one spoke there. The Renfrews stared ahead silently; the two others, myself and a harried looking human, exchanged glances. Everything was hushed as velvet, opulent and curlicued.

We stood there pretending to be furniture as the gamblers played. Now and then a player would signal, and his servant would dart out from the crowd, wipe his brow, fetch a new drink, or whatever small service was necessary.

My lord's table was nearby, a cluster of vampires and him, sitting like a terrier amid a crowd of smiling cats. I couldn't hear them at first, but I nudged my way through the crowd to stand nearer. None of the Renfrews objected, though one sneered as I shouldered past him and another smiled and licked his lips at me, a sneaky little taunt that would have earned him a punch in the face out in the street.

Three of the vampires at the table were of little account: hangers on, the inconsequential scum at the edge of this pond. But the vampire my Lord sat across from was Wilfrid von Blodam.

Von Blodam was slight, turned at an age when his trim little blonde beard was barely past peachfuzz. He dressed immaculately, expensively, and had not one servant in attendance, but two, a pair of matched twins, who stood ready to anticipate any need. The most powerful vampire in Cannes, rumored to be working his way up the power chain as the vampires solidified their hold on the continent.

Before they spread out over the world, I thought, and then thrust that thought away as quickly as I could. Some of them are telepaths.

But how can any of us avoid thinking about the covert war? Great Britain, where the fairy strongholds are based, holds out, and the various African power groups have worked together to do so as well. And the vampires will have to work hard and long to take America, with its vast stores of phlogiston. But already the vampires, aided by a few renegade dragons, have spread so far from their origin point that some have gone eastward to nibble at Russia's edges.

My lord signaled. I refreshed his whiskey. The air at the table felt grave-cold, despite the heat in the rest of the room, and the smoke seemed to clear around the table, rendering it a clear bubble in the hazy interior.

My Lord studied his cards.

"Do you know," von Blodam drawled, "where the little journalist went to, the Miller girl? I kept seeing her around the station, asking questions about the trains."

The twitch of my Lord's shoulder would have been as apparent to the vampire's keen perceptions as it was to me, who only saw it because I knew him so well.

"That one that always wore that little blue hat?" he said lightly, still studying his cards. "I was wondering that myself. Took her out for a drink and thought I'd do it again but the bitch vanished on me. No one seems to know where she went to." He glanced at me. "Don't hover, Smith, it's damned annoying."

I retreated to my cul de sac.

Von Blodam kept playing on the theme throughout the night. "As the Commandant of this zone," he said, "I should be tracking these sorts of people better. I tell you, what, Lord de Vulff, I'll let you know if I hear anything of her."

My lord kept playing, but he was losing steadily despite the medallion at his wrist. You could practically see the money flowing through his fingers, all that labor, hours of coal mining, transmuted

into coins that he spent like water, without even thinking of it.

The rich don't think themselves rich. They count themselves hard up to practice economies such as a single carriage instead of two, or foregoing buying more land or another factory to make them richer. It's easy to hate them for that, and nowhere had I seen it played out so excessively, so freely, shows of wealth that would have been vulgar if they didn't manage to subdue that quality through sheer amount. One man was beggared and dragged away after he bet what he should not have.

Von Blodam saved his taunts for when my lord was about to make decisions, and while my lord's face remained impassive, I could read the emotions there, the confusion and fury. Von Blodam wanted him to attack, I thought, wanted to taunt him into action so he'd have an excuse.

With that realization, I tried to will my lord to come away, to keep calm, tried to put my own thoughts in his head, though there wasn't a chance of that, as though through sheer force of will I could somehow make him do what he should and back away.

Cold sliced through my heart as von Blodam turned ice blue eyes towards me, studying me like a half-dissected specimen. "Your servant came with you from England, did he not?" he asked my Lord.

My Lord's back could have been a steel rod, but his voice was leisurely. "Smith of Smithfield. Their family has been serving mine for generations now, haven't they, Smith?"

"Yes, my lord." My voice creaked from disuse. He gave me a dismissive nod before turning back to the table and pushing the conversation down a different alley. "I understand you've got one of the new Bentleys, von Blodam. How does it run?"

But von Blodam was not done with me. He beckoned, and I went to him, not looking at my lord.

"Good English gnomish stock," he mused, reaching out to trace a finger along my cheekbone. "Tell me, Smith, is there anything that

would shake your faith in your master?"

"No, sir," I said. What else could I? The fingernail on my skin was dagger sharp; it sliced the flesh and I felt blood spring to it as he withdrew his hand.

"No? Nothing? But what of English honor, Mr. Smith? What if you discovered your lord had been trying to cheat at cards?"

The air pushed in on me and his eyes were like stars. I focused on my breathing.

"My lord would not do such a thing, sir," I said, forcing the words out.

"Not for money or … love?" he pressed.

"Never, sir."

He chuckled, slouching back in his chair. "Very well. Let us resume our game." The vampire beside him began to deal as I retreated.

The evening wore on. Fortunes were squandered and re-won, and then squandered again. The cigar smoke haze thickened to the point of oppression, and the air grew stuffy except when someone entered or exited the car, bringing in a night breeze that cut through the heat like a saber stroke.

I tried to keep any thoughts from betraying us, but I could not help wonder. The vampire knew my lord was cheating, he was threatening to say it openly, and there was only one end to it if he did make that accusation: they would kill my lord then and there.

But my lord seemed oblivious to his impending fate. He sat there playing and chattering away, an endless stream of blather that was his damned-silly-English-peer act, playing to the crowd with a touch of whimsy now and then. But underneath it all, he and I and the vampires knew, he was a werewolf, and while they had the numbers, he could at least account for some.

Lost in these thoughts, I swam back as the Renfrew beside me stepped forward to provide and light a cigarette, then retreated into his

former position. My lord was talking about cars.

"Rover claims their new model goes faster than Le Train Bleu," von Blodam said.

"That's nothing special," my lord asserted. "I could leave with the train from here and my Delahaye could get me to my club in London before the train hits Calais."

Von Blodam raised an incredulous eyebrow. "A bold claim."

"It's good English technology," my lord said, and the edge to his voice was the same as though he'd bared his teeth, by the way the tension jumped in the room. Two Renfrews sidled closer.

But von Blodam laughed. "Then perhaps we should bet on it. You will race Le Train Bleu, and if you win, I will give you the prize of your choice."

"And if that prize was to answer a question truthfully?" My lord's eyes burned but could not melt the room's ice.

Von Blodam smiled, and I could feel disaster looming like an iceberg. "Very well. Three questions even, answered with absolute truth, on my honor. What would you put up against something like that, my Lord?"

"Name it," said my Lord softly. "For it's clear that you are angling at something."

The toothy smile broadened. "Very well. A reward of my choice, if the train reaches Calais before you are at your club."

"A reward of your choice," my lord said.

The vampire's eyes lingered on me.

———

Outside, I piled him into the cab and started speaking even as the door swung close.

"What were you thinking?" I demanded. "They won't let you win."

"They don't know anything about cars," he said contemptuously.

"They make their Renfrews drive them about. They won't be able to catch more than the dust we leave in our trail. And I've driven that route two, three dozen times now, half of that in the Delahaye."

He was flush with alcohol and triumph. He was young and rich and callous. How was he different, battening on the labor of honest workers, than any of the vampires?

And how could I possibly change his mind on this? No.

No, I would let him go to his fate. And, as was my hereditary place, I would accompany him.

I could do no less than that.

At 5:45 p.m., we heard the whistle of Le Train Bleu, departing. My lord set down his drink with a leisurely smile, saluted the watching well and ill wishers, and sauntered over to the waiting car, gleaming in the late afternoon sunshine's warmth.

He straightened his jacket and wound a white silk driving scarf around his neck. I could have killed him. We were losing precious time.

But as soon as we were out of eyeshot of the crowd, his entire demeanor changed. "Here we go, old fellow," he said. "Hang on."

The French countryside is beautiful, they say. I caught little of it in the mad rush to Muchy Breton, where we had to search for the pharmacy in order to secure petrol. It took some amount of explaining to the clerk, who was the pharmacist's assistant, and bemused at the idea that our car would require anything at hand in his storeroom. At last, he fetched the pharmacist, who turned out to be an automobile enthusiast, with a shed full of petrol, old tires, and a blacksmith shop's worth of tools.

When I emerged, I found my lord on his knees beside the rear wheel, cursing.

"Someone's slashed the tire," he said. "Dammit all. I turned my back to go take care of a moment of natural business. Low, to stoop to that sort of behavior while a man's relieving himself."

I fumbled with the trunk and took out the spare. "And this," I said. A penknife pierced the thick rubber.

But we were in luck. I turned to the sleepy pharmacist.

The next obstacle presented itself a few miles further on. Fog covered the road, and the car swam in and out of it, a submerged salmon leaping through foamy water, curls and tendrils swirling in its wake. My lord drove slower, but barely, and more than once we swerved to avoid an incautious cow or deer. I tried not to think of how many things stood too low to be spotted through the fog.

We ascended to a hilltop and saw a basin of fog in front of us, an immense white bowl. I started to say something about the odd flapping noise that was just starting to creep up on my consciousness but before I could begin, my lord shoved me sideways, then rolled in the opposite direction himself. A massive claw flashed in the space between us and rasped against the metal before the dragon swooped back upward.

"Hold tight!" We leaped down the hill and into the fog.

My lord steered with face tense, watching the road flash by mere feet from our front wheels, not slowing. Overhead we heard the flapping of the wings.

A train hooted off to the right, somewhat ahead.

"What are you thinking, sir?" I asked. "That's not the Blue Train. It's the train to the western coast."

"I know," he said. "But the crossing is up ahead, I can hear it."

"But not see it." Fog thickened and lessened around us; sometimes I could see his resolute face, other times he was lost to me. Overhead those wings flapped, and sometimes fire coiled, once a great wash of it directly overhead accompanied by a foul, sulfurous stench. My cap had blown off my head many miles ago, and I felt the hairs atop my

head singe and vanish.

"Hold tight!" my lord yelled over the roaring of the wind and if he added anything to that, it was lost in the howl of the train and the sudden flap of wings and then somehow we were soaring through space just ahead of the train, so close I could count every bar in the cowcatcher in front of it and there was a vast scream and crash as the dragon and the train collided, and then a whoosh of flame, exploding outside, that cleared the world of mist and revealed chaos.

The train, one of the great black trains, lay folded and crumpled, intermingled with the thrashing of the dragon corpse, which reminded me horribly of a chicken I had seen once with its head removed, still dashing itself against a wall in search of the escape that it was far past. The train had been pulling three vast tanks; two had broken, and black liquid was spilling out, pooling.

Or was it black? The moonlight gleamed on it as black birds swooped down, a cloud of them, the ones that had been following us, transforming into humanoid forms, to kneel beside that vast pool. We both stood, speechless, at the spectacle of the vampires lapping up the encarmined landscape, the moon glowing emptily behind their eyes.

All those trains had a hidden purpose. Carrying tanks of blood, harvested from God knew where. Not just gallons of it—an immeasurable amount.

The parasitical rich, embodied, literally drinking the blood of the poor.

"Go!" my lord said urgently, pulling me towards the car.

Reunited with the Delahaye, we hurtled through the night. My mind raced. Supplies—the trains would allow the vampires to take the world. A group of them could overwhelm a city, and the trains would let them travel any distance to do so. Despair held my heart so tight I could hardly breathe.

We made it to Calais, scrambled aboard the ferry in the nick of

time. My lord did not speak all the way as we moved over the sea, and the moon made nonsensical images with the froth atop each wave. I stared into the water as he paced back and forth, chainsmoking and unable to rest.

He was thinking of the lost girl, a face he'd only seen once or twice. He wasn't thinking of anything or anyone else.

If we did not reach the club in time, the vampire would claim his prize. Surely my Lord understood von Blodam's intent. He'd wagered my life without thinking about it, considering it just another commodity to be spent. A bag of flesh containing the good gnomish blood that had whetted von Blodam's appetite.

Wasn't he as bad as the vampires? At least they were honest as to how they saw us all.

—————

How did von Blodam get there before us? Some trickery, or perhaps a direct train. But he did, even as we pulled up with five minutes to spare.

There was irritation in his gaze as he said, "It seems you have won, Lord von Vulff. I regret to say the French authorites intend to fine you for racing on public roads."

Amusement in his gaze, but something else … anticipation, perhaps.

"Indeed," my lord said.

"Then claim your reward." Von Blodam's teeth glinted in the moonlight.

"What happened to Marguerite?" My lord's voice was hoarse as though he had run every step of the way here.

He stood there, the embodiment of the system I'd served all my life. How could I still care for him? But I did. I'd known him all my life, how could I not? And did it matter, that he'd risked my life, when he'd

thought there was no question but that he would win? I wanted him to be happy, despite it all. And I thought to myself, oh maybe, maybe.

"I believe you might have seen her along the way," von Blodam drawled. "Some part of her."

My lord stared at him, the beard on his cheek ragged and unkempt, his clothing in shambles from the trip's wind, as though willing him to say more. He was the abstract of what I hated and I could not hold it against him, standing there against its physical embodiment.

But any further answer the vampire gave was not in words: he simply licked his lips and smiled as the street traffic came and went around us and the webs of blood and iron spread and we stood in the future ruins of our world.

Afternotes

This story was inspired by a call for dieselpunk. I didn't end up writing a story for the anthology, but in the course of researching, I ran into the true story of Le Train Bleu and an actual famous race, which I decided to snag for my story.

Translating such things is always a perilous task—there are so many places to step wrong in history, but you also run into interesting bits that add to the story. Pharmacists were in fact the purveyors of motor fuel in early automotive days. The trains full of blood being shipped to vampires, however, is entirely my invention and there are, to the best of my knowledge, no dragons in France.

The hero, my werewolf lord, owes a certain amount to Dorothy Sayer's excellent peer/detective, Lord Peter Wimsey. I love the notion of a foppish peer who is actually hard as nails and quite clever underneath it all, and "Karaluvian Fale", appearing elsewhere in this collection, is another such story.

I have a strong suspicion that the narrator, my Marxist gnome manservant, will be playing a part in the novel featuring Desiree referenced in the "Clockwork Fairies" note.

So Glad We Had This Time Together

JB: I'm submitting my resignation, effective immediately.

I CAN HEAR THE DISTANT HUM OF the building's heart, the slow steps of a janitor cleaning its chambers with wafts of pine and ammonia, strong and harsh. I'll track him down and kill him when I finish. Leave a message scrawled in scarlet under one of the pastel landscapes adorning the belly of a corridor.

Years ago, when I was an intern, I loved coming into the office late at night. After I was done answering e-mail or polishing a PowerPoint presentation, I'd roll a chair up to the window and lean my forehead against the glass, relishing the coolness. Looking out across the avenues of streetlights, I'd wonder who else was awake and watching the night. I'd look at my reflection, backlit by neon, and see a skinny white woman, dressed for success in navy blue with a touch of red, and starting to climb the career ladder of professional television. Then I'd go drink a triple latte before heading to the gym.

I'm writing this in my office at 3 a.m. It's a rainy autumn night, warm and wet, and sideways slashes of raindrops mark the window, but I don't try to see my reflection in it. I just keep typing.

It's been a pleasure working with you, and I thank you for the advice and assistance you've given me.

From my earliest days, a career in television was all I ever wanted. Two working parents left me to be raised by the airwaves, from the moment I got home from school to when I unrolled the plastic wrap from my microwaved dinner with a gust of steam. Letterman's cadences swayed me to sleep every night. The TV was family. There was a local variety show host I loved; he'd smile at the camera and thank me, the viewer, for inviting him into my fine home, and then he'd introduce the friends that had come with him, the new friends I'd meet that night.

There has to be a better place to start. Perhaps with gratitude.

Thank you for selecting me to act as a co-producer of Unreality TV. I know we created quality television there, of which we can all be proud.

When Kurt first proposed the idea, I jumped in full of smiles, because I didn't think he could pull it off. If he crashed and burned, it meant one less at the conference table for a while and whoever came to replace him would be at an automatic disadvantage. Maybe even a possible ally.

JB picked me to assist Kurt, so I shrugged and figured I'd been bitten on the ass by my own scheming. Karma does that sometimes. Now the only chance I would have would be to give Kurt's series wings and make it fly.

I didn't think about the most important aspect of his proposal. None of us did. I don't know if we could have, if our minds were even

capable of it, or if they'd already put some sort of block on that avenue of thought.

"Consider the possibilities," he said, throwing up a flurry of animated rain that faded to reveal his next slide. "Reality television taken to the next level: Unreality TV."

We waited.

He obliged with another burst of droplets and a slide that read "Unexploited Creatures of the Fantastic." Underneath, smudgy photographs were heavily pixilated and hard to make out.

"A vampire, a werewolf, and a demon," he said. "I've got a lead out on a good psychic. A couple of regular humans for contrast. And their location? One of the most unreal places on the planet."

His next slide appeared: a red-roofed, several-storied mansion, surrounded by flowers and froths of blooming hedges.

"The Winchester Mystery House," Kurt said, licking his lips with a surprisingly delicate pink tongue. "San Jose, California. A 160-room building, planned and commissioned by Winchester's widow Sarah, on the advice of her spiritualist. She told Sarah that the ghosts of those killed by the Winchester rifle could only be held at bay by the sound of hammers. Accordingly, builders worked on the house around the clock for the next 38 years. There's stairs leading nowhere, a whispering chamber, doors opening onto other doors, an entire section blocked off by earthquake and not seen in years … in this setting, our participants will live and compete. Compete for one million dollars—and a chance to become part of human society."

⌒····⊸◌

We all know the Hidden World exists, full of ghosts and vampires and other supernatural creatures. Nonetheless, the only ones documenting them are the scientists and the scholars. Aside from a few

public channel documentaries on Bigfoot and the weekly haunted castle showing on Fox, no one airs anything about humanity's dirty little secret, that We Are Not Alone.

Despite this silence, we all know that in every major and minor city, at least one district is theirs, full of demon bars and stores with merchandise to suit their specialized needs. Every spring, a group of college kids goes slumming on a dare and ends up in an alleyway, dead. But we don't document that either—there are no shows shrilling about the Bloodsucker Menace or selling kits to save you if you're bitten by a werewolf. Doesn't that seem strange? Outside the norm? It's like we all have blind spots in our heads where They are concerned.

"One of Tim Burton's apprentices will be decorating the sets. We have free license from the Winchester people to do whatever we like as long as we restore things to their original condition when we're done. Think "Fear Factor" with more blood. Think "Survivor" with life or death. Think "Punked" with ghosts."

Everyone was watching JB's face rather than paying attention to the words spilling like water from Kurt's lips. JB nodded and smiled, and the harvest of approvals swelled before anyone got down to nitty-gritty details.

"Angela, I'm tapping you to help Kurt out with this one," JB said. His face was flushed with the sunlight pouring into the conference room, but the depths of his eyes were air-conditioned.

I could have screamed in frustration, but I kept on smiling. Kurt let his face falter for a moment, just to make sure I knew how unwanted I was, but he paid the cost—JB's eyes slid over and noted the twinge of expression. I kept smiling at Kurt. We beamed at each other like competing spotlights over the wooden expanse of the conference table.

NOR THERE

From the first, I knew we had a phenomenon on our hands …

When we started, I thought Kurt was bringing in ringers. Then I thought they were so convincing because they thought they were for real. Then I realized that they were. They were for real.

Where did Kurt get them? I don't know. He wouldn't tell me who his contacts were, no matter how much alcohol or cleavage I plied him with. Their hooks must have been into him deep.

… mainly because of the outstanding people on the show.

The first day, a gray little man stood outside the door.

"What do you want?" I asked. I thought he might be part of the crew. Steel hair combed over a flat white scalp. Wire-rimmed spectacles. A smooth jaw line, bare of stubble.

"Invite me in," he said. I didn't understand until Kurt rushed up.

"Master, please, please enter," he said with a breathless exhalation. Aside to me he said, "Vampires can't come in unless they're invited."

"That's one of them?" I asked.

"Mr. Smith is our vampire, yes."

"Looking like that?"

We stared at Mr. Smith, who returned our gaze with placid steadiness, the round circles of his glasses gleaming in the fluorescent light.

"I would suggest," I said, remembering that we were partners on the project, "that you have Wardrobe glitz him up. Give him some dark flash and sparkle. Glamour."

Kurt looked at Smith with an anxious glance, but the man let himself be guided along. Wardrobe coughed up a glossy black cape and slicked back his hair. Somehow they gave his skin a ghastly undertone that could be conveyed by the cameras. But he remained, at the heart of it all, a gray little man.

The werewolf also disappointed me. He was a fat, hairy individual, who came with a pet hedgehog in a box under one hirsute arm. Make-up trimmed him down to lend a subtle touch of menace to his swarthy face.

But the demon-possessed was satisfactory. His features were riddled with enough piercings to defeat airport security, and tattoos covered his arms with sleeves of writhing dragons. We used the design for our advertising, scaled serpents winding in and out of the logo, made from the rusted iron of a garden gate: "Unreality TV".

Which left our humans. The medium was a forty-something with merlot hair and silver jewelry jingling along her hands and arms. Then we had one jiggle-bunny who'd driven the ratings up in Playboy's "BunnyCam"; a college student who'd won our "Live Unreal" contest; and a handsome, hunky, heroic type whose closeted sexuality might make for a startling revelation somewhere along the way.

We started filming in May. Burton and his crew did us proud; the interior was half Beetlejuice, half Addams Family. The choice of the Winchester House was smart. Its parquet floors, gold and silver chandeliers, Tiffany glass everywhere all lent to the effect. During those early days, we used to play Count the Fireplaces. There were supposedly 47, but we never could make the count come out right. It changed every day.

There were, as there always are, technical difficulties. Sarah Winchester had been 4'10"; we found it hard to set up equipment in the places scaled for those proportions. And some rooms seemed to affect the cameras; they'd stop working after a few minutes or, worse, distort what was being filmed. One long conversation between the medium and the werewolf was fine except for the sound of a baby wailing that inexplicably crept onto the soundtrack.

I had bad dreams every night, in my bed at the Courtyard Marriot ten minutes away.

But it was great TV, I admit. Nielsen ratings like you wouldn't believe.

NOR THERE

I know you were pleased and surprised, as we all were, at the ratings.

Pleased and surprised and ... puzzled, I think. JB said he hadn't seen anything like them in four decades of television. He kept asking me what accounted for it. I didn't have any clue, but I spun lame possibilities into gold and made them plausible.

In the first episode, we introduced our cast. The medium, Tina, wouldn't talk to Tommy, the demon-possessed teen. We had a hard time persuading her to sit in the same room with him. For a while we played around and showed her reaction shots whenever he spoke. A camera zoomed on her forearm, showing the goose bumps. Great TV. Spectacular TV.

Tommy was spooky, I admit. No one liked to be alone in a room with him, ever. You'd see him looking at you sideways in a way that might have been thinking about the center of the universe or else simply how your liver would taste, fresh and warm from your body.

Everyone loved the werewolf. Fan sites went up across the Internet. I'd thought him a fake until I saw his reaction to a silver bracelet the medium was wearing, and the blisters puddled across his skin. He inspired one of the humorous episodes, where we let loose with the comic relief and fed the ravenous cast nothing but stew, mashed potatoes, and pudding, all with no utensils.

When the college girl got turned in the sixth episode, I wanted to pull the show. But Kurt insisted on airing it, and JB backed him up. The vampire appearing in the doorway, her blank and glassy-eyed stare as she came to him, as she tilted her neck for him ... must-see TV.

That was when my nightmares started, after I'd seen the shot of him raising his face to the camera, his eyes as red as the blood dripping from his mouth. It beat out Janet Jackson's nipple as the most Tivoed moment in history.

126

And the following episode, when she rose and he fed her the housekeeper? Some southern states refused to show it; bootleg copies sold like counterfeit crack on eBay.

By the end of it all, I was proud of our creation. I'd forgotten, somehow, that it wasn't my idea, and that I didn't want to be working on it. There were too many juicy, almost too hot to air, moments. Tommy, making the walls weep serpents. The medium and the werewolf sneaking off to bang. The first full moon. Bringing in the exorcist. The séance where tiny Sarah Winchester appeared and screamed at us to get out, to get out of her house.

We'd filmed and wrapped it all, ready for release in September. Only two casualties, both caught on film, and the Survivor Act meant we were free and clear on all legalities there. It was all over except for the parties. I still didn't like the vampire, but he was standing by me when we watched the credits roll by in a darkened room. In the back a group of stagehands and techies cheered, and someone staggered by in a waft of vodka and lime.

The light from the screen fell across the vampire, the grave-toned cosmetics removed and the skin restored to its dull and unremarkable hue. His dark gray suit was an excellent, expensive cut.

"A good piece of work." I said, making conversation. "I wonder what the public will think."

"I do too," he said. He smiled. The first expression I'd seen him display. "So kind for the viewers to invite us into their homes."

When I looked at his face, I understood the smile.

They have to be invited in. Have to be welcomed. Through the mechanism of your family and mine, the television.

If I'd kept my deadpan, he wouldn't have known that I understood his little joke. But something in my eyes tipped him off.

I wish I'd gotten my own turning on tape.

Nor There

We're forming our own network, JB. Taking the name Unreality TV. Kurt says he retained the rights to the name but you'll want to check that. I've appended a list of the people you'll need to replace. Not everyone watched our initial show, but we have strong faith that our network will have something for everyone, eventually.

I know what we've done, JB, even if you don't. You and Kurt and I, we opened the door to the Hidden World. Not realizing that they might object or, worse, that they might come through it. Not realizing that maybe there was a reason why so many people had refrained from filming it in the past.

Ten years from now, they'll be featuring the last humans on a show. Visions of what the world was like before the Hidden and the Seen merged. That's what Smith told me, at any rate.

I look forward to hearing your reaction to our programming, JB. Kurt sends his regards, but is currently indisposed. It takes three days for a vampire to turn, so he'll be up and raring to go on Monday. We'll be by with our proposal then.

Until then, I hope you'll be watching.

Afternotes

I will confess that I have a fondness for reality shows, particularly the really outrageous ones, and this was greatly inspired by several seasons of Big Brother. *I workshopped it my final week at Clarion West for Michael Swanwick, who cheerfully tore it to bits in workshop and helped make it much better in the process.*

"So glad we had this time together" is the song Carol Burnett used to sing at the end of her show, which was a staple of my childhood. Mr. Smith might or might not have a slight resemblance to Tim Conway in my head.

Snakes on a Train

ELSPETH FOLDED HER HANDS IN HER LAP, trying to keep her brows from knitting. She hated trains.

They were dirty, with bits of smut and coal blown back from the massive brass and aluminum steam engine pulling them along, and engrimed by successions of previous passengers.

They were noisy, from the engine's howl to the screech of the never-sufficiently-greased axles as they rocketed along the steel rails with their steady pocketa-pocketa-pocketa chug seeping up through the swaying floor.

And they were oppressively full of people, all thinking things, all pressing down on her Sensitive's mind, making her shrink down into the hard wooden seat as though the haze of thoughts hung like coal-smoke in the air and if she sank low enough, she'd avoid it.

She glanced over at her fellow Pinkerton agent, who returned her look with his own slightly quizzical if impersonal gaze. All of the curiosity of their fellow passengers was directed at him, perhaps the first mechanical being they'd ever seen, with silver and brass skin and curly hair, eyebrows, and mustache of gilded wire.

"They shouldn't be keeping us back here," she said for the third

time in as many minutes. "If we're his assigned bodyguards, they should let us up to inspect his compartment."

"The porter said he'd tell them we were here," Artemus said in precisely the same tone he'd used the first two times he'd said these words.

Elspeth sighed. Even as she did so, the porter entered the car and signaled to them.

"You go up two cars," he said, and pointed.

They made their way through the creak and sway of a car identical to theirs, then the narrower corridors of a sleeper car. Artemus knocked on a doorway and they poked their heads into a compartment where their package stood with his daughter.

That package, one Joshua McCormick, was a short, brawny little man who held himself with a terrier's alertness. His hair had retreated from the majority of his freckled brown scalp, but still tufted over his ears, which supported the frames of two brass-rimmed spectacles, the left one wider rimmed and more elaborate than the right. His daughter Belinda was unpacking McCormick's trunk with an assistant's familiarity. As Elspeth watched, she unfolded a trunk and set it against the wall so the myriad of tiny drawers and bottles it held were accessible, held in with straps against the train's constant jostle.

Artemus said, "Sir, do you intend to undertake experiments here on the train?"

Professor McCormick shook his head, brows knitting. He folded his arms and glared over at his daughter. "Belinda. It's true. I won't be doing much on the train. If you unpack all of that, it'll just be in our way."

The daughter's stiff shoulders told Elspeth of the unspoken resentment. But she relaxed as the lack of emotions battering against her mind confirmed what they'd been told was a the case: the girl was a psychic null, whose thoughts could not be sensed and who would be able to withstand most mental powers.

It was one of the things she valued about Artemus—the absence of thoughts twitching her one way or another. She was looking forward to spending time with Belinda McCormick, if not her father's roil of pride and greed and anger.

The Professor wheeled to address Artemus just as roughly. "I've told your superiors that your presence is unnecessary."

Another thing Elspeth appreciated about Artemus was his ability to keep his voice modulated where Elspeth knew irritation would have wasp-whined her own tone. "I'm sure that's true, sir. But there are definite and established dangers and not every train headed from Baltimore to Seattle has made it to its destination. Your expertise is important to the War Effort, and so we've been hired to make sure you get there as quickly and smoothly as you can. If you relax and let us proceed in our efforts, you'll find the journey goes quickly and with a minimum of fuss."

The Professor's attention swiveled ponderously between the two of them.

"What sort of dangers have presented themselves?" he demanded, brows beetling in suspicion. "Not the made-up panics from the papers, mind you. The real dangers."

"There have been instances of werewolves, which were responsible for the recent derailment of a train. And lizard-wizards, more than one."

"Snakes?"

"That is the name some call them by, yes." Artemus's voice remained glassy smooth. "We have twelve hours before we reach Kansas City. I'd suggest you get settled and then go to sleep as early as possible. I'm told many people find the rattle of the wheels soporific."

McCormick looked offended by the reminder of Artemus's mechanical state. "And what are you? Is someone operating you remotely?"

"I'm automatous. This is my partner, Elspeth Sorehs."

"A Hasidic." The Professor's eyes assessed Elspeth frankly, and his thoughts pawed at her. She forced down her reaction. He couldn't know that what he was thinking was offensive. That was what almost all men did, thought in terms of what they would have been able to see if the fabric and stays were stripped away, how cupable her breasts, how thickly fleeced her thighs, this one no less than any other. She looked down at the floor.

"You will be in the cubby across the way?" the Professor addressed her directly, staring into her face.

"I will," she said. "Mr. West …" She stressed the honorific and surname in a way that ratcheted the older man's brows further upward. "Mr. West will be watching the corridor outside your cubby. He is unsleeping." It would be a rare creature indeed that made its way past Artemus.

"The train will serve a late dinner in forty-five minutes," the Professor said. "You will join us." He turned and went back into the room where his daughter stood.

Elspeth rolled her eyes at Artemus. She stuck her head in their own compartment, eying the tiny bunks.

"Well, it's snug," she said. She sniffed at herself, ruefully noticing the sour tang to the fabric. That was the worst part of traveling, the lack of bathing facilities.

"There'll be a bathhouse in Kansas City, and a four-hour wait there, plenty of time," Artemus said. "No need to act as though we were venturing into the heart of the wilderness." His eyes glittered phlogiston-blue in what she'd learned to call his pranksome mood. "I'll bet you that he says three things to offend you before the soup arrives. What do you think, my dear Hasidic?"

She sighed. "All in a day's work," she retorted. She retreated into the compartment. At least there was time to change before dinner.

She wore sea-green to the meal, a silk-cotton blend that maintained

its shape better than most garments when traveling. When she saw Belinda McCormick's pale brown silk taffeta, trimmed with Bruges, she wished she hadn't bothered, particularly when the professor's eyes flicked over her, assessing the color against the dark hue to her skin, pronounced after a month in Baltimore's sun.

Swarthy little girl, but sometimes those burn the hottest, he thought with a mental picture that kindled fire in her cheeks.

The table's center held a wire and ivory basket for a spray of fresh flowers and the condiments: cut glass containers of red and yellow and green sauce, tiny shakers of salt and pepper. She fixed her eyes on that. To her right, Belinda was a welcoming, quiet void. She found herself leaning and glanced over to find the girl looking at her with steady, inquisitive ... invitation or naïveté? So hard to know, sometimes.

The other passengers spoke and chattered as they ate turtle consommé, a special Coast-to-Coast salad, and chicken-fried steak. Glasses of sherry were served round, though no one at their table took any. The Professor spoke primarily to his daughter, checking to make sure she knew the details of his trip, and what days and when he would be where. Artemus maintained his usual polite detachment.

Elpseth did the same. When a fat man lurched up from his table, at first she didn't react, lulled by the train's motion into a half-doze that barely noticed the warmth of his anger. Artemus, though, stood with immediate grace, interposing himself between the newcomer and McCormick.

"Necromancer!" the fat man spat at the Professor, who looked up but continued to chew his steak, placid-jowled and incurious as a cow. "Our President is not content to have sent the dead into the field against their own brethren, but now you assist Abraham the Unholy by raising the dead to bind them into machines." He pushed at Artemus, who budged not an inch. "Whose soul is bound into you, demon-machine?"

"No one's but my own, I assure you," Artemus replied.

Someone at one of the watching tables laughed and the angry man blushed, taking a step back. The steward appeared, taking his elbow to guide him out. The situation stopped ticking with menace as Artemus returned to his seat. The windows rattled in their frames, coffee cups clinked in after-dinner saucers, and they sped on along the prairie.

Elspeth removed herself at one point, vanishing to the johnny-car and returning with cheeks flushed.

Artemus leaned over as she sipped coffee to murmur, "What happened?"

She leaned back into her chair, trying to look official as she whispered into Artemus's aluminum-cast ear. "A woman wanted know what you were like in bed, offered me money for you."

"And?"

"And!? Should I pimp you out in order to make a little extra income along the way?"

He shrugged. "It's all data."

"You don't even know what to do, let alone have the equipment to do it!"

He quirked an eyebrow. "I am given from certain 'blue' materials that digital and lingual stimulation is sufficient. It's not as though the act would be about my own pleasure after all, other than the frisson of new experience. Still, I am told it is a valid way to persuade a witness or ally."

His tone remained impersonal but his eyes flickered an amused blue. She jerked away from him and turned her attention to Belinda.

"What do you hope to do in Seattle?" she asked.

The girl toyed with the food on her plate. Elspeth thought she'd eaten a few bites at most, perhaps even less. "I will continue to act as my father's assistant, of course," she said hesitantly.

"Of course you will," her father interrupted. His own plate shone;

he'd used a roll to scrub the last of the gravy from the cold white china. He stared at Elspeth.

She doesn't keep kosher, his undermind said. I wonder what else she is ... unconventional in.

After dinner, Elspeth lingered, sniffing hungrily at the draughts of cigar smoke that wafted her way.

"Think it's safe enough?" she overheard at her elbow. She craned her ears to listen.

"There was a werewolf attack last month, but since then they've put up silver," the other man said. The deck of cards riffled before he dealt them out. They whispered across the white linen tablecloth.

"And Snakes?"

"Snakes?" The other man spat out a laugh. Black stubble hazed his jaw. He caught Elspeth's eye and gave her a vulpine grin, sizing her up. Raising his voice, he said, "Snakes are what they use to scare passengers into behaving. Don't go anywhere by yourself, because you might get et. That's just a way to keep pretty ladies from getting lured into shadows for kisses from nice men."

Elspeth refrained from joining the conversation. As a Pinkerton agent, she'd met plenty of supernatural creatures. She knew there were a few werewolves, or rather shapechangers, that lived in the wilderness in small families. She was less worried about Snakes, even though the semi-mythical creatures were blamed for nearly every disaster that claimed human lives.

In either case, this wasn't like England, overridden with all manner of creature, including werewolves, fairies, and vampires.

The Professor sat puffing a cigar, working it with tight jaws. When it finally had burned to an inch's worth of stub, he caught Elspeth's eye

and nodded at her to follow him as he rose. His mind revealed nothing other than the last of the tobacco's perfume and a weary readiness for his bed.

She followed him through the several cars housing those unfortunate enough not to have the price of a sleeper, relegated to the hard wooden benches fastened to the walls. They smelled of sweat and cheese and garlic and stomach gas and she sensed herself perceived by minds sleep-clouded by motion and time spent staring forward waiting to arrive.

Outside the two compartments, the Professor paused.

Elspeth waited.

He looked everywhere but at her. "I want you to speak to my daughter."

"About?" His embarrassment burned in her stomach, incandescent as lava.

"She has always lived with me. Her mother died when she was three. Our domestic situation has made her isolated in a manner that has warped her."

"Such as?"

"She has become forward in unexpected ways," he said. His pink skin deepened in tone and he wiped at his brow with a crumpled silk handkerchief.

"The suffrage movement appeals to many young women who feel their own lives are circumscribed," Elspeth supplied. She'd seen this struggle before, including in her own family when she'd announced she planned to become a Pinkerton agent.

He shook his head. "There are many movements affecting the young nowadays. I was thinking more of the …" He hesitated, picking the words as carefully as making change out of a purse. "The movement that some people call Free Love."

Elspeth tried to school her face into a lack of expression, but a

brow crept upward despite herself.

"She wishes to practice Free Love?" she said, very carefully. Where was Artemus? But her partner had said he wished to check the rest of the train. She wondered if he was looking for the woman who had offered Elspeth money for a couple of hours with him.

The Professor's hand flapped in the air like a trapped bird searching for windows of escape. "Tell her … tell her that things are not as simple as she would like to think when it comes to defying societal mores. For women there are consequences and they come when least expected or desired." He sighed.

There was something in his mind around all this that made Elspeth uneasy, but she nodded. They exchanged slight bows and retired into their compartments.

Artemus was back within a half hour, ready to set up watch. Elspeth did not question him as to where he'd been. Her partner's inability to sleep was a definite plus. It made simple sense to always have him be the one watching in the small hours of the night, when his human counterpart might fall prey to drowsiness.

So many pluses to partnering with him. Before him, she'd been assigned to a former Army colonel who had never quite gotten over the shock of working with a woman. For Artemus that had never been an issue, and chivalry was impersonal with him, a matter of his metallic brain and body outshining any human's, gender notwithstanding.

They'd spent a week last spring in the Pinkerton Academy and she'd had a chance to speak with other female agents, despite how few and far between they were. Chloe Louisiana was a mulatto and former slave who always partnered with another woman, a half-Shawnee who'd been raised in England and whose name was Persephone Godschild. They were all united in their hate of the only other female agent present, a southern sharpshooter, Belle Cheatham, whose disdain they had all dealt with in the past.

"You're lucky to have Artemus as your partner," Chloe had said. She glanced over at Persephone, who'd nodded. The three of them had been sitting in a classroom, comparing notes and waiting for an instructor in ballistics to arrive.

Elspeth hadn't understood. Back then she'd seen it as punishment, assigning the odd psychic to the only thing capable of dealing with her. She went back and forth on whether the assignment was punishment or praise. It felt like either with equal frequency.

———••••—••©

She lay in bed. A thought occurred to her and she pulled herself out of the narrow bunk to press her face up to the cold glass of the tiny window. Outside the vast plains were silvered with moonlight and the train's long shadow raced beside them. Faint clouds seined the starry sky and somewhere a wolf howled.

Artemus shifted in the hallway. He'd heard her, she suspected, and wanted her to know her he was there if needed, without saying it outright.

Another one of the little gestures that seemed so unmechanical.

She returned to bed and lay there. The train said chuggadiggity-chuggadiggity-chuggadiggity and she dropped into sleep counting the syllables of that complex beat.

Someone scratching on her door woke her. She gathered her wrapper around her nightgown and slid the door open.

Belinda, in her own wrapper, embroidered with pale blue flowers and uncoiling ferns. No Artemus in the corridor, but the light in the other room suggested he was there with the Professor.

"Do you smoke?" Belinda said in a low whisper. Her eyes sparked as Elspeth nodded, and she held up two cigarettes in a conspiratorial way. "They're talking. We'll go indulge."

Outside, they set the cigarettes alight with phosphorus matches in the doorway's shelter before moving to stand on the swaying platform as the dark world hurtled past.

Belinda exhaled. The smell of the tobacco flickered in Elspeth's nostrils. "You know what I want in Seattle?" she said.

Elspeth shook her head. It was so refreshing not to be able to pluck the answer out of the other's head, mystifying and giddying all at once, trying to figure out answers from clues as fragile and fleeting as cigarette smoke.

"I want to have a friend. Maybe several," Belinda said. She reached out with her free hand and scraped the back of her index finger along the soft flesh of Elspeth's inner arm.

Elspeth's heart jumped in her throat. In her mind, the Professor's voice said: ... *the movement that some call Free Love.* She didn't react to the touch and after a long moment, Belinda leaned back against the railing and took another puff from her cigarette.

Elspeth had opened her mouth to reply when something lunged out of the night, a snarl of claw and tooth and gray fur striking from the ground to land between them.

Belinda recoiled, colliding with the glass of the door even as Espeth's foot snapped out to catch the beast in the throat. She thanked her Pinkerton training, all the work she'd had to do to prove herself.

With a gabbled whine, the creature fell away. Elspeth grabbed Belinda and pulled her inside the car.

In its confines, the younger woman swayed, hand at her throat, eyes wide and fixed on Elspeth as her knees buckled.

Elspeth stooped to the floor as well, feeling the rocketing rails underneath through her shinbones, grappling Belinda to her.

Belinda's lips tasted of tobacco. Her heart hammered against Elspeth as Elspeth drew her into the compartment and the narrow, moon-washed bed.

⸻

She woke tangled in Belinda's arms to the sound of knocking on the door. Artemus' characteristic shave-and-a-haircut-two-bits.

"What is it?" she called.

"The Professor."

She gestured quiet at the wide-eyed Belinda as she pulled on her nightgown. "What about him?" she called through the doorway.

"His doorway is locked but he's not answering."

⸻

Artemus looked to her before fingering the lock. He was not supposed to pick mechanisms unless there was a human present.

She hoped that Belinda would have the sense to wait until they had entered the other cabin before making her way out of Elspeth's compartment.

The lock clicked open and Artemus's hand fell away. He flipped the handle open and swung it inward cautiously, as though afraid of waking the Professor.

Who was unwakeable, lying as he did in a pool of crimson and surprise, face agape.

As they stood there in the doorway, Belinda appeared behind them and gasped. "Papa!"

"I must ask you to stand back, Miss McCormick," Artemus said. "Elspeth, would you take her to a quiet place close by?"

"Like my cabin?" Elspeth said.

"That would do, certainly."

Elspeth escorted the wide-eyed, shocked Belinda back into the cabin and petted and soothed her for a few moments before returning to Artemus' side in the other compartment.

He stood frowning in the middle of the compartment. "I don't see it."

"See what?"

"The professor was carrying the formula for his work to the War Ministry."

She looked around the tiny space. "It's not here?"

"He has his case there, and another trunk full of presents. I believe for his host's children."

"What makes you think that?"

"I took the liberty of opening them. One is a puzzle, another a set of fables, and the third a board game, 'Snakes on a Train.'"

"So the killer must have taken the formula."

"Belinda is the most likely suspect."

Elspeth hoped Belinda would remember the brief story Elspeth had coached her with an order to cover their liaison. "She went for coffee to the dining car but found it closed. He was alive when she left."

Artemus's expression ground into disapproval. He didn't like activating that portion of his face's mechanism, she knew, preferring to keep it a bland and unthreatening smile.

"I don't think it was her," she said firmly, and left it at that, hurrying on to say, "I think it'll be someone who gets off at the next stop."

"When is that?"

"For a major stop, one that is more than fuel? A few hours."

———•••——•◗

Summoned, two wide-eyed porters helped drag the body back several cars, wrapped in a blanket and supported as though it were an under-the-weather passenger, back to the refrigerator car.

After that, the Pinkerton agents canvassed the train to find the individuals planning on getting out at Kansas City. A young married

couple, the Emersons, planning on joining Mrs. Emerson's brother's homestead nearby; a school-teacher headed into the Territory; two traveling sales-men, one in patent sun hats and soaps, and the other in tin-ware; two former soldiers headed to get jobs as cattle drovers; and a veterinarian who had just purchased a practice in Kansas City in the mail.

Neither Artemus nor Elspeth could extract any reason why any of these individuals would have reason to kill the Professor.

Artemus' expression was still disapproving. "The daughter ..."

"It's not her," Elspeth said. "I think it's a wolf. We saw one when we were out there. One could jump onto a platform and come along a corridor."

"And have hands to open the door?"

"Were-wolves," she pointed out. "Shape-changers. Skilled ones can manage halfway forms."

"If there were such a creature then it is long gone," Artemus said.

"Let's question everyone," Elspeth said. "The man who called him a necromancer, for example."

That man turned out to be a Portland bound minister, Alexander Knolle. Roused from his own sleeping car and questioned as to how he knew what McCormick had been doing, he pointed out that it had not been much of a secret, since McCormick had spoken in several lyceums in the Baltimore and DC area in the week previous to boarding the train.

"He bragged on it," the fat man said sweating but adamant, gaze trembling between the two. "On how his formula help suit machinery and morbid flesh to each other. Morbid flesh, that's what he called it. Dead things. I fought in the war last year. I know what comes of that." He shuddered and retched.

―•••―•◐

The rest of the night, Artemus spent on the platform watching for wolves.

Around two in the morning, Elspeth went out with him. The stars stretched overhead, brilliant as diamonds, lights that seemed close enough to reach up and pluck one.

"Is Belinda settled?" Artemus said over the rush of the wind and the rattle of the train.

"For now," Elspeth said. She tilted her face away from him, knowing he'd be able to read any rush of heat to her cheeks. She said, over her shoulder, "When we were first assigned together, I didn't like it. Now I wouldn't have any other partner."

She wasn't sure whether or not he was aware of Belinda's scent clinging to her, of the phantom pressure of hands that clenched at her skin. Perhaps he'd think her blushes the result of her verbal confession. Either way, she wanted him to be reassured. "There's no one else I'd rather have." Silence stretched between them and she said, struck by it, "Can you say the same?"

"I am used to you," he said, but she thought some other emotion glinted far below the living light of his eyes.

Someone knocked on the partition. Belinda, pressed up against the glass.

"Someone's in with papa's things," she said. "I heard them knocking about."

They crowded in, Artemus first. The heavy musk of wolf musk hung in the air. Where they had searched through the Professor's things but kept them in order, someone else had exercised no such caution, but rather flung drawers open, tumbled cases on the floor, and dumped belongings out onto the floor. The puzzle pieces lay underfoot mixed with a scattering of tea bags and the delicate bones of some bird's wing, mingled with some reptile's coiled spine.

"Looking for something." Artemus picked up a copy of a book and

laid it on the bedspread.

"But what?" Elspeth said.

"The formula still."

"So it's whoever killed him but they still don't have the formula." Elspeth looked around the compartment. "Either because it's here hidden among his belongings, or because he's hidden it elsewhere on the train."

"Or because he never had it," Artemus pointed out.

Disappointment clenched at Elspeth's gut. "What makes you think that?"

"It seems as possible as anything else," Artemus said. He looked around at the mess. "Someone believes it's here, at any rate."

"If it's a werewolf, they'll surely try one last time before we hit the next town," Elspeth said. "How is he or she managing to keep up with the train?"

"They are supernatural creatures, endowed with uncanny amounts of speed and endurance," Artemus said. He didn't add that one of his appeals for the Pinkerton Agency was his ability to match those uncanny abilities.

They waited in the darkness. Artemus was braced in the cupboard space; Elspeth crouched near the door. Belinda was bundled in Elspeth's bed again with orders to bar the door and not come out for love or money. After those instructions had been given, the two Pinkertons had taken up position. They didn't speak.

The hours jolted by, the train slowing and speeding up. If she were the wolves, she'd wait for one of the curves where the train would be forced to deaccelerate, she thought. Even as it occurred to her, the axles squealed as they leaned left.

She tilted her head, listening, but also extending her other sense outward, searching for thoughts. There it was. *where? where?* was not the thought of any passenger but the frustration of someone looking for a specific thing, returning to search again. *river/camphor/dust* flared in her senses and said they were familiar, long familiar. She heard a sound she couldn't decipher, lost between the outer and the inner perceptions.

"They're trying to get into your room," Artemus said, moving to the door.

She followed after him in the darkness, wishing they'd told Belinda to wait elsewhere.

Sparks flared, a shot rang out.

Artemus shouted.

She struck a light in the silence to see him holding a lean and ragged wolf by the paw/wrist. Green eyes glinted, considering her. The toothy jaws opened and croaked out, "Hnake. Here. Kill Hnake."

She looked at Artemus, but his gaze confirmed her own senses. Sincerity.

They backed into the other tiny bedroom, debris and puzzle pieces crunching underfoot.

"You're looking for a Snake," Artemus said. "You sensed it, presumably."

The heavy muzzle dipped in a nod. This close, Elspeth found that every instinct of her body screamed to get away. The green eyes blinked in amusement, considering her.

"It's Belinda," Artemus said.

"This again?" Elspeth said. "I know you don't like her."

"That has nothing to do with anything. She's the Snake. She's taken the actual daughter and disposed of her along the way. As a master illusionist, she's able to cloud your mind and make you think she's just a null."

Elspeth ran through matters in her head. The sheer weighty reluctance of doing so convinced her that Artemus was right. Something was very wrong with Belinda.

"Something more," Artemus said. He knelt and picked up a handful of puzzle pieces. "Look at the backs."

She turned over the carved wood with dawning realization. "Pencil marks on the back. It's his formula."

Artemus' blue eyes shuttered. "If the knowledge goes to the War Ministry, they will make machines from fallen soldiers. So will anyone else who learns it." He methodically plucked puzzle pieces from the floor. "They are very flammable, these pieces."

This was why they assigned a human to the mechanical, to think out questions of judgment and justice. In theory. But it seemed he no longer needed her.

She took the pieces from his hands and shoved them in the waistband of her shirt. "If we just throw them out, there's still a chance someone could find and reassemble them."

He nodded. "The engine is three cars up."

———•

But when she reached the engine, Belinda was there.

"Ahhhh," the young woman breathed out regretfully as she saw Elspeth's face. She spread her hands in a helpless gesture. "I take it the jig, as we say, is up?"

Elspeth took a few steps forward, looking at the door to the boiler, small and square and securely shut.

Before she could move again, Belinda's form blurred and interposed itself. Elspeth felt the hard muscles against her own.

"Would you like?" the voice buzzed, half out loud, half in mind. *Like to see what I really look like?*

146

She breathed out assent and the golden curls shimmered, gave way to a hood of shimmering scales, purple and pine and scarlet, and eyes that stared at her tenderly. She was enfolded in coils, and Belinda's mouth hovered over the vein that pulsed in her neck.

I will not touch your blood, the voice said in her head, *not for all the world, beloved, but oh, if I did, it would be right here*—the teeth dipped and grazed the skin in a circle of freezing pleasure that ran from that point down to her very core, where it warmed and made her loins heavy with desire—*right here* and the lips caressed the skin as though licking some flavor from them.

Even as that pleasure burned, Elspeth grappled the door open and threw the puzzle pieces in to flare up in a cascade of sparks. Even so, the arms held onto her waist, the warm breath caressed her shoulder. *It is a bad thing for anyone to hold, and there will be other power, given time,* the internal voice hissed, and suddenly nipped, not breaking the skin but making her gasp aloud with the intensity of the pleasure.

The orgasm shook her, drove her off her feet, and the arms released her to let her slide against the wall as the Snake backed away, green eyes amused and regretful.

We will meet again, you and I.

The door opened and the figure was gone, fallen out into the dark night.

———••—◦

"It is," Artemus said, "something that we can explain to the War Ministry. The professor died telling no one the formula. It died with him."

"You don't want to say that the emissary of a group of magical shape shifters killed him for it"? Elspeth asked.

Artemus shuddered. "We would face questioning for weeks." The amusement faded. "We'll have to find the group ourselves."

Nor There

"If they don't find us first," she said. She heard the voice again, *beloved, and then there will be other power, given time.*

She looked to Artemus.

We will meet again, you and I.

And what will happen then?

Afternotes

I freely confess that this story came from the title, which seemed like a no-brainer. Once I had that, and knowing that it had to be steampunk, I pulled in Artemus and Elspeth from "Her Windowed Eyes, Her Chambered Heart" and then figured out what "snakes" referred to.

Some readers will see a contradiction in the love interest here and that in Her Windowed Eyes. That is true, and I'm working on another story to reconcile the dichotomy, set down near the Mexican border, which has let me explore another region of Altered America.

This originally appeared as a Patreon story.

THE PASSING OF GRANDMOTHER'S QUILT

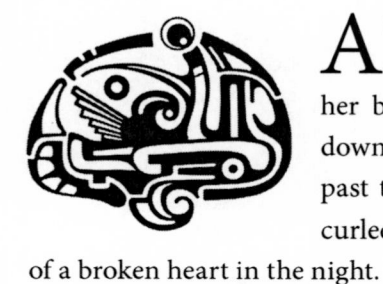 A FEW WEEKS AFTER MY GRANDMOTHER'S death, her quilt began crawling from her bed in the early hours and roaming downstairs. You'd hear the rustle as it went past the door, and in the morning find it curled somewhere, like a dog that had died of a broken heart in the night.

The quilt had been made by my great-aunt Mabel. It was a crazyquilt, and a fancy one too. While Mabel's eye for color might have been a little off (the predominant shade was orange), her expert craftsmanship and the fabric she'd used made it exceptional. Bits of velvet were soft as mouse ears, laid between strips of satin ribbon, and embroidered flowers bloomed along every careful seam. Smaller than most quilts—Grandmother had been a diminutive woman—and Mabel had made it to fit her narrow widow's bed.

Finally one morning I went down in the morning's early hours. The quilt lay beside the window, spread out as though basking in the moonlight, while across the room its counterpart swam in the watery mirror under a cold white rectangle.

I felt I was intruding, but I was tired and the quilt had been keeping me awake.

Thus my words were not particularly kind.

"She's dead," I snapped.

The quality of the silence in the room changed. I realized that the quilt had not known this. She had died in the hospital, after all. To the quilt, it might have seemed that she had gone on a visit somewhere. Only when days had turned into weeks had it begun to worry.

"I'm sorry," I said. The quilt remained quiet, unmoving.

Turning around, I went back upstairs.

When I came down in the morning, the quilt still lay there. But as I came closer, I saw that it was a layer of pieces of cloth on the floor, pieced together, but with every seam or stitch gone, undone.

The pieces fluttered as I opened the window. They rose up in a great swirling mass and poured out like a swarm of butterflies, leaving only bits of twisted thread behind.

Afternotes

One of the things I remember from childhood is the quilt my grandmother Nellie made, a crazyquilt with lots of bits of satin and velvet, embroidered with flowers and butterflies and bits of fancy stitchery.

The quilt, alas, itself died in a house fire, and my grandmother has passed on as well. She was a stellar craftswoman, capable of taking an object and figuring out how to replicate it; I still have two of the vests she made me in high school because I can't bear to part with them, or with the old pressure cooker that I use pretty constantly. She made a wedding cake for me that was without parallel, and put enormous effort into its creation, all because she loved me without question. She was in many ways a thorny and cantankerous woman, but she will always have a very special place in my heart.